NEW AMERICA

NEW AMERICA

John Mamone

LIBERTY HILL PUBLISHING

Liberty Hill Publishing
2301 Lucien Way #415
Maitland, FL 32751
407.339.4217
www.libertyhillpublishing.com

Paperback ISBN-13: 978-1-6628-3092-1
Dust Jacket ISBN-13: 978-1-6628-3093-8
Ebook ISBN-13: 978-1-6628-3094-5

PREFACE

In 1981 a group of men from the U.S. and Britain plotted to install a leader and government of their choosing in a small and underdeveloped country in the Caribbean. Their intentions were not honorable, and they eventually were caught by U.S. officials while attempting to execute their plot.

The incident was forgotten, and the two countries never again thought about it, except as a footnote in the history of the Caribbean country.

Events slowly developed over decades that made the idea come to the surface again and this time with a sense of urgency.

Fifty years later, honorable men and women have presented to the people of this same island nation a new proposal.

Much like their ancestors before them, they too are escaping from those who would persecute them for their beliefs: The belief in true independence and the idea of the truly sovereign individual. They are departing a land that they loved and many of them had fought to defend. Not because of some foreign invasion. Their enemy was much more insidious. It was the product of generational erosion of their core. It was a dilution of what the generations before them believed in their souls, that America was the land of the truly free. But now there is an immutable paradigm shift, and that belief will be put to the inevitable life or death test.

NEW AMERICA

THE YELLOW AND BLACK DINER SIGN WAS glowing through the early morning mist. It was busy and the parking lot was close to full. Typical for this metropolitan new south city. Utility trucks and Cadillacs, dually pickup trucks and a Maserati, Lincolns, and Smart cars. The parking lot made quite a statement.

Through the front door came four middle-aged men like so many others that morning.

Whatta' ya have boys, the petite waitress with the company visor asked?

Christy, I'll have two poached well, dry wheat, Russ said, and grits.

Tom, what 'bout you? Aww, Christy just the special.

What for you, Jake? Just coffee, Christy.

And for the stranger, I don't believe I've seen you here before?

Well, no, my dear lady, I do not believe you would have. This is my first meeting with these gentlemen, but I do rather think you will see me again. My name is Charles McGavock.

Well, pleased to meet ya Charles, Christy said, letting just a little bit of her west Texas twang show. Where's home, Charles?

She couldn't help but ask without trying to be too nosey.

Well, I've spent time all over the world, but I would say the Cayman Islands is home for now.

Oh well, fancy that. I guess you will be having hot tea with lemon then, chimed Christy.

1

Very good my dear, Charles responded.

How did you know? Just as smooth as she could muster, you didn't seem like a Dr. Pepper man.

The men made sure they had the corner booth; they knew the conversation was not made for public consumption. Measured tone was the operating procedure for this morning.

Gentlemen, have you given much thought to the literature our organization sent to you?

I realize it does represent a large commitment on your collective parts.

Commitment is not the word I'd use, blurted out Russ. More like an exodus.

Russell, we admit with this organization, there are changes that must be accepted and one must be prepared to execute, Charles responded, as though he had said this many times before. Not practiced, but as if he had had to face this situation often.

You gentlemen must have been concerned about the present situation or you would not have put forth the effort to seek me out.

Jake looked up at this point and began, look Russ, we've been through this a hundred times, there is no point tryin' to get around it. If I stay here any longer, I'm going to have to sell what I can and walk away from the rest. I just have what I'm planning on taking down there and that's it!

Tom didn't really want to talk, but he began slowly,

Fellas, we've all grown up together; we've been through lot of B.S. and crap and helped each other when we could, but dammit, this is different!

We're going to be affected and there is nothing we can do about it! I am going to go and that's it!

I haven't told Leslie yet, but I am getting ready to move all we can when we get the confirmations. I just have to decide if I want to leave a little just in case it doesn't work out.

Charles piped in at that moment,

Thomas, I just do not think you will find much to come home to. What I mean to say, well it just is not going to be the same. I am sorry to say, I believe what you remember as your quaint hometown will soon be gone.

Tom didn't at first say a thing; he dropped his head, not wanting to look up. It was like if he looked up at Charles, he would know it was over. But the truth was it had been over for months now, the insiders had already implemented Charles' organization's plan. They had retired early. They sold out. They just packed up and went on vacation but did not come back.

Finally, people didn't ask anymore where so-and-so had gone.

They had moved on, was always the answer.

Maybe Florida.

The background din of the diner overcame the last words of their conversation. These men who had been friends all their lives now had come to their biggest crossroad. The hardest part was dealing with denial, now it was just time to accept the facts and to go.

I expect you gentlemen will need a month, two at the most to finalize your affairs, Charles dryly commented. We really cannot proceed until we receive your individual wire transfers and confirmations.

Tom finally looked up and nodded, as did the others. They all understood it would take at least that long or so to burn bridges and cut ties.

HANNOVER STEAM

THE TOWNSHIP OF HANNOVER ROOTS TRACED back to 1650's. Those roots were not lost on the townspeople and many labored to keep the heritage and history alive.

The historic homes that lined the original colonial pathway that was an old post road stand preserved and stoic against time. Many of the great homes were built by the founders of manufacturing companies that flourished in the nineteenth and most of the twentieth centuries in the nearby city centers of commerce.

But besides the wealth that had come to many in the region, the township and surrounding area had a natural beauty with forested rolling hills and fields filled with wildflowers.

Nearby, the great river flowed through the gentle fertile valley where shade tobacco was grown for cigars makers, made its way to the Sound and on to the Atlantic. And the weathered rock faced cliffs from ancient mountains were within a short drive of the town.

Each landscape's beauty changed with the time of year. Each season reset the attraction to the township of Hannover. Spring would bring the rebirth of tiger lilies, iris, and forsythia. Followed by the unfolding of leaf buds on mature trees and the fragrance of honeysuckle and fresh mowed grasses.

Summer warmth and sun grew the tunnel like leaf canopies of ancient oak and maple trees covering the old roadways. The towns swimming holes were well used by kids of all age.

And weekend day trips down the old river road through the historic villages that dated to the 1700's with their immaculate town squares and white churches topped with ornate spires. And there was the country lane that crossed the river on the still operating ferries to the nearby state parks and beaches, not even an hour away.

In early autumn, with the changing color palette from shades of hunter and sage green to brilliant yellow, gold and crimson brought the season of apple cider from local orchard's roadside stands, county fairs and stacking of firewood to steady against the coming north winds and nor'easter storms.

A highlight of the long winters was the tradition of placing small candle lights in the windows of the historic homes that fronted the old post road every Christmas seasons.

The falling snow on the tall pines and spruce trees with the scent of freshly cut pine wreaths and of hearth fires of apple and oak drifting through the crisp air would bring out the Santa in even most hardened Scrooge-like curmudgeon.

In the evening, the warm glows of the candles from the windows cast their soft light onto the pine boughs bent down with the freshly accumulated snow to only magnify the atmosphere.

But it was more than the holiday charm that endeared the towns people to the area. Change came slowly to this part of the world and people liked it that way. They resisted the overdevelopment that other parts of the region encouraged.

Their town had traditions and a quality of life that most hoped would continue.

Hannover became a quiet town next to the cities of hardware and tool manufacturers along with the insurance company that had established Southern New England as their home base of operations. Over the decades, Hannover continued to slowly grow but the manufacturers, one by one, moved south or regions that lured away their businesses.

For many years, the town fathers faced the challenges of the paradigm shift in their local economy. State and local government became the major employer for many. Others reluctantly came to grips with the fact they would have to leave the area that they loved to restart their lives.

But with changes one exception remained, the quality of the education provided by the schools. The Board of Education saw to it that the funding required to maintain the quality of education was always available and that the students of the township had the opportunities to excel.

One shining example of their foresight was Hannover High and the Center of Science, Technology, Engineering, Arts and Mathematics or Hannover Steam. It was a hybrid of other school's formats whereas other systems had separate schools for the arts and for the sciences.

Hannover had decided to combine the two advance studies centers. The theory was by combining the centers, students would be exposed to other advanced studies classmates with other interest and by doing so might germinate creativity that might not have otherwise developed. This eclectic mix of students could have a possible leg up in the competitive exercise of acceptance and admission in the universe of higher education.

The classes were challenging and varied:

- Advanced calculus and cellular microbiology.
- Astrophysics and Computer aided design and manufacturing.
- Theatre, stage design and production.
- Music, production, and recording. (in the school's recording studio)

These were just a very few of the advanced studies.

One of the classes that filled quickly was a computer graphics class.

While the course itself was required for many students, It was the teacher whose unorthodox style of teaching attracted interest and was appreciated by the students.

Mr. Goodrow was a tall gray-haired gentleman. While he was in his fifties, he still maintained a full mane of longish hair. He was always impeccably dressed and could easily fit in any corporate boardroom meeting or off a page of a British spy novel.

He was refined, yet cool and casual in his manner. He had the uncanny ability to maintain command of the class yet present the day's material so that it would be easily absorbed.

Mr. Goodrow was also an avid jazz and jazz fusion fan and a collector of rare vinyl recordings. He would regularly bring a few of his favorites to class and after he had presented the day material, he would "educate" the students to the genre. And of course, play the recordings on his own stereo system with a turntable. It is the only way the quality of the recording can be presented, he insisted.

One day he would play recordings of Stan Getz and Dave Brubeck, or John Coltrane, the next Les McCann and Eddie Harris or Thelonious Monk and Diana Krall.

The students would soon learn to appreciate his selections.

After a few weeks, one of Mr. Goodrow's students asked if he would allow the students to share with the class some recordings they liked. The student was James Mc Brian. James played several musical instruments, like his parents did as well. He explained his parents had stacks of recordings from the sixty's and seventy's. He suggested that the recording could play in the background as the students worked on their assignments just as Mr. Goodrow had done.

Mr. Goodrow knew it was just a ploy to update the play list, but he agreed.

James first choice was a band from the sixties called "Buffalo Springfield."

Fellow classmate, Ian McAlister brought in "Led Zeppelin II". His next-door neighbor and friend, Russ Simpson had a "Tower of Power" recording. A recent enrollee to Hannover was Bob Steele. He had a unique collection and his favorite addition was "Dan Hicks and his Hot Licks",

Mr. Goodrow shook his head and rolled his eyes after classmate Jake Leland played Captain Beef Heart and Frank Zappa recordings. He was overheard saying, now I know why I liked jazz!

Within a few weeks, most all had taken turns playing some recording for the class.

Even Mr. Goodrow was impressed and surprised by the wide array of interesting music.

After school some of the classmates would continue with the musical exchanges and introduce their friends to others and their friends. And the circle of friendships grew even larger.

Many of these friendships would endure the years to come and the test of time.

ONLY THE BEGINNINGS, ONLY JUST THE START

THE THREE NEW FRIENDS, IAN, JAMES, AND BOB rambled up the path from the backyard to the nearly finished semi- treehouse kind of tarpaper shack.

Come on, guys, I 've got to show you, my project! I have been working on it all spring.

I gotta get some more wood to finish the second floor. It was more like a hut on steroids.

There's a couple of houses being built down the hill, If I can maybe get a couple pieces of plywood, I can finish the roof.

The architect of the structure was Ian McAlister. It was more than a project for the spring, it was his personal quest. Today's enlistees, although they didn't know what they were in for, were to secure the last bits of wood for the roof.

Bob, just grab that corner of the sheet, they've got extra, they won't miss it, announced Ian. In an hour the final piece was in place.

Good, now let's dig out the wine cellar, which was just a two foot by two-foot hole in the dirt to keep future beer cool.

Ian had already planned out the evening with a list of tasks, each to add glory to the newly named retreat. "The Shack" was scrawled on the tarpaper-covered door in chalk.

After we add the skylight and the "roof top lounge," which was nothing more than a few pieces of two by four's nailed in place to keep tipsy visitors from the fifteen-foot fall to the ground, we should celebrate, added Ian proudly.

The sweet scent of greening woods and flowering laurel was almost like a sweet birch beer, and it filled the twilight air. It was now just warm enough to stay out later without a chill at night. It was nine p.m.; the sun had just gone down in this quiet little New England town. It felt perfect. They weren't old enough to be caught up with the world's events but old enough to drive.

Ian uncovered from the corner of their building project a six pack of Narragansett he had "borrowed "from his dad. The brewery's popular motto "Hi Neighbor! Have a Gannsett!" was employed and all savored the evening's reward. It was just the first of many to be shared that summer at" The Shack."

* * * * *

Jake Leland and his fellow audio and visual aid partners, Bob Steele, and his friend, Tom Lukas had pulled off their most brilliant scheme of all time in the history of morning announcements of Hannover Steam.

For weeks they had been adding their own brand of humor to the otherwise starched, staid, and dull P.A. announcements. Their opening monologue was accompanied by the "Sounds of Wall Street" that Louis Rukeyser's Wall Street Week used at the beginning of his program from the 1960's and 70's. It began, tick, tick, tikka, tick to the sound of the ticker tape machine of decades ago Wall Street's stockbroker's offices.

Jake, who's on Principal Long's list of ,"*did not appear for class*", at Hannover' for June 4th,

Tom asked of his partner in crime,

Well Tom, it appears this morning's list invites an appearance at the Main office and that includes a special guest spot for Brian Germaine and Candy Hoffman.

It seems the closed-captioned security cameras have captured for all time, the two riding off into the rising sun in Candy's new Jeep from the school parking lot on Friday morning.

How could this be, Tom, queried Bob as though a major offense had been perpetrated. That is an exceptionally good question Bob, and I'm sure inquiring minds and Principal Long would like to ask the very same thing, he responded in his best Groucho Marx impersonation.

The ticker tape sound carried on for a few seconds uninterrupted.

But on with other news, segued Bob, this just in from the office in the circular men's room high atop the RTB school of Dance, it's this weekend updates!

Tom turned on a recording with Frank Sinatra singing" *Strangers in the Night"* and turned the volume so it played just loud enough to fill as a background to their narrative.

Saturday' night's dance features the dulcet tones of R.K.S. Otherwise known as the "Rabid Knights of Swing."

Bob casually remarked to Tom, say, isn't that the band that started that commotion at Belden's Place? Why, yes, I believe it is, genuinely nice to have them back for a return performance! That soiree is to take place in the tastefully decorated gym, at eight p.m., does it not, Bob?
I believe you are correct, Tom.

And those in the senior class that assume they are graduating, don't forget your orders for caps and gowns must be returned to Ms. Johnson by end of school tomorrow.

I'll lay odds there are going to be a few surprises coming out of that graduating roll call, what do you think, Jake? Tom dryly added.

Bob, piped in Tom, aren't you forgetting something?

Ahh, that's right, Tom, all seniors who are interested in senior skip day to Rocky Neck State Park, report to the parking lot at eight a.m. sharp tomorrow morning.

Well, that wraps it up here Jake.

Good morning, Tom.

Good morning, Bob.

Good morning, Jake.

Tom turned off the recordings. The three of them looked at each other and tried to make it into the hall before bursting into fits of laughter.

As the morning announcements faded from the speakers in every single classroom in Hannover Steam, a new high-water mark had been established for the group of friends.

The morning had gone off without a hitch. Tomorrow they would see if their planning had paid off. At first there appeared to be no outward signs anybody was listening, No one approached them to ask what was going on tomorrow. No one had pulled them to the side to demand, what exactly are you kids doing?

There wasn't the thunderous, "Tell me you're mocking me," Principal Long would bellow when some infraction had been thrust against the school's rules and regulations.

No ruffled feathers, could they have just gone unnoticed? Nothing was said.

All settled into the automatic glide path of the last days of school.

* * * * *

James had noticed her before. Abbey Quinlan was the sister of a new acquaintance James had befriended from Mr. Goodrow's graphic design class. She met James before when he had offered her brother, Dave, and her a few rides home after school. She really was on her way to bigger things and knew where she would go after Hannover.

He knew he would see her between Art History and Ancient and Medieval History classes.

Hi, Abbey, his approach, casual and low key was the plan, just to see if there was an interest.

Hello James, she responded, nonchalant but pleasantly as she walked by.

He stopped for a second to glean any reaction. Did she smile? *If she would have stopped for a second, maybe I could tell*, he thought. *Maybe for just a second is all*. He turned away and figured this was a dead end. Within a few steps he felt a tug on his arm.

James, is it your band playing Saturday night?

Yeah, I'm afraid so, Abbey. What do you mean, afraid so, she said, like she was unaware of the band's history. Well, you know, people thought I was involved in that trouble at Belden, James quietly responded.

I was there, Abbey replied. I know you didn't have anything to do with it. It was that gang banger at school, Brian, and that sax player, he was a real dickhead.

Yeah, I know, that's what I call him, James quipped, Johnnie the Dick.

In one fell swoop my first chance to play in front of all my friends was destroyed by an anger management class drop-out sax player. What an assclown, James sighed.

At this point, Abbey's smile said all there was to say. I'll see you there, James.

It was all he had hoped for that morning.

* * * * *

The weather was perfect. It would be at least eighty-five degrees and not a cloud in the sky. The early morning parkers seemed a little busier than usual. The guys who had sport cars, muscle cars, cars the owners had just repainted midnight metal flake, or just got a set of the newest BBS forged wheels had to be there.

The early parkers got to park on the street parallel to the cafeteria. This was crucial because the cafeteria had floor-to-ceiling glass windows, and everyone would see your ride during the day. Your status for that day depended on how early you could get up and park.

This morning the early parkers had filled the road in a line of cars that had formed around the corner. Nearly thirty cars, all filled with seniors and a few underclassmen.

Russ was near the beginning of the procession in his monkey shit brown 63' Olds.

Guys, it's seven-thirty. This thing is out of hand, we need to leave ahead of schedule or we're all going to get caught. James had gotten in line about midway and had Ian, Bob, and Jake with him.

The Pontiac could hold one more. James was sitting on the front fender when he was startled by her voice, it was Abbey.

I told my mom I wanted to go, and she said it was okay, do you have room?

James reeled around and looked at Bob.

You're in the back.

Five minutes later they were on their way.

* * * * *

James awoke with his head leaning against the window of the 747.

"Ladies and gentlemen, this is your captain. We are twenty-five minutes from Hong Kong. Please prepare all immigration papers if you have not already done so. The flight crew will come through the cabin one last time to gather any newspapers and trash. And thank you for flying Cathay Pacific."

He was mad at himself for dosing off thinking of her again. It was so many years ago, for God's sake. That world then doesn't exist now. And didn't exist then. It was over before it started. What a fool believes is so true. But she was like a song in his head that played over and over until it almost made him crazy.

He was surprised and stunned when he saw her those few minutes, ten years ago. But one thing was certain: he saw the indifference through her half smile and the indirect gaze of her eyes. What did he want from her, anyway? Maybe just avoid that awful ennui, he reasoned.

Those painful awkward pauses were one thing that killed the beginnings of a relationship. James thought it was a curse, words that did not come casually. But he did have a knack for one thing for sure: saying just the wrong thing at the wrong time. Especially with Abbey. All he wanted to do was move on; it was the memories that wouldn't evanesce.

After the plane landed, James knew the routine. Take the Number 25 bus over the mountain-like hills to the other side of Lantau Island to Mui Wo. Go to the Silvermine Hotel and take a shower and head to one of the open-air bars for a couple of Peronis.

He loved the little village, and it was just a short walk from the hotel over an arched stone bridge that crossed a little river to the ferry boat landing and village center.

It might seem a little strange to come all this way to drink Italian beer in China. But Mui Wo was the perfect place for it. It was festive, yet serene. The gentle lights of the seaside restaurants and bars that lined the bay were all within steps of the ferry boats to central Hong Kong.

The nighttime spray from Silvermine Bay and the South China Sea filled the air and the gentle breezes with the aroma of freshly caught seafood being grilled or steamed just feet away.

If you could close your eyes and be anywhere in the world with the love of your life on a perfect night, this would be the place. James would say, it was that night when you would say to yourself, this is the best it could ever get.

In the morning he would take the slow ferry to Central and head to the main office of the Bank of Hong Kong and wire transfer the required funds. He would call his brother, Joe and make sure there were no last-minute changes. They kept four separate accounts in four different countries. The instructions had to be precise. Their small office near the Admiralty had already been rented. He would swing by to make sure there were no last-minute issues and say good-bye to some of the former staff. Later that day he would take Ferry One's fast ferry back to Mui Wo.

It was early June, and the Dragon Boat Festival would begin in a few days. The highly decorated crew boats with large dragon head bows were lined up on the sandy beach within the shelter of the village's little harbor ready for their crews to man them. The village was abuzz with activities and the preparations for the start of the races. People from all around the world had come to witness and take part in the festival.

Waist high walls made of rounded stone lined both sides of roads and walkways made with skillfully placed cobblestone meandered over arched bridges to the village center. The walkways were filling with visitors catching glimpses of the boats lined up on the beach front preparing for the upcoming racing events.

It was a shame, but James couldn't witness the races. Tomorrow he would have to take the taxi over the mountain to the airport. He would be back in the U.S. by nine in the morning. The day you live twice because of recrossing the International Date Line, you end up arriving back in the States the same time you left China. It was always taxing on your head and body, and you never arrived back without a couple days of serious jetlag.

* * * * *

Sir, this flight is not full; I can upgrade you from your frequent flyer account points you have acquired; would that be all right? Oh, hell yes that would be all right! James said, forgetting where he was.

Excuse me, sir? The agent said and smiled. Oh sorry, yes that would be quite all right.

Window or aisle?

Oh, window please, James responded although he didn't know why, you can't see anything for most of the trip. Except for that few minutes over the central coast.

Just because she lives there doesn't mean you need to see it.

It's going to be a long flight, just settle in, he said over and over. And I'll have to get past the jet lag and meet the group in Savannah in three days.

* * * * *

17

Ian and Jake's flight had just pulled up to the airway at Savannah's Airport.

The feel of a coastal southern town was omnipresent, warm, and friendly.

The scent of salt marsh and the nearby Atlantic Ocean permeated the humid morning air.

They would soon meet up with Russ and Tom and review Charles' company's progress. They were not surprised the company was calling itself," New America."

After ten minutes, the idea was obvious. The company, which was really a partnership, offered permanent ownership in what the founding fathers had envisioned all those many years ago. Self-reliance, individual sovereignty, the least amount of government possible. In this system, the individuals owned a share of the country. It was in their shared interest to have effective and efficient government. Trade and technology were the panacea, world class technology and global trade were the goal. Taxes were based on the very minimum the country required. There were no social safety nets. Taxes were based on what was consumed, not on income made.

We have the final reports of numerous studies, and we are certain the more money you have, the more money you can spend, and you will want it to be spent here. This is the basis for our tax system and our engine for growth, confidently explained Charles.

The minimum entry price to participate in ownership of "New America "is one hundred thousand dollars, U.S. per share as of a date certain. Afterward we will endeavor to establish our own currency; it will be based around the price of a fixed fraction of a troy ounce of gold and tied to the Swiss franc, because that is, in fact, the world's most stable currency, Charles matter of factually added. We will also endeavor to then explore the possibilities of block chain systems and a crypto currency as an additional option.

In our proposed country, you are free to establish businesses that will add to the common good of all. We have labored diligently to draft laws that must be adhered to unquestioningly. None of the participants wants this endeavor to mutate into a lawless Wild West situation. All business activities must provide for the growth of New America but must not be deemed a hindrance or immoral or harmful by its fellow shareholders of the country. All shareholders are required to have input on all decisions that affect the country. Noncompliance will be deemed as non-interest, and therefore voiding voting rights, privileges, and residence in New America. We are planning to include retirees who wish to participate, but only after the infrastructure that may be needed is complete and in place.

Ian was the first to ask. Okay, I understand the principles, but why one hundred thousand dollars a share? Charles responded, I am afraid to say, but for this to work, you must have some place to relocate and have skin in the game, as you Americans like to say. We have established that the governments and citizens of two island nations are willing to review our system as possibly a better alternative to their present system. One, we must invest to establish a binding foothold, and the other is willing to invite us to improve their currently underdeveloped system.

What we have begun is to negotiate with the Commonwealth of Dominica and the Island of Pico in the Azores.

The Azores are an autonomous part of Portugal. We have asked the Portuguese government if we can approach the residents of Pico to meet with the founders of New America and listen to our proposal. The assemblymen and local officials have expressed interest in a meeting and may be willing to talk because their citizens will be grandfathered into our system. Each one's acceptance is equal to one half share; this is their payment in kind. Citizens prior to the agreement can participate under this agreement. For the islanders who participate but cannot add to the system because of age or physical limitations prior to the agreement, a generous monthly dividend will be paid.

Dominica's situation is such that we have proposed to the elected officials one half share each and invest with each Dominicans ten thousand dollars the first year. The remaining four years will be the same amount and will be credited to their individual share. They have priority hiring and training to a job of their preference, but they must state in advance this is agreeable. They are encouraged to buy into the system as soon as possible. We would like all involved to participate and add to the overall system. Ownership is the key because we want all to feel like they are part of something in which all benefit, and they have a sense of pride and accomplishment to be involved. Much will be needed to invest into Dominica.

The island of Pico has fine soil for their vineyards and some established infrastructure. We think the potential for the island and the surrounding other nearby islands in the triangle area, as it is known, are tremendous. We anticipate this idea to be well received throughout the area, and if the system proves agreeable, we will want to talk to the other nearby island surrounding Pico.

Because we will feel there will be the need to have more area for the expected applications from the U.S. and Europe and possibly South America and Asiana, we may approach the elected officials and people in other island nations to see what their ideas may be for their future. The idea is the sooner an individual participates, the more the individual shares can be worth. The glory of this system is that it does not have to be an adjacent border. The member islands belong to the same system.

All areas participate in the same growth system. All involved add to the same interests and enrichment.

Wow, said Jake, this is like Berkshire Hathaway at fifty dollars a share! Ever since the Feds skyrocketed the taxes, I knew it was time to get out. I'll be damned if I'm gonna keep giving away two thirds of everything I make for these stupid ass taxes!

I'm afraid it's time to decide and I know now is the time, quietly added Tom, who really did not want to believe what he knew was obviously true. I'm in.

Russ was still almost in shock. It had taken all he had to come this far on faith. Even though he had invested thirty years in becoming a senior partner in his firm, after these new tax increases, he had barely enough left for everyday expenses. With three kids in college, one at Yale, he was afraid he might lose the house, even with his wife working again. He kept muttering, If it weren't for those damn tax and fees increases, things would be different,

These new taxes and fees are everywhere and on everything now. They killed our chances for any kind of future. The hell with it, I'm in!

*****

The next day, James arrived in Savannah to meet his lifelong friends. The meeting place was an outside patio of the Hyatt Hotel at noon. The spectacular view of the colonial era city with the calming effect of the slowly meandering river removed the stresses of any issue of the day. Guys, I'm sorry to put you through this, but I couldn't forgive myself if I didn't at least show you another way. I have got to tell you that Joe and I have put in for four shares each. We are officially cashing out. I have lost faith with the system and these two-faced politicians, we just cannot make it if we continue the old way. I'm telling you this is it for us. We are going to restart there once we have the official word.

Charles McGavock had accompanied the four friends before James had arrived. He was a tall, stately figure with wisps of salt and pepper hair and full greying beard. The weathered lines of age had started to be more pronounced with his now tanned visage.

He had made it a point to be conservatively dressed regardless of the situation.

Today was humid and sunny. Charles suggested, as he dapped a handkerchief across his brow, it has gotten quite warm, why don't we meet inside and discuss the progress at length?

I believe there is a wonderful lounge that overlooks the river. Why don't I meet you all in, say, thirty minutes?

With the background of container ships and tour boats plying the river and the tourists filling the Riverwalk, the men met up again. Charles began, gentlemen, the company's goals are proceeding to develop, soon you will know, officially, we have established our agreement and binding contract with the first island participants. Please keep abreast of the situation. We will only ask you to forward the balance of your ownership fees after the official announcement. You all have the packets with instructions. I expect to see all of you again, but I feel we might all see the world differently when we meet next.

And James, Charles added, with a smile beaming across his face.

Yes, Mr. McGavock? James' gaze shifted from the huge passing ships to the group.

Would it be a Peroni or a Tsingtao beer when we meet again?

James thought for a second and replied, If it's Pico first, then a Peroni. If it is Dominica, then a Tsingtao. He didn't know it, but this would be the code they would use for the next few months.

* * * * *

It was the first of September when James had received the email from Charles:

James, final negotiation nearly complete, it will be Tsingtao. Stay updated to our email news announcements. James replied, received, and thanks.

THE POINT OF NO RETURN

THE CABLE NEWS STATIONS WERE TRYING TO SPIN the just announced plan from the newly appointed Treasury Secretary Ralston.

Andrea Cooper was laboring to put the best face on the story. The Treasury Secretary began his explanation of the executive action. Well, this currency devaluation will save the government about thirty percent per year in interest payments towards the now acknowledged fifty-five trillion-dollar national debt. However, your cost of living is now going to skyrocket.

Inflation will inevitably accelerate. It could be five percent a month increase for as far as the eye can see. My advice to you on a fixed income is to save those coupons.

I think if you are retired, you may need to consider returning to the work force.

If you are working full time, I might apply for a second ... or third job.

I might consider the pay rates at one of the big box stores or one of the on-line retailer warehouses as the additional source of income you will need to survive.

I can tell you, my fellow Americans, none of this will be easy. I must tell you this financial situation will not go away anytime soon. Ignoring the debt has now manifested itself to the point that its effects are now to be felt at every level of our society. If you are religious, pray for our country.

That night on PBS, Treasury Secretary Thomas Ralston, was interviewed.

Let me ask you a question, Mr. Secretary, the interviewer began, why exactly are you back at this post? Well, someone had to take the reins in Treasury. My understanding is many nominees kept refusing the appointment.

Mr. Secretary, the commentator exclaimed, you can't be serious!

The Secretary nodded with all the seriousness he could. I'm afraid so.

Well, Mr. Secretary, it certainly seems like you have your hands full this time.

How does it feel to be back in your old office?

Honestly, he paused to make sure he knew exactly what he was about to say.

Awful, this is a real mess.

The next day the New York Stock Exchange average fell below ten thousand for the first time in decades. It had dropped steadily in the past weeks, but this was a big psychological point. If it continued like this there would be no support again to five thousand. That would represent tens of trillions of dollars in equities vaporized.

* * * * *

Protesters had started to show up in front of the White House and the U.S. Capital Building. At first it was only a handful. As the weeks started to tick away, the lines and the volume continued to grow. Only Newsmax and Fox Business News would show up regularly to interview the protesters. The mainstream print media would only carry a few lines about the

The only time a major network did the six o'clock news live shot was when a Native American Tribal Counsel office was closed because of lack of federal funds. There were several dozen people in the office. Some of the now unemployed arrived at their former office in tribal dress. A few had formed small circles and began their tribe's chants and dances in front of the now closed office. The news crew believed the three thousand people in the area were protesting against the closing.

The only individual from the closed office that was interviewed did not realize so many other people had been protesting at the same time. You know, I'm not sure if all of these people are associated with our tribes, the interviewed stated.

I'm not sure either, responded the reporter. But there sure are a lot of support people here regardless!

In the days that followed, the crowds would sometimes form at the Washington Mall.

It was a warm mid-September Sunday afternoon. The crowd was estimated to be over fifty thousand. They had come from almost every state in the country.

Retirees simply could not survive on what now were almost worthless retirement pensions. Now that Social Security was only being paid to those seventy and older and now reduced by thirty percent, the safety net income they had counted on never materialized. With government health care gone bankrupt and President Delacorte's new Hail Mary Health Care plan sucking the last gasps from an already running on fumes economy and U.S. Treasury, anyone with any kind of medical condition was in real trouble. Most had resorted to moving in with whoever could find room for them. And hope someone in the family knew someone with had medical connections.

A parade of concerned businessmen and politicians tried and failed to address the masses with words that were not only soothing and hopeful, but inspired credibility. But that well had long ago run dry The crowd had finally had enough.

An elderly woman approached Congressman Gordon, who many in the crowd admired and respected. But this was different. Even the respected congressman could not appease the fuming masses.

Why should we believe you, congressman, a snow-white haired woman, well into her eighties, screamed, almost breaking into tears. You have promised us it would never get this bad, why should we believe you now?

Gas is now eight dollars a gallon and you voted down drilling and fracking for more oil where the people in my state are begging for the jobs!

Where are all these electric cars factories you said was gonna be built?

Where are these **new car battery factories you promised?**

It doesn't matter to you they were supposed to open in my state and never did!

We can't afford any new electric car the government says we have to have now anyway!

You forbid any new pipelines! We still need the oil and jobs.

And you damn fools outlawed coal mining. You won't put any money into clean coal.

You'd rather throw people out of work and tell them to learn how to do something else for a living.

What the hell is wrong with you people!

I dare you to follow me to Kentucky or Pennsylvania or West Virginia; we'll fix your no coal mining ass, you damn morons!

And now you want to tax us out of existence!

So now you voted to save some damn jumping prairie mouse we used to shoot and feed to our cats. So now we can't use that land to feed our cattle.

What the hell is the matter with you?

I can't even grow tomatoes in my back lot because you say the run-off will kill some damn geese! And if I shoot the goose for filling my back yard with piles of turds and sticking it in the oven, *I go to jail!*

Do any of you morons have any damned sense at all?

I do not give a damn about your damned spotted owl.

I do not give a damn about your damned geese!

I give a damn about my children and their children and the way this country used to be before you incompetent morons took over everything and thought you knew better than we do!

What the hell is wrong with you! **Why should we believe a single word out of your mouth?**

You allow this administration to piss away trillions of dollars we don't have and will never pay back. Now we gotta suffer because you can't afford the interest on the money you pissed away and didn't have in the first place!

Is that about right!!

How the hell did you dumb asses ever get elected, you can't even run a damn merry- go-round!

Now the elderly woman was shaking her fist and was now even more visibly very irate.

As she screamed, her grandson who had accompanied her, put his hand on her shoulders to keep her from falling and attempt to calm her.

The crowd responded and repeated in ever-increasing volume,

Why should we believe you!? Why should we believe you!?

Over and over, as if that were the only action they could muster that would have any effect on their lives. The congressman looked for a friendly face and signaled he would have to be hurried off the stage. The crowds now started to push into the stage. They had to take their frustration out on the nearest official they could find.

Why should we believe you!!? Why should we believe you!!!?

Then muffled by the volume of the crowd was an unmistakable sound. *"POP."*

A middle-aged woman in a bright yellow dress, standing on the stage, moved to help him off the stage, reached out toward the congressman but fell limp in front of him. The bright red of her blood began to show against her dress. The woman just grazed him as she fell, and for a second, he turned to help her. Then he heard firecrackers and felt the shock and pain. Then he collapsed on the stage floor.

A look of stunned surprise swept over those closest to the stage. At first, no one knew from where the shots had come.

A single shot had already hit the woman in the yellow dress, two more hit the congressman on the stage. *"POP. POP."* Two more, but none were hit.

The wounded woman collapsed into a hanging backdrop drape that was part of the stage. As she fell, the drape and the supports that held it collapsed and covered her. At first no one in the crowd moved. They stood there in total disbelief.

Then someone screamed in horror,

Oh my God! they killed them!

Some in the crowd yelled out and pointed to a figure running away in a military looking uniform.

Oh my God! they killed them!

The crowd pointed toward the figure running toward the White House. The crowd then surged past the stage toward the ellipse and in the direction of the White House.

The point of no return had been breached, like a dam that exploded under the pressure of too much flooding water. In a millisecond, the nation was never going to be able to return to the way generations remembered America.

At the Smithsonian Museum of Natural History, a well-known local television and radio personality and two work associates were leaving after recording a spot about a new addition to the museum. They were to have lunch and head back home.

Within feet of the exit, they watched in horror as the crowd overtook the stage in front of them in a burst of pent-up anger and frustration threatening any government officials in sight. The crowd stretched past them and the ticket booth adjacent the Washington Monument, toward the Ellipse, gathering almost by instinct. Tens of thousands started toward the White House.

The crowd was screaming, **They killed the old lady! They killed the old lady!**

The senior of the three work friends, Neal Brockton, was still at the museum entrance.

He pulled out his cell phone and began to record the event.

My God, I can't believe this is happening! He was in total disbelief.

Belinda, can you get a shot of this with your phone? This is going to get ugly!

Belinda yelled to her friend right behind her, Royal, are you okay?

Yeah, I'm right behind you! Royal yelled back. Neal, are you getting this?

They knew they were witnessing history. Royal steadied Neal as the last of the crowd pushed by.

Neal, I hope you got this, because no one will believe this is happening.!

Just wait until we get this to the station, he kept saying, still not wanting to believe what they knew they were seeing. The crowd kept yelling louder and louder:

Why should we believe you!!? Why should we believe you!!

The shouts were echoing through streets. The sirens of the police cars were just starting to be audible. The crowd approached the gates of the White House. They were stopped momentarily by the new higher and reinforced iron fence. This situation had triggered a new security protocol planned the year before. First, an ever-louder humming, then a bright blue flash illuminated the block. At that moment, anyone holding a cell phone or video camera, or other handheld device dropped it to the ground. It was a mass of smoking plastic and metal that covered the ground. All vehicles within five -hundred feet stopped dead. Then the hum slowed and stopped altogether.

This stunned the crowd at first and it appeared the situation could be controlled. But then the first of the crowd started to climb on one another's shoulders, then another and another. The guards on the grounds ran toward the on-rushing crowd, but very soon the numbers were too many to control. The Marines on station shot warning volleys in the air, but it was too late. The crowds would not be stopped.

Twenty-one were wounded before the tear gas subdued the crowd. The scene was like out of the killing fields. On the metal fence, like some grotesque scarecrows, hung three young men, impaled after they were wounded. Two had died.

The military and the police rushed in to seal off the area. Before the wounded and dead were removed to a secured facility, the area was sanitized.

Neal and his friends had escaped the crowds in the confusion, but his phone had captured the scene and carnage from just outside the security perimeter.

* * * * *

31

The President was not there that afternoon. He was with the Treasury Secretary on a mission to entice the Pacific Rim nations to buy a new round of Treasury notes.

The Chinese said they had to have eleven percent returns before they would risk any more Chinese RMB. Chairman Ho Jintao reminded the President that the U.S. dollar was at its lowest point ever. And dropping. The Chairman scolded all in the mission, pointing his finger like he was trying to finally make them understand.

The United States cannot expect to just print money without consequences. We cannot risk our currency on such a bad investment. If your administration's wish is to spend the world's money so recklessly, I suggest you should ask the world if they are willing to participate.

When the President received the news about the Washington incident, he persisted for another ten minutes and concluded the sales job. No sale today, he said to an aid before boarding Air Force One. Now what's all this rabble rousing at the White House?

* * * * *

Within hours, a hastily arranged briefing for only invited press members was assembling.

Mr. President, how did you feel when you heard that one of the wounded was actually ex-Congressman Brown? Helen Thomason, the long-time White House reporter, asked the President at the impromptu press briefing.

Is he a Democrat or a Republican, the President half-kiddingly replied. Those who worked for the mainstream media broke into laughter.

A look of disbelief fell over a Newsmax press corp reporter. He stood up and shouted,

Mr. President! what the hell is the matter with you?

Over twenty people were wounded, with two dead, and you're making jokes!

He slammed his reporter's pad to the ground and stormed out of the briefing.

Within seconds, the briefing was stopped.

The lights were immediately shut off and those remaining were escorted out of the briefing room, but not before they were told that if they ever wanted their press credentials renewed, they would not televise or report this incident.

A NEW DIRECTION...WHETHER YOU LIKE IT OR NOT

RUMORS OF THE EVENT HAD TURNED INTO A TORrent of cell phone video clips of the reporter storming out of the press briefing. True to form, no one in the briefing would comment. The press corp reporter had decided to meet with the network legal staff before commenting any further.

The incident at the White House grounds had been sanitized quickly. The President said he had personally seen no such incident.

They don't call it plausible deniability for nothing and say as little as possible about the incident, Mr. President, cautioned the White House legal counsel. But the rumblings had begun.

Who is this man that is so blind!? screamed Michael Savage during his late evening broadcast. What are these rumors we keep hearing? Why won't anyone comment for the record?

The cell phone video that three friends had produced and delivered to their radio station was being examined and confiscated by the FBI.

It came to the attention of the FBI by way of the NSA.

Neal's conversations with the radio station had been "monitored" for quite a while, it was discovered.

After all, he was known for his radio rants and pronouncements about governmental waste and abuses that had caught the attention of the staff at one of the public broadcast monitoring groups and several concerned congressmen and senators. Although there was no recourse for the moment, there also were to be no questions.

The Attorney General's assistant, Mr. Golden, was sitting in the radio and television station owner and president's office. He beckoned to release the video clips to him.

Mr. Golden approached the popular talk show host.

Neal, I'm sorry, but we all agree here you cannot under any circumstances comment on this weekend. We consider this to be a matter of national security and that gives us quite a bit more authority.

Neal blurted; *You can't do this! Who's authority?*

Mr. Golden put his arm around the tall, lanky talk show host's shoulders and said firmly, but just loud enough for only him to hear,

Yes, yes, we can, and we are profoundly serious about it.

But it wasn't until the assistant A.G. pulled on his shirt sleeve and pulled him toward him and whispered quickly in his ear. At that point Neal turned white as a ghost.

Please don't make us react to any untimely leaks to the public, the Assistant A.G. added.

What does **that** mean? Royal quipped.

Mr. Golden only raised his hand like he was finished with the conversation. There was no further communication with the A.G.'s office to be made.

Belinda hurried over to Neal and asked, What did he say to you? Neal pulled her to the side and replied in shock,

He said he knew where I lived and that he would not want anything to happen with a slip of the tongue. Never in forty years have I ever seen anything approaching this.

The now shaking veteran kept repeating to himself, what is happening to my country? How did this happen? **How could this have happened?**"

REALITY IS A DIFFCULT THING

ON THEIR WAY TO THE BEACH, HE KNEW HE WAS in trouble. He never had felt anything like this. He asked her, Abbey, where are you going to change? You don't have your bathing suit on under your clothes, James commented while downshifting off the exit toward the beach.

Yeah, I know, I was so surprised my mom let me go, I forgot they don't really have a place here.

James thought about it for a second and said, I can find a gas station and you can change there.

No, I've got a better idea, she said. You just stand there, and I'll change in the car. No sense wasting time when we can hit the beach.

The others went ahead to stake out a spot, while James held back, guarding the front of the car.

Everything all right? he asked her.

Yes, be ready in a second. She couldn't have sounded more alluring. She had a white bikini and it fit her like a glove. She was the most beautiful girl he had ever seen; she had the silkiest dark brown hair and the face of an angel. He knew that image would always be burned into his memory.

The rest of the day James felt like he needed to watch over her. After all, she was his responsibility, and he felt a little funny and almost tongue-tied with her. She was so very cool, and she seemed to know just what to say. He knew it was over when she got up to cool off in the water. She reached for his hand to join her. He had just then surrendered to her, there was no going back.

With the incoming tide and the late afternoon sun, accompanied by pink-red shoulders, nose, and cheeks, they group headed home. James dropped each off at their respective homes but stopped at Abbeys home last.

She beckoned him to come inside the home she shared with her siblings and parents.

It was a large two- story white colonial with stately brownstone chimney and a wraparound porch. There was a great room with a huge bay window that overlooked the meticulously maintain flower and herb garden that was outlined by cedar and blue spruce trees. Tucked in amongst the trees was a small clearing that was like a private sanctuary where you could lay in the thick grass and get lost in the moment. This little sanctuary was bordered on one side by an addition to the old house called the ell. Abbey's room was in the ell.

They gathered the blankets from beach trip and spread them in the thick grass.

Abbey brought out some aloe vera lotion and pointed to her back and shoulders for him to gently cover her smooth but reddened skin.

James kidded her that her nose was beginning to resemble Rudolph's and that she should lead the route back to the house. She elbowed him playfully and he made a fake wince and laughed.

That night she placed the first of three of her vinyl recordings on her turntable. They both sat on the floor as the records played. He sat behind her and wrapped his arms tenderly around her waist. James kept thinking to himself, *This is the best it will ever be, this is the best it will ever be.*

When the last album," After the Gold Rush," was finished playing, she slowly got to her feet and kissed him.

It's late, and you should go home, she murmured softly while walking him toward the doorway of the ell.

The next day they lay down in the secret little hidden garden outside her room. She was soon to get ready for her trip to France for most of the summer on a student exchange.

Five weeks, it's too long! James lamented, but he had also planned out his summer.

The band was booked in advance, and he would be playing quite a bit. He knew he would be moving soon to an off-campus apartment with a few of his buddies from school that they had already rented. College was just a two-hour train ride away. James would be able to see Abbey on weekends.

It might just work out.

* * * * *

The next few weeks were busy for James, but he missed her terribly, She did write a letter a week and all seemed like it should between two people trying to keep the romance alive.

She'll be home in another week, he kept thinking. He would visit and hang out with Dave, Abbey's brother, who he had befriended before meeting her.

The warning didn't seem to sink in at first. Dave casually remarked one evening while he was showing James his collection of vintage guitars, be careful around Abbey, she can change like the wind. He added, I guess you like her. James responded, I've never felt like this before.

She's got me in knots, I can't even think straight around her. He finally admitted, I miss her so much, it's crazy, this just can't be good. Dave said to him again, believe me, I know her, be careful!

She returned home in early August. At first everything seemed great.

Abbey, this is too much! James was surprised by her gift. It was a suede jacket she had bought for him. He was at a loss for words. They stayed up past midnight as she was telling him all about the south of France.

Abbey finally said, You've got to go home, you can't stay here, and my folks just wouldn't go for that. He left that night with the winds starting to pick up.

Hurricane Doria was bearing down on New England, the first in two dozen years. It was just the beginning of the stormy weather he was about to endure.

FACTS ARE STUBBORN THINGS

CLIVE JOHNSON HAD BEEN AT HIS POST AT THE American History Museum that Sunday afternoon. At his security station, two dozen security camera panned the grounds and key locations in the museum itself. As he was beginning to settle in and take a sip of his coffee, he looked up to see a woman fall on a temporary stage that had been set up that morning, just across from the main entrance. The camera had captured the event. Before panning to another location, Clive could see a figure in a uniform or dark suit hurry toward the camera a few seconds before the crowd outside rushed the stage.

Clive was sure he saw something that did not belong there. Was it a pipe or a gun barrel? Almost by instinct, he made a copy of the camera recording and put it in his jacket pocket at his workstation. He knew something was happening, but he was trained not to leave his post unless a supervisor authorized him to, or another guard was there to replace him. He had to stay where he was.

At six p.m. the museum guard locked all doors and made sure all visitors had exited the building. Clive secured the doors and finished his shift. It wasn't until later that night the three men from Secret Service had requested to see recordings from the cameras.

On Tuesday, Clive returned after his day off. His supervisor asked him if he had seen anything unusual that Sunday afternoon. I do remember some commotion outside, but it never reached inside here, sir. His Alabama roots were just discernable in his voice. The incident seemed to be closed, the supervisors seemed satisfied with the reply. It wasn't until that evening that Clive remembered the recording. Unsure what to do, he stuck it in his backpack along with his Contract Law book for his class that evening.

Before class, Clive was becoming aware of what had happened that afternoon. His classmates were speaking in hushed tones about the rumors starting to filter out of the Capital.

How many were hurt? Clive asked. We're not sure. I keep hearing over twenty, but everything is buttoned up tight, responded one of his classmates. I've heard it was worse than that, but **no one** is talking officially.

Clive, now aware of what he might have seen, asked quietly. Did anyone hear about any shooting? Donna Loomis, who was in their study group was surprised Clive had asked.

You know, I have a friend who works near the Washington Monument. I think he was working Sunday; I'll ask him.

The professor entered the room, and all attention was shifting to the lecture.

I'll be sure to call you tomorrow, Clive, Donna whispered back to him.

WHY NOT A BETTER WAY?

CHARLES MCGAVOCK HAD PROVEN HIS WORTH to the new organization. He had far exceeded the best estimates the founders had hoped for in terms of potential "citizen share-holders" for the corporation.

He waited in the ante room of the founder's private offices. The founders had both been pioneers in media and both were extraordinarily successful. Their combined audience and popularity made them very much a threat to the policies of the present administration. The straightforward, commonsense approach to the world around them had helped millions to understand their values and ideas. In the heyday of radio and television, these men, and women and many like them maintained their vision of what they believed the founding fathers had expected the country to become. For many years, this was an agreeable format and all prospered.

*****

A group of recluses had survived in the communal life camps their parents had formed in the cannabis-saturated counties of the central west coast. The development of this quixotic commune life seemed more appealing to these sincere yet ever increasingly socially withdrawn remnants. They did have one obsession and concession to the modern world outside their confines, the internet; they soon became masters at embellishing and spinning the societal bliss they had created in this imagined social utopia.

After a few years, a network of these like-minded offshoots had started to influence others who were falling prey to their daily spin of life removed from reality.

They had organized into a network targeting and influencing the naïve, the under-experienced and unseasoned of life's true lessons. The promise of a nirvana-like life path was throwing out spores like a fungus ripening in the wind. These socially progressive philosophies flourished in the liberal ground zeroes of the colleges, universities, and institutions, many in the northeast and west coast.

From the cocoon of tenure, the cogs of these elite institutions influenced tens of thousands of malleable students to succumb to this siren song. From their protected, predictable, and unchallenged lives came a resentment of those whose paths in life were not parallel to their own.

Some of these malleable students become savvy in the further development of the internet and what was to be software platforms of social interactions and its companion platforms began to grow into something no one had envisioned. The world now had instant access to information on anyone and anything that could be imagined....and manipulated and controlled.

Often their targets of displeasure and scorn were the very foundations of the economy. While some of the criticism held kernels of authentic concern, the criticism mutated into conflict supported by underground groups that had malevolent agendas. While often these televised actors in these conflicts were just paid inciters to stir up a mob and violence, the product was a social divide that only grew more pronounced.

When the episodes of televised violence and senseless destruction became a daily event, many of the unfortunate targets of this agenda were the blameless independent middle class business owners.

These were the risk takers and achievers who sought to leave a legacy for their family and employees. They built their businesses by the sweat of their brows. They built their small and large businesses by inventiveness and innovation. They built their business with the knowledge attained from the College of Hard Knocks. They were allies in a capitalistic system. They believed an individual's ability and desire was his only limitation. A sovereign individual was the goal to their way of life.

Eventually this philosophy of independence could not mesh with the collective mindset of the progressives. Whether it was the progressives' inability to deal with individuals who they did not care to debate and understand, or just the base envy of those who had produced and were beginning to reap the rewards of years of dedication, a conflict of ideals was on an imminent crash course.

The progressives had spawned a generation who were involved with other *"causes du jour"* and filtered into the rough and tumble world of politics. Many became speechwriters or policy advisors for ranking government officials. They, drop by drop, began to change the direction of the topics. The course of what were the most important issues of the day was being directed by the new generation of wizards behind the curtain.

THE SHOWDOWN AT THE U.S.A. CORRAL

HOW DO WE CONTAIN THESE PEOPLE, THE AIDE to the California congresswoman complained. I've been pulling my hair out over the amount of water these farmers are diverting from the river basin. The aide, Ms. Venus Hurlewicz-Jackson, was a hired consultant for the congresswoman from the Bay area.

Congresswoman, you need these new voters in your district if you are going to get re-elected, and they are passionate about the spotted yellow darter and the purple climbing mussel. We must protect them if you expect to stay in office.

But Venus, the congresswoman replied, the farmers need that water if they are to have produce for market.

I don't care about the damn farmers, she shouted back angrily.

You need to get re-elected, and those damned farmers are not in your district. We need to side with the new voters in those blocks in your district, and that's it. The vote to reduce water to the irrigation canals is next week. I need to tell these people you are with them and the darter and the mussel.

What about the farmers, what do I tell them, the congresswoman questioned her hired gun.

Tell' em to kiss your ass, you got the Feds on your side, I know it's going to be law and if they don't like, they can kiss your ass, they Ms. Hurlewicz-Jackson fired back.

Okay, already, okay. Tell them I'm with them.

Venus screamed to no one in particular, *those damn talk radio jockeys. I've got to shut them up. If they didn't get hold of this issue, we wouldn't have this problem, I'll fix their asses!*

The farmers did not get their water and the crop losses amount to four-hundred eighty -five million dollars and over eleven thousand full-time and temporary jobs were lost that season.

The next year, a new school of yellow spotted darter was found in Oregon and another in Northern California. The urban outdoorsmen and homeless encampments that surrounded the area discovered the purple climbing mussels on the occasionally exposed rocks in the river.

Before Fish and Wildlife employees had come to check on their population, over half of the known inhabitants had been picked clean by the members of the encampment with impromptu clam bakes. No one was ever held responsible.

After the water was diverted away from the irrigation canals, the farmers and their employees started to flood talk radio and letters to the editor and the state house. The polls were eighty percent in favor of the farmers. The local talk radio stations were getting to the reasons the individual elected officials had voted in the manner they did. When they finally were able to interview the congresswoman, she claimed the Federal ruling as she understood it to be.

The trouble was there was only a temporary ruling in effect. There was no reason the water had to be completely diverted away from the farmers. Ms. Hurlewicz-Jackson was unceremoniously fired but the congresswoman had been reelected.

It was only two months later that an opening at the FCC came to the attention of Ms. Hurlewicz-Jackson. She knew someone from her college days in the department, and four weeks later she was moving to Washington, D.C. but now she was Ms. Hurlewicz only.

Her husband had been having an affair with a farmer's wife.

VENUS GETS HER REVENGE

OKAY, EVERYONE, THIS IS VENUS HURLEWICZ, Commissioner Campbell said to the group. As you know, I am replacing Commissioner Mc Dowell, and we will have a lot of work ahead of us. I've brought in Venus to help in our determination if a reworked Fairness Doctrine is appropriate. I believe this is our biggest task at hand, so I would like to start on it, ASAP.

After the meeting, the commissioner pulled Venus to the side. Listen Venus, we've known each other since college. I'm going to be tied up with this internet hacking incident of the Department.

Damn, this is a real mess, and I don't know how long I'm gonna be tied up with it. Can't these people figure out a damn security protocol?

I'm going to count on you to take the lead for me on this renewed Fairness Doctrine crap. Honestly, all those radio guys have a right to their opinion, and I got no problem with opinion, but I'll go by what you decide. Just pass on your findings to the other commissioners and send me your final report, he casually said as he was leaving her office and closing the door behind him.

This is going to an easy job, she thought. *I'll pretend to go through stacks of reports and charts. I'll give myself a couple, maybe three months, and then,* she chortled, *I'll pull the plug on those bastards. I'll spend a couple of years here, get a pension, then I'm outta here. I'll show these sons of bitches,* she added with a chuckle.

Within six months the reworked Fairness Doctrine was reinstated. But not only reinstated, it was amended that in order to maintain a public broadcasting license, the individual broadcast entities had to hire a government-approved monitor, full-time, to make sure they did not "upset the fairness balance."

With the Supreme Court now tilted left, the outcome at best was challenging and uncertain. A few radio personalities attempted to ride it out. Even the smallest markets were commanded to bend to the FCC's new stricter rules.

A few major cable news outlets and major syndicated radio talk icons succeeded in taking the ruling all the way to the Supreme Court, but with the death of Judge Johnson and his replacement by long time left leaning, H.R. Clayton, the decision was decidedly in favor of the FCC's ruling.

The Fairness Doctrine had reduced the once-popular format to now as entertaining as watching paint dry. The public revolted and protested and had rallies in support of the old format. It was not going to be undone.

A few had private subscription on satellite service, a few were online. But the old business model was now unable to overcome the imposed changes.

The true story of how and why the decision had been made was brought to light by someone at, ironically, the FCC.

George Lopez was actually a big fan of talk radio and an occasional caller. He was shocked at the so-called in-depth decision made in his office. He knew it had to do with the hiring of Venus, because no one else agreed with the decision but they were afraid to confront the new commissioner. George wanted to get to the bottom of this.

He reasoned, *I'll ask Venus to dinner and see if she is willing to talk about it.*

After three glasses of wine, Venus exposed the truth like an exotic dancer with a $50 bill in her face. George had a prepared statement when he was called to reveal what he had learned. He relayed how Venus consulted with no one in the office, and because of a personal vendetta against talk radio networks, had manipulated the studies concerning any positive roll the format was providing for the public. She was transferred to the IRS, at a higher pay grade. However, it was decided not to reverse the ruling for five years or until the next administration decided to review it, whatever was first.

THAT'S ALL I CAN STAND;
I CAN'T STAND NO MORE

THERE WAS A SMALL AIRFIELD IN RURAL VIRGINIA between Fincastle and Troutville, just off route 220. It was part of a private club built back in the fifties. Rumor had it the big "families" from up in New York and New Jersey would "visit" sometimes for months when a group of senators or a congressmen would decide to use them as their "target" to get re-elected. The families would be unavailable for comment during these times. And no one could find them.

The club had changed owners several times over the years and been upgraded for various reasons. The present owner was a well-known head executive of a national network of radio and television stations. He had all the facilities installed if ever an occasion for an emergency radio or television broadcast needed to be aired.

After the actual story of the flippant decision on the reinstatement of the Fairness Doctrine had been uncovered, a pall fell over the industry. Then anger and disgust and finally, resolve. A movement emerged to take control of their situation. If the government could carelessly, single-handedly destroy these owners and their empires, then there was little protection afforded to any who dared to protest the system.

On a chilly autumn morning, the airfield began to filled up with a variety of small twin engine private planes and jets. From the aircraft emerged a mixed group of men and women. Most were dressed as though they were planning to attend a top-level executive meeting.

Roger Murphy, a barrel-chested mountain of a man, spoke first to the privately assembled group of over four dozen owners and personalities.

"Some of you may know me already, I am Roger Murphy, he started. I am the founder of Media and Broadcast Incorporated. I thank you for appearing on such short notice on this brisk autumn day.

Let me start by saying I love this country. I love the opportunities once afforded to me and the chance to build this company with the help of some of you here today. Others of you have organizations that might even compete with us, but you are welcome here. I welcome you because together we face a struggle, dare I say unbending antagonist, that we cannot defeat.

This adversary has by its own incompetence and megalomania damned the rights that are supposed to be God-given. For over two hundred sixty years, this country has protected a man's peace of mind to know that an individual's labor and effort could lead him to the path of success. These people would place much on the line and sometimes risk all to further the goals they had set for themselves.

What is the threat that they pose to this adversary? The threat is that they exist, their beliefs, their raison d'etre. It is to create, to build, to think for themselves, free from the demands and weight of those who had not learned the rewards from self-accomplishment.

I cannot and will not live in a world where am I damned for producing and then singled out and persecuted when I decide to benefit from some of these fruits of my own labor.

Roger slammed his fist on the table where they had gathered.

I cannot continue to live in a country where I am the enemy. I cannot continue to operate in an atmosphere where my God-given rights mean nothing!

This new philosophy, where coddling the unmotivated and perpetuating the inept is alien to me! Overruling the lessons our fathers and grandfathers have taught us of hard work and constant self-improvement is inconceivable to me. I, for one, do not wish to be a party to this deranged syndrome. Unlike some, I do not wish to spend the time I have left on this earth convincing the inconvincible. I, for one, do not wish to be party to those whose main objective is to, through some perverted social osmosis, live off the results of my sweat and labor.

A country where this is the rule cannot last, and I, for one, no longer want any part of it!

Gentlemen and ladies, I have fought in two wars for this country and have the scars to prove it. I have had to watch as some of my best friends died just feet away from me.

I never thought I would see the day when I would not do or give everything I humanly could for this country.

My friends, he paused as he tried to regain his composure and quickly wipe away the beginnings of a tear.

This is not a country I recognize anymore. We have little by little lost what we understood the founding fathers intended for this country.

To you who are gathered here today, I pledge to begin to restore the vision our forefathers fought and died to preserve. And to honor all those whose blood was shed to give the promise of freedom and the promise to prosper with no limitations or interference from an overbearing and myopic government. From this day forward, I am dedicated to the formation of the concept of **New America.**

It will be as the framers intended, it will be as the founding fathers envisioned. It will be for those who wish to control their own futures. It will be unfettered by the mediocre and incompetent. It will be a haven for those who wish to advance by the efforts of the sweat of their own brows and the rewards that only God gives to those who have come to learn that lesson. It will be a rebirth of the individual and the freedom to be so.

I cannot promise to you I will be able to achieve this without your help. I cannot promise you I will be able to achieve this at all. But it will be soon time to decide. It may be the biggest of your lives, but decide you must, and it will be made if we are to expect to carry on the dreams and wishes of our forefathers.

We have been, as have others who have accomplished much, singled out by those who cannot fathom or will not try to understand what was sacrificed to pursue our dreams. We are expected to bear the burden of a system that has eroded to the point of near non-functioning. Yet our yearly homage to the modern-day mighty Rome is now unbearable and increases without forethought.

Gentlemen and ladies, this is the direction I plan for myself. I hope some of you here believe as I do and can agree with my decision. I will plan to prepare for your input and to meet with all interested parties. I will advise you to the details pending your responses."

The group agreed to meet in a month. They knew they were the critical mass. If it was decided to proceed, they might not be able to resume the businesses they had built. The revenge for separating and daring to assert their new independence might forever label them persona non grata. It could very well be the decision that generations might thank or curse them for making.

* * * * *

Roger Murphy had retired to his study with a few close associates who had been with him from the formation of the media giant. A large stone fireplace blazed with the hardwoods of apple and hickory. The aroma and the glow of the fire almost removed the seriousness of the moment. Roger had been saving this Napoleon brandy for an occasion that had now arrived. He opened it with all the care he could as if he were handling a newborn baby.

My friends, please share with me a toast to the endeavor we are about to begin. I believe in all my heart we will begin to blaze a trail that many of us will not see finished. He paused. This torch we are about to carry will be handed off to many, each bringing it closer to the goal we seek and farther from where we came. It is to those who have caused us to start down this road I offer these words:" **Pugh E Mahone.**"

They clinked their glasses and finished the brandy.

THE DIE IS CAST

THE FIVE FRIENDS HAD EXPERIENCED THE JOYS and travails of nearly forty years of friendship. They had gone their own ways and had settled throughout the country. But they all seemed to share the same conclusion. Things were not looking all that good for the future.

Tom had already retired after twenty-five years with the police force. He had invested wisely and was doing okay, but the additional new taxes and fees on his income and dividends were beginning to hurt. The increasing inflation had now begun to make everyday items more expensive. He had not anticipated these events at this stage of his life.

Ian had become a master mason and loved working on old houses. He would always say,

Every stone tells you a story, just look at it and it will tell you where it wants to go.

Even though it was a tough New England economy, Ian always had work. He spent years restoring his eighteenth-century home. Every board had to be as close to period correct as possible. Every stone in the walls had to be native. It was just his way. He loved his work. And his customers kept him busy.

Russ had found his way down south. He was new to the company that had just been in existence a few years. They were establishing themselves as a consulting and managing company for large arenas throughout the country. The company was flourishing, and Russ was climbing the corporate ladder quickly.

Before the end of his second decade with the company, he was a senior partner and was able to open his own division office. Life had been kind to the big fellow so far.

Jake had learned the ropes and wires of being the maintenance supervisor of a high- tension transmission line crew. If it wasn't over one hundred fifteen kV, he wouldn't mess with it. He had put in twenty years and now had five crews to manage. He had a few more years and kids to put through college and he would be home free.

Within six months of the new administration's change in direction of established policies, there were signs of serious trouble in the now seriously weakened economy. The inflation that the Secretary of the Treasury had predicted was hitting rates not seen since post-war Germany in 1920. The dollar, which was already as buoyant as a brick, was sinking even faster.

The public refused to participate in any more money-losing Treasury bill schemes. In fact, many Asian and European countries were considering cashing in a trillion and a half dollars' worth and letting the chips fall where they may.

Hell, they might end up with Manhattan, the way things were going.

The specter of trouble began to manifest itself in a myriad of ways for the friends.

First, Jake and the crews were laid off, and then when they were called back it was for only three days a week.

Ian's mason work abruptly stopped, cold, end of story.

Russ found that the public arenas were farming out all work and management to a company based out of India. The Indian company was sending twice as many people in to manage the facilities for half the cost. After years of personally building relationships with the customers, it was the almighty dollar that had put him at a disadvantage he could not overcome.

Tom was managing to hold on, but when the stock market lost over fifty percent of its value in such a short time, he sold out most of his positions and tried to regroup and rethink his plan to survive.

All were terrified they would end up losing all they had. They contacted each other over the following weeks to check to see how each was dealing with the increasingly worsening situation.

MEETING AT BAD SODEN

James and his brother, Joe, had taken over the family business. It was an old-line business and at one time had offices throughout the world. Now most of their business was in Asia and the occasional trip to Europe.

During the last trip to Frankfurt, James met Charles McGavock. They had both been staying in Bad Soden, a small village about twenty miles from the center of the city. It was beautiful, clean as a whistle and the air in February was crisp and clear. The walk from the Tyrolian styled hotel brought them down a hill through the center of the little village. The story book like village was filled with bakery shoppes and cafes and restaurants of all kinds. The villagers would stop at the cafes before catching the morning train to the center of the city.

"Guten morgen," the baker greeted all his regular customers. It was early in the morning and James and Joe were on the way to the Frankfurt trade fair for their business. The morning air was crisp and invigorating when they stopped for coffee and rolls. There, at the next table was Charles McGavock.

Good morning, gentlemen, Charles pleasantly addressed the two.

Good morning to you, sir, James replied, but how did you know we were not locals?

Oh easy. I have been visiting this village for quite some time and usually it is only during the trade fair do new faces make it out this far. I love it out here, it is a wonderful place.

I see by your official badges you must be heading to the city center this morning.

Charles cheerfully added, wonderful event, I've have enjoyed it in the past, so many things to see. Joe piped in, Charles, are you involved in international trade too?

No, no longer, I am afraid. I have a position now where I do get to visit with my old customers from that business, Charles stated matter of factually. No, now I have a mission of sorts.

What type of mission, James asked innocently.

Charles leaned over in their direction, I interview and recruit candidates for a new corporation of sorts.

Well, what do you mean, a corporation of sorts, James couldn't help but ask.

My associates and I have a vision. As businessmen from the States, you may find some aspects of this idea of interest. I will tell you in advance, it may take a while to digest the scope of my associates' plan.

James and Joe were now intrigued by the proposal. They finished their coffee and together boarded the morning train to the center of Frankfurt.

Charles explained, James, Joseph, what we are represents a new corporate structure of sorts, but on a scale not ever attempted before. We would consider those who have the conviction to become shareholders in residence the pioneers of maybe the greatest corporation to date.

James rolled his eyes, Charles, what is this, Microsoft, Apple, IBM, and Berkshire Hathaway, all in one, for five dollars?

No, James, no it's not, it's more. We are the idea of what you have just described and tens of thousands more. We offer more than just stock ownership alone, we offer to those who can see the goal of this corporation, the freedom promised long ago by some incredibly wise men. Ownership in this company promises to uphold and preserve the rights that are God-given.

Gentlemen, I have only provided a primer, if you will, I cannot represent what we in this, well for now, let's categorize it as a corporation, have set as goals. I can only say that as citizens of the U.S., you must by now recognize the dangerous mutations the country has and is still experiencing. We hope to offer a solution or at least an option to those who feel affected in a manner contrary to their true beliefs.

Charles' manner had shifted to serious yet still pleasant. I am planning to be in the States in a week's time. I feel as though we should meet again so we can truly review the scope of the mission I have now dedicated myself . With all the faith I can muster, I genuinely believe in the goals of the corporation.

Charles smiled and reached in his suit jacket pocket for his business cards. I only give out just a few of these, he said only half-joking. James, Joseph, how may I plan to contact you?

They both hurriedly reached in their wallets for their cards.

Charles replied, fine, gentlemen, I will plan to confirm with you no later than, say, the end of the month. Does that sound agreeable?

Agreed, they said in unison.

They all exited the train at Main Station, Charles toward the airport and James and Joe toward the train to the Trade fair.

CLIVE'S CONNECTION

DONNA LOOMIS DID CALL CLIVE AS SHE PROM-
ised. I talked to my friend, and he was working at the Washington
Monument on Sunday, she said. He was there in the afternoon
about three when he took a ten-minute break. Donna continued,
Then he said he was walking back to work when he heard a
firecracker or something. Then he said 'all hell broke loose but
I couldn't find out what had happened. I think somebody must
have shot something off, but nobody knew for sure. He thinks
it must have had something to do with all the people protesting
but he isn't sure. But the strangest thing about it he said was
when he asked his supervisor about it the next day. He got a
strange response, like what did you see and where were you and
what did you hear, like he had something to do with it. And
then the strangest thing of all happened. He said the supervisor
looked at him like he had just run over her dog.

If you were smart you would forget you heard or saw anything,' she said, as if she didn't want to be bothered by any of
this story.

Clive, what do you think happened, she asked, like she
had stumbled over a dead body. This is scary. Clive responded,
Donna, I don't know, but I'm just as sure as I can be something
bad happened, but It just doesn't make sense.

Then Clive told Donna about the tape he had made and
what he saw that afternoon. She was afraid for him.

She quizzed him; Does **anybody** know you recorded this?

Just you and that's it. He knew her concern was genuine.

Is there anybody you can trust in town to take the tape to and show it?

Clive knew of only one man he could trust in town.

He had helped his father back in Tuscaloosa. It was Senator Silsbee.

Richard Silsbee had been a country lawyer in Alabama, He eventually was selected to a judgeship in Tuscaloosa. That was where he met Henry Johnson.

Henry was a tall black man with a deep voice like God would have. Henry was a farmer with eighty acres outside of town. When a big box store wanted to come to town, they decided part of the farm Henry owned was land they needed for their parking lot. Henry agreed to talk to them, but their offer was not nearly the price Henry could accept. The big box stores lawyers tried everything they could, include throwing him off his land.

That was when Henry met the judge, in his courtroom. The judge understood Henry's situation. This was not the first time a big chain of stores had tried this. The judge came down on Henry's side.

Judge Silsbee said, If this national concern wants this property, then they will satisfy Mr. Johnson. If not, Alabama is a big state, I am certain they can find another location.

The judge and Henry had been friends ever since that day.

Clive was concerned and nervous that the senator would not remember him or his father when he called his office to ask if they could meet.

Why of course I remember Henry Johnson, the senator said on the phone. And how are you, Clive? I hear you are in law school now, is that right?

Yes, sir, I am, thank you for asking ,Clive replied.

You know, I saw your father when I was back in town over the holidays.

How is he, son, I hope he is well.

The senator had concern in his voice for his old friend. Oh, don't you worry sir, he's doing fine. Well then, son, what brings you to my office?

Clive tried to recite the events of Sunday afternoon in a calm manner. But when he told the senator about the tape he had recorded, he could see a look on the senator he had not seen before. The Senator's face was flushed, and he became nervous and genuinely concerned.

Clive, have you shown this tape to anyone, anyone at all?

Shown the tape, not shown, no sir. Clive insisted. But I have told one girl in class about it.

He was almost embarrassed to admit. Clive handed him the recording.

Until we examine this tape, do not speak a word of it, and for God's sake make sure your friend doesn't either. I'm not sure what you may have recorded, but this could be extremely important, the Senator said firmly. I'll stay in contact with you. If you don't hear from me in a day or so, please stay in touch, but call me at this number, it is my private line. The Senator wrote down the number on the back of his card.

Clive felted a wave of relief sweep over him. He still didn't understand all the repercussions of the event. But he was sure he had contacted the right person. He had to make sure Donna did not say anything to anyone. He had to see her right away.

A CHANGE IN THE WIND

Abbey and James were sitting at the large tavern table overlooking the garden. Through the bay window the sun was starting to filter into the great eighteenth century house.

I need to drive up to Boston for an interview, said Abbey. And I'm a little nervous about it.

The drive or the interview, James asked. Maybe both, Abbey responded.

James looking up from the local morning newspaper, smiled and said, Hey, it's no problem, I'll drive, I haven't been to Boston since I visited my sister when I was sixteen.

It was a great weekend. She took me to this old Irish bar called The Plough and Stars,

I was drinking Guinness with her in one of the back booths, it was great.

Abbey gave him a funny look and said, get real, I've got an interview at Radcliffe for college, and I don't really know what to expect.

Abbey, James interjected, you are one of the smartest girls I know, you'll do great.

She gave him a glance that said with her eyes, I don't believe you, but thanks.

* * * * *

The interview went off without a hitch, but Abbey was concerned.

Why would they ask if you would rather live in the country or the city?

What did you tell her, James asked as they were walking back to the car.

I just said I don't really know, I just felt so stupid. Abbey was worried, it was her first big Ivy League interview. I blew it, she sighed. James couldn't resist.

Abbey, I'm afraid you're right, this is the kind of remark that will follow you the rest of your life. I'm sure the next interviewer is sure to see that you could not decide between the country and the city. Oh well, Miss, we'd like to hire you for this position, but we see you don't know where you want to live.

She whacked him on the arm and smiled. After a moment she asked,

Have you ever been to Hampton Beach?

James looked at her. In Virginia?

No, you big dummy, in New Hampshire! she replied.

There's a beach in New Hampshire? he answered.

You know for a senior and what are you going to school for, engineering?

You're not too smart. Yes, there's a beach in New Hampshire, she playfully fired back.

Get in the car, I'll drive.

* * * * *

Hampton Beach wasn't much of a beach; it was more like a big rock pile with some sand mixed in.

I used to love it up here. After work I would sneak into this music hall and listen to the bands, Abbey told him. She pointed up the beach to an old dance hall and bar.

James looked at her. What do you mean, work?

Oh yeah, last summer I was a maid at one of the beach motels.

James was really puzzled. Let me get this right, you were up here all summer working by yourself, last summer, weren't you like only sixteen?

What's wrong with that, she responded like she meant to say, I can take care of myself.

James thought about it for a second and replied, Nothing, I would think it was unusual for a young lady to be here by herself for so long. No, it was fun; I wish I could do it again.

James could only reply, well, good for you.

But the truth was, James was extremely impressed, her hook was set in him, deep. She was smart, beautiful, and independent. He was in trouble.

The remaining summer days and nights were heaven sent. They would drive to the beach at night just to sit together on the sand and hold each other. The nights were made for them, and this was their time.

* * * * *

September had come as he knew it would and yet while they were together all was right in the world.

It was the night before he would move to college, and he needed to tell her how much he had tried to control the feelings he had for her. He wanted to never let anything ever come between them, but he needed to let her know he had lost that battle. He cared for her very much and wanted to see her as much as he could.

She spoke at first softly. All things do sometimes come to an end, we had a fun summer and I care for you very much, but this is not the time. I will someday want or need the love you have for me, but you and I have our lives ahead of us. I need to be out in the world more before I can accept what you want to give to me. I am not ready for the gift you have placed here. Maybe someday, but not now. She kissed him as she had before and walked away.

James had seen her just a very few times over the years.

He eventually moved from New England to the South like so many others. This was where the fast track and the business had found a new home. It was way past the time to get dug in.

THE FORMAL SEPARATION

COME ON IN, CHARLES. ROGER MURPHY SPOKE to him from outside his office. Charles, how have you been? Roger seemed upbeat, more so than he had seen him in a long while.

Very well, sir, thank you for asking, he replied, feeling more at ease now. In the room with Roger were John McManus, one of the major cable television figures, and Ross Liden a major syndicated radio personality and co-founder of Media and Broadcast Corp.

Charles, Roger started, I am sure you understand that we all have been working intently to fulfill the goal we have set for ourselves. I wanted to be the first to tell you we have an agreement with the present governing officials in Dominica. We can transfer to them their ownership stake and certificates in New America as of the first of the month. Because of your dedication and the teams, you have assembled, we have the initial funds to make agreement payments to the Dominicans who are to be founders in New America with us. Roger was beaming.

Your teams will now need to contact the parties who have given to us the deposits and update them as to when we will convene in Dominica to discuss the initial needs for them to prepare to become citizen stockholders. I have contacted the committed hotel chains and they will begin construction as of the first of this coming month. The airfield in Roseau will begin the three-thousand-foot extension to the main runway and improvements soon after.

John and Ross both patted Charles on the shoulder. Good job, good job, Charles.

He could at last see the progress he had hoped would come to fruition.

Gentlemen I think our new offices in Dominica can be readied in ninety days. We should be prepared to make our formal announcement soon after that. Roger started to explain the details ahead of them that needed to be addressed.

As fellow founders of New America, I feel as though we must be ready for any unexpected reaction from this government as we complete the transfer of stockholders and resources. We may need to transfer as much as we are able prior to the formal notice. I will plan to meet the present Prime Minister in Roseau to coordinate our announcements and to address all founding citizen stockholders in New America. We will meet again with the present Dominican people to reaffirm their acceptance of becoming citizen shareholders. I want them to understand all that is being done is so all can go forward, so all experience the best everyone can contribute. We will need their skills and cooperation of all to prosper. We also will need their voices and input to ensure the future of New America. I hope they understand that every individual is important here. Without the Dominicans supporting our individual efforts, this plan may fail from the start.

One priority is to inform the banking citizen shareholders to begin establishing their branches and offices. We will need to begin our banking system immediately and start to convert to our own currency. We will need above all stability in the currency. We can't allow ourselves to be affected by any further downdrafts in the dollar.

Gentlemen, that's it for the present, let's keep moving forward. Let's meet Friday morning of the twenty-ninth before we fly to Roseau.

John and Ross agreed. They all were looking forward the event.

HOTEL WASHINGTON

JAMES REACHED FOR HIS CELL PHONE AS HE walked into his office. Hello, is this James or Joseph, the voice on the other end asked.

This is James. Well hello, James, this is Charles McGavick.

Charles, my old friend, how are you? Fine, fine, and Joseph, how is he? Good, he's good.

Well, I needed to contact you and your associates, we have an initial commencement date in Dominica. As such, I will need to meet with you and your associates to finalize ownership. As a condition of our agreement with the officials in Roseau, we can only allow a maximum of ten-thousand new citizen owners a year to be able to relocate. So, after the maximum is reached, you will have to wait until the next available relocation date opens. I strongly suggest that we meet in Washington D.C, possibly the first week of next month, and make final all the documents. Would you prefer I contact your associates to finalize the process?

No, Charles, let me handle that and I will confirm with you on the first week of May.

Very good, very good, I have reserved rooms at the Hotel Washington; it is close to the monument and the Smithsonian Institution. I'm sure you will find it most agreeable.

Great, I will contact the others and confirm.

Very good, my friend, very good... wait a moment, hold on a second, James. Then there was a long, almost painfully pause.

Uh, oh, oh my, I didn't think this would transpire this early on, Charles said over the phone, not realizing he was talking to James.

Then Charles' voice changed. James, I fear you may want to turn on the telly. There is an announcement from your President and the Treasury Secretary. This may influence our plans.

Oh, okay, Charles, call me back in a half an hour if you would.

James turned on the television in his office and sat down to watch. The announcement was from the President. He was beginning to outline his executive order EO 21876-A. At the same time, a split screen showed the Dow Jones Averages and all markets beginning to react to the rumored wording of the order. The averages were dropping, and fast.

The Dow had dropped five hundred points in ten minutes. It now was breaking news on all major broadcast networks. As the news began to filter out, people stopped in their tracks and watched on their cell phone or TV or listened to a radio. The phone did ring thirty minutes later.

James, I'm afraid your President Delacourte is going to accelerate our plans. I see the markets are already reacting terribly to this announcement. I just never imagined anyone would ever be so bloody foolish, Charles said, almost incredulous to the initial statements.

James was in near shock. Well, I'll be damned, this is absolutely unbelievable. Do they have the first idea what they're doing? They can't think they can pull this off.

By the end of the day the Dow had fallen nearly two thousand points. The overseas markets would confirm if those markets were just as surprised and shocked. Within twenty-four hours, the financial markets would confirm what Charles and his group foresaw and prepared for.

James would begin to prepare for the transition. He would contact the others and coordinate for the meeting in D.C.

It wasn't needed. Within the hour, they had called him. Russ asked if they could meet earlier, possibly next week. As did they all.

Charles, James began, what if we speed up the meeting, maybe next week?

James, I understand you and your associates are anxious to begin to protect yourselves, but I have appointments and meeting in place. We might meet on, say, the first Saturday and finish our business, and then you may take a farewell tour of the Washington area. You may enjoy it even more, knowing you already have an exit plan. We will meet on Saturday instead on Monday, but that would be as much as we can allow.

Well, okay, I will pass along the plan then, James replied.

Very well, my friend, the first Saturday in May, we can plan for twelve noon.

Charles was trying being a calming influence, but he could tell the tension was building everywhere.

FIRST SATURDAY IN MAY

James was used to getting up early. When he went down to the lobby of the Hotel Washington, the coffee shop wasn't to open until six a.m. There was plenty of time to walk out around the Mall and the Ellipse and the Washington Monument. The mist and the fragrances of the early morning would still filter through the just rising sun.

James slowly observed the sights and the magnificent buildings. It was such a shame that buildings that were once the symbols of freedom and opportunity now were just empty shells that long ago had lost what greatness they represented.

As he made his way back to the hotel, James noticed a few buses had lined up in front of the hotel and the lobby had begun to fill with guests lining up at the registration desk to sign in and check out. He made his way through the crowd and headed to grab a table at the coffee shop. A man in the corner booth motioned to him. Already seated was Russ.

Always get up early do ya, he half mumbled through the porcelain coffee cup.

Well, it's force of habit, all those years of getting up at dark-thirty, James quipped.

Yeah, yeah, have some coffee and let's get somethin' to eat, already.

Where is everybody, James replied as he poured from the coffee carafe.

Ah, giv'em another ten minutes and they'll be down.

James was reaching for the sugar bowl when he thought he heard a familiar voice. He whirled around to see who was in the lobby. The lobby was now filled with tourists and young children. Others were mulling around, waiting for the bank of elevators to take them up to their rooms. James scanned the lobby for a second and went back to his coffee cup and his now fully awake friend.

What are you looking at, Russ asked. Nothing, nothing, I guess, I thought I heard something.

James remembered how he had embarrassed himself on one of his trips to Hong Kong. He thought to himself, *That woman could have been her twin.*

He had come up to a woman sitting at the airport bar and tapped her on the shoulder. He was so sure it was her.

Abbey? She whirled around and knocked her drink all over. **No, not Abbey!** If she had a knife, it would have been in his chest.

I'm so sorry, James replied and would have been glad if she had plunged it in him.

I'm so sorry. He stooped down to help wipe the spilled drink up off the table and floor.

I thought you were an old friend; you look just like her.

Well, okay, but as you can see, **I'm not.**

Her female companion, who was almost as mad, jumped in, Come on, Melissa, let him clean up, we gotta catch our flight.

The feeling that everyone in the terminal had now turned to stare and mumbled in unison, what an asshole, was just beginning to diminish when he passed her again on his way to his gate. Every dagger she could shoot out of her eyes had cut through him a hundred times as she walked by.

This was enough to curtail any more of this type of inquiry.

James and all his now assembled friends were discussing the morning plans and meeting with Charles.

Well, Russ and I are gonna head over to the Washington Monument, started Ian. Then we'll meet up with Jake and Tom around eleven back here.

Sounds good, said James. I'll meet you back here then.

James headed up to shower and put his feet up for a while and got ready to meet Charles. He had all the confirmation information he needed to give to Charles in a manila envelope and that would be it, it would be done.

At around ten minutes to eleven, James headed back down to the lobby. As the doors to the elevator opened, he started out, looking in his blazer pocket to make sure he had all the documents for the meeting.

Walking toward the restaurant in the back corner of the hotel lobby, he was sure he had heard a familiar laugh. He stopped for a moment and glanced around the lobby, but by now the area was busy and groups of people had come and gone in just minutes.

Just in front of the maître d' station was Charles and the now gathered group of friends.

Good to see you, James. Shall we take a table and review recent events in Roseau?

That would be great, I am anxious to hear the latest.

Well, I am sure you will be pleased, I have some of the latest photos of the expanded airfield and the Old Towne center. The group moved to the maître d' and asked for the corner table away from the rest of the guests.

Gentlemen, Charles began, I could never foresee the events that are unfolding before us. When I was approached by Mr. Roger Murphy and his associates, I was sure that it would be several more years before we reached this point. The pure amateur foolishness of this administration has certainly exacerbated and accelerated the financial and constitutional crises. None of this was predicted. Charles' words were words that seemed to almost underestimate and understate what the group understood.

Gentlemen, I am relieved that we have had the foresight and courage to take this undertaking to its conclusion. While all here understand our task is just beginning, I know in my heart we have made the absolute best decision we could. I know you all will have concerns over what you are leaving. I can only offer to you, do not, I repeat, do not, look back with regret. The ones who are responsible for this situation are now faceless. This country's condition was not the product of one administration alone, although it may have been avoided with competence in this current leadership.

Mr. Murphy knew at some point there was a point of no return for the country, and that this new undertaking, a restart from the ground up, was the only option. We will take to heart the painful lessons learned from the mistake of the indifference to financial reality.

Gentlemen, I trust you have confirmation of your wire transfers for the last payments for your portion of ownership into New America. If so, we can take the opportunity of this meeting to finalize the documents. Charles was filling with pride at all that had been accomplished.

We have a commencement date of Monday, August 1st. On that date the legally binding contracts with the citizen owners will take effect. You will be free to transition as you wish, although conditions here may encourage a more accelerated process. Gentlemen, please let me sign off on your documents and propose a toast.

To all, "Au salute." Charles beamed cheerfully.

Glasses were raised and clinked together in toast. "Au Salute."

* * * *

Sunday morning the group was heading back to catch their respective flights. James had decided to stay a day or so longer. He had a feeling the opportunities to visit here again would most likely be nil. There were things worth seeing and so he would relax and walk around town and make his peace with the country that had at one time offered so much but now seemed intent on stripping most of it away.

It was not much of a decision to leave behind all they had spent most of their lives building. It would only be difficult to say goodbye to all the people they had worked with for all these years. They had only received offers on the factory and office building of half of what it was worth. They took what they could get for the assets and closed. There wasn't much sense of trying to soldier on because most of their customers had gone out of business or retired. The largest customers still open knew they could make demands that were great for them but left little or no profit. Now with the dollar losing value and components more and more expensive, it was just a losing game.

The last of the inventory would be sold off next week. Then the closing on the building and that would be it. It wasn't the end of the company; it would be just restarted. The 150-year-old company would live again, just somewhere else.

THE SAGA OF ROCCO'S AUTO SUPPLY

It was 1948 and a young man from Naples, Italy, Rocco Mastrianni decided he would listen to his cousin and move to America. He would book passage on a steamer heading to New York. He planned to find work and then bring his family as soon as he could.

With the help of his cousin's family, he was able to find work in one of the small restaurants on Mulberry Street in little Italy. Every morning he would clean the fresh fish and shrimp, then make the pasta and bread dough for the evening dinners, and at night he would move to the double sink and wash the evening's pots and pans. Twelve hours a day for weeks at a time. Only the holidays gave a day off.

Rocco was working in the kitchen one morning when an old paisano from Naples stopped in and looked him up. Giovanni Romano had come to America a year earlier. But unlike many, he had landed in the Los Angeles area. He was doing very well repairing and replacing auto body parts. He had discovered he could use the skills he learned repairing ship hulls in Naples and apply it to the ever-growing auto repair needs in the now sprawling L.A. area.

Rocco had worked with Giovanni before deciding to move to America, so he had some of the skills in demand. Giovanni promised him he would make the money he needed to get his family to Los Angeles in weeks, not months or years.

Two weeks later Rocco found himself in a small apartment near Venice. His job was to scour the now filling up junk yards and scrap yards, looking for fenders, hoods and door panels that could be repaired and reused. With little or no cost for panels, Rocco and Giovanni could use their skills and bring new life to the previously unwanted parts. They could in turn sell the repaired parts to do-it-yourselfers and used car lots wanting to save money.

The endeavor soon was very profitable. Within six months there were ten other metal workers, banging out dents and straightening hoods and trunk lids. Rocco's family, his wife and three boys were able to come to Los Angeles soon after that. The two entrepreneurs decided a larger facility was needed, and in 1954 they opened a new facility in Pasadena just off Colorado Boulevard. The business expanded into new parts and servicing the new "hot rod" scene. By 1963, their business had outgrown the Pasadena location and moved toward the expanding inland empire and moved to City of Industry. Here they bought a larger plot of land, over ten acres, and built a new one hundred thousand square-foot warehouse and office. They hoped this would be the last time they would need to move. For years they had poured in their sweat and labor and tears. The American dream was real, and this was a typical example.

In 1968, Californians had suffered enough of smog and air pollution. The regulation and rules began to slowly affect the auto business and changes were coming.

The newly formed EPA in the seventies began to flex its muscles. It began to force junk yards to close or control the runoff from all the decaying autos. Property taxes were soaring to pay for the expanding state-sponsored programs. The once profitable business was starting to suffer.

The families decided it would make sense to concentrate just on the performance and off-road part of the business and close the repair end. The large facility was broken up and space was rented out to other business. Now at least they could maintain the cost of expenses and still make a small profit. But the shadow of any further increase in taxes or fees could change all that overnight.

When Rocco Sr. passed away in 1997, Giovanni decided to sell his portion of the business to the children of Rocco. Although Giovanni and his wife of fifty-one years, Maria, were in their seventies, they decided to would move to the Old Country and spend his last remaining years in Villa Franca in Tuscany. Many of Maria's family lived just a few miles away in Pontremoli.

The mountain air and the nearby vineyards would be all he would need. The village of seventeenth century stone buildings and the small-town square with its open-air cafes and bakery shops would remove much of the traces of the stress of the last decades. If he felt as though he needed to visit Milan or Pisa, the train station was just few miles or so past the stone eighteenth century arched bridge that was part of the village center. They had already found a small townhouse just up the mountainside. The little twice a day bus service had a stop just down the road from the medieval looking stone homes.

Giovanni had maintained a strong relationship with his relatives in Italy. One of the advantages to this was that it made it easier to get an Italian passport. He and Maria had gone through the process, and both had received one. He had also opened an account at the local branch of the Banco di LaSpezia. None of the families knew it, but this would become particularly important in months to come.

The trip to visit the bank was a little difficult for Giovanni. To enter the bank, he had to enter a cylindrical rotating glass entrance. He stepped into the entrance way, stopped, then the glass cylinder spun so the opening exposed the lobby of the bank. He then walked into the bank.

This might be the best way to keep the bank robbing down to a minimum.

Buongiorno! Mister Romano, come in, come in, Rosa d 'Loretta beckoned to the elder gentleman. Good morning, Rosa, he responded to her. She looked like an angel, her dark silky thick hair glimmered in the morning light and her sweet voice made him wish he were fifty years younger.

Ah, yes, I see your wire transfer has come in from America, two hundred fifty-two thousand Euros, is that the expected amount? Yes, I believe the first wire was that amount, he responded, trying to hide his excitement. Now he could finally relax. The relatives would be glad dinner would be on him tonight. Life would begin anew at seventy for them.

The next morning as the sun had just peeked over the snow-covered range of mountains behind them, the telephone rang. At first the couple couldn't figure out what the noise was as the ring was so different.

Maria, it's the phone, pick up the phone.

Hello, hello. Rocky? Is that you?

Rocco Jr., or Rocky as the family called him, was calling from California.

Aunt Maria? How are you, how do you like it over there so far?

Oh, it is lovely, Rocky, I wish you and Stephano were here and all the family could be together for a while.

Well maybe soon auntie, maybe soon.

Bueno, Bueno, she replied, excitedly.

Lem'me talk to Uncle G. for a minute.

Uncle G. was Giovanni's favorite nickname and the kids called him that like it was his given name.

Hey Uncle G, how's it going over there?

Well, you know, it's not too bad. I think Maria likes havin' all her relatives around, so what's up?

Listen, the state has just reassessed all the property and the building with this new emergency tax these assholes decided they gotta have for the next couple a years, Rocky told him, trying to keep from losing his cool on the phone.

Well, what'ya gonna do, Rocky?

Stevie and I are thinking about comin' over for a week maybe a little less and talking to yous guys.

No shit! that's great! He pulled the phone away for a second. Hey, Maria, the kids say they're comin' over to visit! Okay, that's great, lem'me know when.

Okay Uncle G., I 'll let you know for sure in a couple three days.

After Rocky had hung up, he wondered out loud, hmmm, somethin's up back there, I don't know what, but it can't be good.

Giovanni was right thinking something was up.

*****

Stephano turned to Rocky, Hey if it wasn't hard enough before but now this HCA tax bullshit on top of it? Afanabola, those augauts!

Rocky, why are we bothering anymore? These goody-two-shoes in the capital are gonna make it impossible to make the money we used to make.

Listen, we got enough now, and this place is too full o' fruits and nuts with a broom uppa their ass over old cars. Rocky took the words out of his brother's mouth.

Yeah, I know, it's time to bail.

I know it's time too. It's been time for a while. Uncle G. has just made it easy for us.

Okay, let's sit down and pencil this thing out. We can see what we owe and how much we still gotta on the books.

If it's as bad as I think with this reassessment and HCA, we're toast, Rocky conceded.

DOMINICA

DUST FILLED THE AIR AT THE FAR END OF THE
1960's era airfield. Melville Hall Airfield had been barely able to
accommodate commercial aircraft. The tower and the facilities
desperately needed to be upgraded and modern facilities built
for the increase in traffic.

The airfield did, however, have a warm inviting feel that the
tropics provided.

The construction had been under way for several months
and in just a few more weeks the first of the commercial jets
should be able to touch down non-stop from the U.S.

Keeping the local charm of the old airport, the original
building had been converted to a first-class restaurant and bar
with a modern terminal built alongside. The grounds around
the building were covered neatly with the flora and fauna native
to the island. The roadway to the airfield from the newly completed Melville Hall Airfield Boulevard was landscaped with
palm trees, bird of paradise and orchids. The parrots and
conures had gathered around the fruit and banana trees at the
entrance, squawking in unison. It was just the right size. It was
inviting and warm yet functional. It was the proof that New
America would be a good citizen to the island.

The first few weeks would be a whirlwind because so much
would need to be done. The offices would be in Olde Roseau.
The streets there were stone and brick, in narrow, neat rows
that sloped up from the harbor along the river that ran through

the town all the way to the foot of the mountains in the center of the island.

Some of the very first to set up offices had selected from the rows of old three-story building near the river's entrance to the bay. From the second floors of these buildings with their balconies there was a beautiful view of Old Towne and the pristine ocean. The constant breeze and the scent of salt water was the best tonic for the hectic pace of the first few weeks of settling in.

All around as shareholder citizens arrived, more and more store fronts and shops appeared. Hotels and B&Bs, restaurants and seaside cafes started to dot the seaside boulevard. The first branch of the Bank of Roseau was now open. Small taxis and buses carried more and more arrivals all over the island by way of the new "South Ocean Parkway," paid for by a toll from the Melville Hall Airfield to Roseau, and now to the cruise and container ship docks in Marigot on the windward side of the island. The Cane Field airport just North of Roseau was also expanding to accommodate turbo prop aircraft from the other islands.

Dominica was growing, but not before the native Dominicans and the shareholder citizens agreed on the progress at every turn. The newly modernized Town Hall had a meeting the first and third Monday of every month. The morning meeting recapped the current progress, and the afternoon was reserved for native Dominicans to review the progress and recap how their shares were growing in wealth.

The Prime Minister, Pierre Boucharde` and Roger Murphy had become fast friends.

The Prime Minister was quick to grasp the genius in the New America. He knew if the plan were administered slowly and carefully, all would benefit. He knew he would need to ensure that the native Dominicans did not grow unhappy with the changes. It was his responsibility to demonstrate that these new arrivals would ensure that future Dominican generations would prosper with the citizens of New America. But it was also his responsibility to encourage the Dominicans to contribute to the new system. Because if they realized the benefits of ownership, they would only help to speed up the development of this experiment, this new nation, and their opportunity for wealth.

The tasks were numerous and the work daunting the first few months. But the progress was breathtaking.

Both the Prime Minister and Roger Murphy knew the island could only sustain a limited population. The areas that were agreed upon by both natives and new arrivals were certain tracts that were mainly on the coastal plains. The pristine mountains were to be maintained as an untouched nature preserve for a water source and to limit growth.

The agreed-to limit on additional population in total was fifty-thousand people. At the current rate of growth, this gave them a five-year window to develop and sustain the new nation.

After that, if all succeeded, other candidates' countries would have to be considered.

THE AUDACITY OF EGO

WHATTA 'YA MEAN THEY WON'T GO ALONG. THEY have to! They are going to! The words still reverberated outside the oval office. Chief of Staff, Jack St. Merde had to break to the President what the casual observer already knew.

The Southern states and most of the Plains states are not going to just bend over and take it, Jack told the President firmly.

Well then, the hell with them, I just signed an executive order, **that** fixes their asses.

Mr. President, I strongly advise you not push this!

Look, Jack, I **won**, the people elected me, that means I can do what the hell I think best! ...it`s for their own damn good.

That's why they elected me! Isn't it? **Isn't it?** The people elected me because I promised them certain benefits, I know they want em! **Hey, somebody`s gotta pay for it!**

Sure it`s gonna cost them, but it`s for their benefit and I gotta tax them! **It`s too damn bad if some of the people get mad!**

Mr. President, a good part of the people think they can spend their money just as wisely added the Chief of Staff. Jack, don`t be obtuse, the President scolded his aide.

The people know we are gonna do a better job than they can. Everybody in D.C. knows that, for Christ's sake!

Mr. President, the Congress will never go along with this. pleaded the Chief of Staff. Other advisors began to move in their seats nervously.

Mr. President, I concur, began the steady monotone voice of Chief Economic Advisor George Van Pelt. The effects on the economy are going to be staggering.

Look George, you are only here because I want you to be, don't make me accept your resignation, got it? Jack St. Mede spoke up. Mr. President, the Minority Leader of the House will finally have something to rally his troops against you!

Screw the Congress...And the Minority Leader, all they've done is block everything I need to do to make this country go forward!

Sure, of course, Mr. President, but the Congress could go to the Supremes...this could go on for years... Tough shit, I'll have all this enacted, then try and stop it, barked the President.

I got the House and the Senate in my pocket, in a couple weeks I'll get them to push this through Capitol Hill, I got the votes. We'll pass it in the middle of the night, and it will be all over but the shouting. Then see if they can undo it, good luck with that!

The paper of record broke the news in the Friday morning issue:

President Delacorte To Order Freedom For Unions Act. Congress Livid. States Stunned

The Executive Order basically stated, to make up a titanic shortfall of the funds needed and available for the implementation of the new single payer health coverage system (single payer HCS) for all social and medical services, a surcharge or fee of twelve percent would be calculated and assessed to the federal income tax portion of all hourly and salaried persons with positions of employment, except for those that were not already unionized, that resided in a right to work state: States that did not maintain a right to work status were exempted from the surcharge, as was the District of Columbia and Puerto Rico.

As the President reasoned in his executive order EO 21876-A, Right to Work states contributed less, as a whole, into the health care program known as the ACA act of 2010 during its existence, therefore the now acknowledged shortfall for his newly enacted single payer HCS must be carried by those state who contributed less in total for those years.

In addition to the twelve percent assessment of hourly and salaried wages, an addition fifty cents federal user fee on each gallon of gasoline and diesel fuel pumped for consumption of a motor vehicle would be added to states that were right to work to aid in the funding. This act would be in effective thirty days from the date of the Executive Order being signed.

At first there was stunned silence and disbelief. Governors of the affected states threatened action against the Feds. But no one knew what to do. How could this administration author such a tyrannical, irrational, and far-reaching edict? A pall of darkness, confusion and uncertainty seeped over the country. It was almost like the days after September 11th, 2001.

No one seemed understand the action by the President. How could he announce and sign an order like this? Analyst began to crunch numbers to see if the President's analysis of the short fall was wildly inaccurate or possible at any angle.

The mid-terms were still over a year away, so there would be no effective action by the Congress because the Senate would still block any bills sent to it by the House. The Senate was still bottled up by the President's most loyal and ancient members. Nothing would even reach the floor for debate, no matter how it affected the country.

Lawsuits to work through the systems would take months, even if they were fast tracked.

Even the British and French media were stunned by the action. There was little criticism by the U.S. media because most news networks were just propaganda arms of the Delacorte's administration. This was confirmed after a media executive was caught in a secret recording confessing to what was suspected for years.

These networks had requested that the federal government place F.C.C. employees in the newsrooms to monitor how stories were covered and selected. This was not for themselves but to control any other networks who would not follow the preferred narrative of Delacorte.

The digital social platforms had long been supporters of anyone like Delacorte and they were already in his pocket, contributing the major percentage of funding for his campaigns.

There were a few shots of people walking into what looked like a government building in the Washington D.C area. The few reporters who dared to interview workers received a "deer in headlights" response, like nothing had even happened. Or worse, they didn't seem to care.

The owners of the media outlets knew their licenses would be pulled in a heartbeat with the mention of the harsh reaction to the President's plan. The largest social media sites just kept censoring messages from posters who were against the executive action. Or closing and suspending the accounts. So much for the freedom of speech.

That night the President met with his closest advisors. That'll show the bastards. That'll show 'em who the hell is boss around here, he kept saying.

Secretary Ralston finally spoke up. Mister President, why the right to work states?

I mean maybe they paid a little less, I would have to check the numbers, but why single those states as the cause?

Tom, he replied back, it's not that shortage! It's that fact that they dilute and divert the campaign funds we need to keep the party in power. If we don't have more bosses in every state injecting the funds to the re-election campaigns, how are we gonna keep the wheels and hands greased? It cost a lot of cash to keep our boot heel on the throats of the other side of the aisle.

We are gonna be out on our asses come election time if we don't. And we're going to need a lot more money. We can't get the Supremes to reverse that damn Citizens United decision yet, so we need a bigger advantage. I want that right to work thing over with and done. That's what I really need. So, make 'em pay through the nose!

Besides, I got other plans to announce and it's gonna take a lot more taxes and fees to get them off the ground. I'm thinking the Universal Basic Income thing ought to keep our asses planted in D.C. for a couple more decades.

The President kept to himself over the weekend. He was confident that with one signature on one executive order he would have his way and after all he **was** elected to have his way with the country, like it or not! They'll understand, they will understand, he muttered.

I am right. I was always right. They are just too stupid to understand.

CALIFORNIA DREAMER

THE SCENT OF HONEYSUCKLE AND LAVENDER poured in her window. Through the shades, the first rays of sunlight filtered into her bedroom. The old house now seemed so empty without him. They had been together for almost thirty years and now he was gone. Why didn't he listen to her about the headaches and the pain?

Abbey had barely overcome the shock of finding him face down in his prized vineyard, cold as a stone. Six months later and she still reached for his hand in the morning when she woke up. She wiped away the welling tears and gathered herself up to face another difficult day.

Now she must face the enormity of keeping the farm and vineyards. They had done so well for so long...until the state diverted the water for irrigation away that came from the river. She had always been a proponent of conservation and the endangered species act. She never thought it would be her that was now endangered. The wells they had dug a few years ago were now almost dry and the ongoing drought had only acerated the lack of available water.

Then the EPA sent the letter that forced her future into a death march. Because a portion of the acres of the vineyard would pool with runoff during the rainy winter, no more grapes could be allowed to be harvested and the vineyards could not be maintained. The fine was $37,500 a day. This was because there was a chance protected migrating birds might flock there, and any activity would disturb them. She thought that she had an agreement with the EPA that drains would be installed, and she would capture the water for irrigation. However, the EPA decided that the act of installing drains would disturb the migrating birds' wetlands, whether they were migrating or not, and any potential runoff could pollute surrounding federal lands, therefore, Abbey must cease the main source of income for her and her two teenage boys. The legal fees to challenge the EPA had exhausted the life insurance money she had when Hal died.

This morning she would get dressed and meet with her old friend at the Citizen and Farmers Bank, Ken Vanderlin. Ken was an old California surfer dude who's now graying hair was pulled back into a ponytail. His bank had seen them through the worst days of drought and somehow Abbey and Hal managed to survive.

Now her future was bleak because of career bureaucrats who could not find the right end of a shovel. If Ken couldn't find some way to rework her loan payments, there would be very few options for her and none of them were good.

* * * * *

Come on in, Abbey, Ken said almost cheerfully. Come on and sit down and close the door Ken, I'm not really good at drawing things out, what did the bank say? Abbey just blurted out. Listen, Abbey, you got to get caught up on the loan, I can't do anything until we are current.

But what happened to the fed money for distressed farmland? Abbey almost incredulously asked.

No more for this year, but... Abbey, he responded, the bank can't do anything, you are at your credit limit with the bank and now you are two payments behind. I don't know what else we can do, except to sell off some or all of the vineyard.

Ken that land was in Hal's family for a hundred years! I **can't** sell it!

Abbey, I understand, I do, but what are you going to do to get caught up? I don't know, I guess I can sell off some of my parents' antiques and some farm equipment, other than that I don't know what we have left, she said almost in a whisper.

Abbey, here's the number of an auctioneer we sometimes use, he said while scribbling down the number. If nothing else, maybe he can help you get caught up a month or so.

Okay, Ken, I'll think about it and call you next week.

Look Abbey, the bank is extremely nervous, it's not just you, nearly everybody here is having tough times. The bank's board is worried the Feds are going to come down on them and this resurrected and reworked Dodd-Frank bill has got them afraid to extend anything to anyone. Understand the bank's hands are tied. Ken was almost desperate to make her understand.

I got it, Ken, I'm on my own and it doesn't look good, but you don't know how to tell me, is that about it? Looking away as he closed the door behind her, Yeah, that's about it, he responded. Good luck were his last words to her and call that number I gave you.

EMERGENCY MEETING...
GREENSBORO AIRFIELD

That Saturday after the President's Executive Order was signed, a flurry of activity began. Starting at six a.m., a series of small corporate jets began to line up for their final approach into the small county airport in Greensboro, Georgia. By the airport, several black SUVs and accompanying state police cars lined up to receive the deplaning passengers. Within fifteen minutes all were whisked to a private meeting place on the shores of Lake Oconee.

Reynolds Plantation became the location that the governors of the affected states agreed to meet to address the issues and outline a course of action. A parade of state troopers and local sheriffs had sealed off the circle leading to the plantation resort. For the remainder of the weekend all twenty-five governors would forge a reply to the President's executive order and elect a representative council in hopes of avoiding a larger conflict with Washington.

Not wanting to waste time, at eight a.m. the hosting governor of Georgia, Governor Miller, had sealed off the meeting rooms and had assembled those directly involved in the response in the walnut and pecan paneled, Sassafras and Tupelo rooms with staff assembling in the remaining rooms. Governor Miller, a tall, lanky man with a shock of white hair and a voice of a hellfire and damnation preacher, began with a prayer.

"Heavenly Father, please guide us through what may be the most serious of events to shape this nation. We beg for Your wisdom to address the difficult and dangerous road ahead. For we are few whose decisions will affect millions. Of this we beseech You, Heavenly Father, aid us with Your blessing that we may take the righteous path and rescuc our troubled nation. Amen."

A loud **"Amen"** echoed through the hall and the meeting began. The first to speak was Governor Cabbott of Texas.

"Gentlemen, Governors and friends, we in Texas were absolutely floored at the announcement of the executive order, E.O. 21876-A. The level of sheer arrogance and divisiveness this President and administration have stooped to is beyond reasonable and rational thought. I am certain we have a Jekyll and Hyde for a President. He has become unfit and unsuitable for the job. But we may not be able to remove him. He has gotten away with so many unconstitutional actions prior to this, and our efforts to stop him have failed. Only this president would openly and boldly call what is obviously a tax, a fee and surcharge just so he can give Congress the finger. He may just get away with this as well. We can attempt to take him to the Supremes, but with the death of Judge Johnson and now with H.R. Clayton confirmed as his replacement, we will never win; it will be five to four as sure as I am standing here.

Collectively, we are twenty-five states, we carry much sway and power together. Our natural resources and newly developed gas fields will more than suffice as a crowbar to help leverage a solution to this inane dictum of this administration. I can only believe that there is a total departure of reason in Washington. I fear the mindset of the embedded elites in Washington. I fear there is no sense of propriety. I fear we may have a situation where the differences and lack of understanding of core values may have induced a permanent rift between our two parties. We cannot sustain our individual budgets and obligations with these new proposed burdens. The probability that we as twenty-five states may need to take inventory of our assets and liabilities may be the next unavoidable step in remedy of our shared situation.

I think a poker player would call the bluff at this point. We should by all rights have the combined leverage to undo this situation. I propose that we speak with one voice, we call the bluff of the President and demand that he rescinds the malicious and inane ruling. We should try to work up a timetable for his response and for once play chess, not checkers, with this administration."

A round of cautious applause and the increasing volume of concerned conversations started to fill the rooms. Not because the assembled did not agree with the speaker, but the sense of ,"what next?" if the chess game went too far. Would the states adhere to the idea of taking inventory of assets in case this did backfire? All did realize they could in fact paint themselves into a corner. Small groups of governors from adjacent states began to form. They began to discuss what their reactions would be if this went beyond negotiating with the President and unwinding the situation.

The governors concluded at dinner that a meeting with as many senators and congressmen as possible of these twenty-five states should convene in concert with the governors.

That night as many congress and senate members were contacted directly as possible. Others were sent emails or texted. The follow-up meeting was for Sunday eleven a.m. in Atlanta at the Governor's Mansion. An exact head count would be known by midnight.

UNINTENDED CONSEQUENCES OF CONSOLIDATION

ABBEY HAD MANAGED TO SELL OFF SOME FARM implements she could no longer use because the EPA had shut down her vineyard operation. She seemed unaffected by it until it was clear some of her family heirlooms and antiques would have to be sold off. When the eighteenth- century highboy was carried off, she couldn't control the sense of loss. She buried her head in her hands, weeping and slowly walked back to the half empty farmhouse. She was forced to lay off the few farm hands she had employed for years. This was very painful for her. She knew the farm hands had nowhere to go. They wouldn't be able to survive and take care of their families. There were very few farming jobs left in the valley. Most farmers had sold out to land developers.

With this she was able to temporarily catch up on payments with the bank. If she could harvest just enough crops from the last forty acres she still owned, she might pull through. She knew there would be little or no water for irrigation. If there was enough water saved from the now overgrown vineyard wet area, plus just enough rain, she might just save the farm.

The winter was usually wet, but all this did was delay the planting. Then the rains stopped. Abbey slowly doled out the water she had siphoned off, illegally, from the wet area of the vineyard. It was enough to keep a few acres growing but it was clear most of the acreage would not make it without at least one more soaking rain. They never came.

The water she saved kept just enough crops to harvest to pay a few bills and keep a small something on the dinner table. She quickly fell behind with the payments to the bank. She looked for more assets she could sell. Only a few things of value were not already gone. Abbey now tenderly removed her wedding ring and headed to the only pawn store she knew.

Abbey got just over a thousand dollars for the ring. She decided to pawn it, but she almost knew she would not be back for it. She headed to the bank to see Ken and pay down what she was behind to the bank.

Ken was surprised to see Abbey at that moment.

Come on in Abbey and excuse the mess. There were a few cardboard boxes and a half-empty office that she walked into.

What's going on Ken, she asked, almost afraid of the answer.

Well, I was going to call you Abbey but you're here now. The bank has been sold to a mega bank and I'm not being asked to stay on. A letter is to be sent out next week to all the current customers. I got to tell you Abbey, the reason I am not staying is because we have too many loans in arrears. These guys have already announced they are coming down on all loans late or in arrears. I know they will make your life miserable, Abbey.

Even if they asked me to stay, I wouldn't. Are you having any more luck in getting caught up?

Abbey just shook her head. Ken, I have pawned the last asset I had, my wedding ring, and was going to get current but I don't see how I can keep this up.

Abbey, I'm going to tell you this as a friend, try and get what you can for the farm, sell some off to the developers and keep what you can because it is clear, these new guys will take it and sell it off to them anyway. There is no sense trying to rationalize how long it was in Hal's family. Do what's best for you and your two boys.

Abbey walked out of the office and didn't try to get current with the loan. Two weeks later, Abbey got an offer for the farm. It was two-hundred- thousand dollars under the appraised value. The developers just said the EPA was keeping them from developing all the land they wanted. Abbey surrendered to the reality of the situation. She had tried, she did all she could. There was no sense in fighting any longer.

Abbey came home to tell her two sons she would have to sell their home. Jeff, who had graduated just last summer had his degree in finance. Jeff was the oldest and was always wiser than his years looked at his mom and replied, mom, the developers always wanted this land. They were just figuring some way to get you outta here; you just beat them to it. Don't worry, mom, I'll get a job somewhere. We'll make it.

But the strain on the family was taking its toll on Jeff as well. He had lost over twenty pounds over the summer. He kept telling Abbey at dinnertime he had just eaten and wasn't hungry. But no one believed him. So many of his friends had already moved away. They had gotten caught in the trap of no jobs in the town or the area for that matter. He was just one of the last still around.

He thought he was mad at her and the reason he hadn't moved on. She was always so worried and now alone. He knew until she had this burden removed, he would be here. Maybe this being forced on the family was the way out for them. Now they would have to leave what had held them here. But where? The last six years with this administration's economy had frozen out any new openings for even entrée level jobs. It was out of state if anything was going to happen.

Abbey was starting to gather boxes at the local grocery store to pack what they had. She figured one more car full of boxes and she would have enough. It was one her last trip to Fred Meyers, she ran into one of the local politician-farmers.

Abbey! He said, relieved like he had found a lost kitten. Is that you?

Miguel Tomez had grown up in the valley. He was a handsome man in his early fifties, with a thick salt and pepper moustache. His voice was smooth like port wine after a long drag on a robust cigar. Abbey, where have you been and what has happened with the farm?

I'm going to lose the farm, Ken was let go and he can't do anything because the bank was sold to some mega bank, she replied, like she had said it a hundred times today. I suppose you voted for the new version of Dodd-Frank too.

No, I wasn't in Congress then, he sheepishly replied. But Abbey, I'm glad I ran into you, he said, like he almost forgot something important. There is a group of ranchers and farmers that are going to Washington to meet with Congresswoman Webber to issue a formal complaint against the EPA for the blatant abuses of power. We want investigations into the individual cases and yours would be very compelling. What do you say, Abbey?

Miguel, where the hell were you a year ago, when I really needed the help? I don't know, I'm getting ready to go to Reno to see about starting over. Who else is going to go to this thing?

There are about twenty locals that are definitely going, Miguel replied.

Twenty, huh? Well, we could give that dried out husk in D.C. an earful if nothing else. When is this happening?

Well, I'm going too, and we leave the first week of May, on Saturday, he replied. We still have room for you. Okay, then put me down and the two boys, we'll make a long weekend of it before making the move.

Atta girl! Maybe we can do something after all!

* * * * *

The developer called his childhood friend who worked at the West Coast district office for "Keep California Green." He in turn called an old understudy at the EPA. The waiver to develop the questionable wet land took an hour and a half and a New York Strip at Ruth's Chris Steakhouse.

THE PRELUDE

OFF HARRIS STREET IN DOWNTOWN ATLANTA
was a relic of days of white linen suits and white gloved valets.
The Capital City Club was the meeting place with back rooms
of cigar smoke and bourbon. The deals behind the deals were
agreed to here first.

But now governors, senators and congressmen could meet
in small groups here away from the gathering media at the official site of the Governor's Mansion. Across the street from the
Club was the Atlanta Merchandise Mart. Because this complex
of three buildings was not open to the public, some of the larger
groups met in the uppermost floors of these buildings as well,
after hours, when business in the wholesale trade was done for
the day. One of these three building had an auditorium suitable
for meetings of five hundred attendees.

With the access of the MARTA subway train and its underground station at this location, a stream of attendees, virtually
unnoticed, could come and go to these meetings, especially if it
happened late at night. A late-night partier or conventioneer at
the Hard Rock Café or Hooters on Peachtree Street, just across
the street, would have no clue the future of the nation was being
debated a couple of hundred feet away.

The first "unofficial meeting" was decided to include the
twenty-five governors of the "RTW," or right to work states.
Some of the northern RTW states found themselves especially unfairly singled out. They were the most affected by this

executive order because they had only recently voted to become RTW. The Governor of Michigan was one of the most vocal. He had many allies in the Southern governors because these governors realized just how senseless this executive directive was. Governor Jordan began.

"Gentlemen and Governors, I am James Jordan of Michigan. I want to take this occasion to voice my thoughts of the beginning of a new journey in the history of this nation and these so-called United States. Gentlemen, I feel as though this nation has been tearing itself apart for years. The fact that an administration and its President would believe it can continue to overrule and disregard the Constitution at will and the fact a surprising number of members of government agree and approve only means this grand experiment in a representative republic is in its death throes.

This executive order is our reason to salvage what is left of the framers' original sacred ideas of the rule of law, liberty, and individualism. Even when this present administration leaves office, the trail of the seeds of their philosophical destruction will continue to grow and flourish. The efforts to reform and resist have been futile. No citizen groups come forward anymore. No one from the IRS was ever punished for attempting to break the back of the Tea Party. No one went to jail. The once concerned citizens just wouldn't deal with the very real threats to them individually from our own government.

The demographics are now too different, and the ideals too removed from what kept this nation together. I have expended all the energy I could muster to achieve RTW status for the great state of Michigan. But we cannot survive as a functioning state with this presidential game of screw you. I have already begun the process of taking an inventory of the state's assets and potential contributions to a new entity.

The legacy of this administration will be that they alone cleaved this nation. Whether it was because of misplaced ego or naive misreading of the public or the continued vote buying from the coddling of the masses that reject self-worth for parasitism. In any case, the damage is done, the debt is irreversibly too large to pay, and the fix is in. We should in some way feel lucky that this administration forced our hand and now we are free to start again and dislodge the lampreys. I may be speaking for the moment for myself, but I for one am **not** afraid to face reality.

Fellow Governors, I speak for many, if not most of the citizens of my state, the time is now to begin again, let the chips fall where they may and survival of some remnant of the country we love will continue."

There was no thunderous applause but an increasing volume of voices. The governors gathered in small groups at first and then began to move amongst each other with nods in approval and agreement.

Just across the street, senators from the affected states met on the twenty-second floor on the Merchandise Mart. And the members of the House of Representatives met in the auditorium in the adjacent building. Spokesmen from each group were appointed and each group would meet early Sunday morning to report on and review the proposed actions and solutions.

Sunday at eleven a.m., the announcement by Governor Cabbott was to be made. The announcement was covered by most cable news outlets, local TV, radio, and printed outlets. There was no coverage by national networks or the grey lady or the D.C. post. Their opinions were this was a Southern issue and therefore not worthy of major coverage. Their message to the local affiliates was, don't call us, we'll call you. At five past eleven a.m. the brown matter hit the whirling fan.

Governor Cabbott addressed the media in front of the white columns of the Governor's Mansion.

"Ladies and gentlemen and members of the press, thank you coming. The events of the past week and the announcement of the President were stunning. We have shock and dismay amongst the members of congress and governorships at the sheer arrogance and disregard for the basic tenets of the rule of law. The constitution is apparently just another fish wrapper to this President. We of the twenty-five Right to Work states that have been singled out because we believe in the equality of opportunity are now prepared to call this administration's bluff. The elected leaders of these twenty-five states will agree in principle to an exit plan from this unlawful and extreme discrimination.

We consider this a warning shot across the bow of this administration. These twenty-five states will from this point forward act with one voice. To defuse this extraordinarily destructive situation, we propose a five-day cooling-off period. In the event of a promise of a reversal of this Executive Order , EO 21876-A, we will extend for the period of one further week the opportunity to negotiate and finalize an agreement. After that further week has expired and no conclusion has been agreed to, we will begin to implement our exit strategy.

The ball is now in President Delacorte's hands. We are prepared to move heaven and earth to reach a conclusion to this situation; however, we will **not** become a scapegoat for the unsuccessful policies of the now desperate and overreaching administration. We are prepared and willing to ameliorate this conflict we find ourselves in, this unprecedented power grab, that includes a cleaving of the affected states. Please understand we are extremely serious about this and understand the consequences of these possible outcomes.

At the end of the next seventy-two hours, we will meet with the members of the press to update you on the progress or lack of progress and will continue to do so until we have exhausted our cooling-off period. We, as the group of RTW states, continue to develop and confirm our pledge to cleave our collective selves from this untenable future. Thank you for your time, but there will be no further questions now, however, we will update you at six p.m. tonight of any developments."

The attending reporters fired off a series of question but were directed to be back at the same location at six p.m.

The seriousness of the threat must have begun to sink in as breaking news announcements began to pepper the major broadcast channels. The mainstream media talking heads began to question the seriousness of the threats and how silly the whole situation was. After all, it was the Right to Work States that **had** underpaid into the yet to be implemented single payer HCA. The Grey Lady editorials condemned these "yahoos" as the remains of the Civil War malcontents. Of course, many of the states were not "southern states" but that did not matter. The blogosphere erupted as Politico announced, "South Threatens Country Again," and hash tag "Southexitsagain."

MSNBC seized the opportunity to gather a panel of All Stars of the Left to predict that President Delacorte would garner support by imposing this executive order. They pointed to a flash poll that showed seventy-six percent of the polled supported the President. It wasn't until the next day, after drilling down into the poll as to who the questioned responders were, was it revealed that of the one thousand one hundred polled, all were from the AFL/CIO, ILWU, SEIU and the UAW.

SAINT TAMMANY PARISH

New Orleans was brutally hot in late spring and summer. Many of the locals used to travel to the north shore of Lake Pontchartrain to experience the soothing mineral springs and cooling breezes. The shores of the lake had many elegant homes and a few elected officials in the parish owned some of the most exclusive and private properties.

Congressman Peter Lefavre was a developer in St. Tammany Parish and the Northshore communities. His home was just north of the world's longest bridge across the twenty-five-mile-wide lake. His home had one key addition, a dock that could handle sixty-foot boats. Along with the ten thousand square foot home there was a private gated driveway.

The county airport just north of Slidell could accommodate small private jets along with Lakefront Airport that could handle larger corporate aircraft. The first of the drafting committees for the 25RTW group decided this would be the best location to gather over the weekend and begin to draw up the initial chess moves to counter the President's expected demands.

The committee consisted of five governors, five senators, and five congressmen. From this meeting the army of lawyers and financial experts would be expected to fill in some of the transition issues and the workarounds to begin the cleaving from the Feds and D.C.

Congressman Lefavre and his family had many of the locals working for them in their various business and political affairs.

The logistics of keeping an important gathering of key officials under wraps and under the radar would be just another day in the life for them. The congressman had basically a small compound with more than enough room for the planned meetings.

The first to arrive were the governors of North and South Dakota. Then Louisiana, Texas and Georgia. The states chosen were based on a wide representation, as were the senators and congressmen. The Dakotas and Texas because of oil supplies, Louisiana because of the upriver control of the Mississippi River at New Orleans and its oil and port establishments. Georgia because of military bases of Fort Benning and the submarine base at Saint Mary's, Port of Savannah, major oil pipelines through Athens and Atlanta and the world's busiest airport. Senators and congressmen were also selected because of strategic assets in their states.

Governor Miller of Georgia had called Governor Delise, of Louisiana, in advance.

Jimmy, this is George, say why dontcha all get some of your oyster and shrimp po' boys made up from Acme or Deannie's and a crawfish boil and a couple cases of Abita beer and I'll return the favor when y'all get back up in Atlanta. We'll take the rough edge off this thing and git everyone relaxing before we get down to brass tacks. What'ya say, Governer?

George, I'm gonna make you an honorary coonass!

You got it!

You do that, Jimmie, you do that! laughed George.

The meetings began in earnest at three p.m. Governor Delise started off.

Everyone knows why we are here, maybe not because we are ready for it, but here we are. I am one who believes this is something that would have had to have happened sooner or later. I can only believe that the impossibility of the repayment of the now fifty-five trillion-dollar debt would never be addressed by President Delacorte. And if the election of bread and circus politicians continues, the end and collapse of the dollar will lead to an ending no one wants to think about. In a perverted sense we should be grateful that this crisis has developed.

What we first need is to decide what reactions we will have to the President. I don't have the first idea what this amateur is thinking and about to do, but whatever it is, it will be bad for us. He must know that the current financial situation will collapse the dollar, the economy, and his ass, along with the country. It is the only sensible reason he is pushing this RTW crap.

Governor Snyder of North Dakota piped in, How in the hell did he **ever** think we would just roll over and go along with this dog squeeze?

Doug, jumped in Governor Cabbot, you know the President has nothing but ass-kissers and asses surrounding him. There can be but two or three people in that whole D.C. crowd that knows one end of a balance sheet from the other. And they are too chicken shit to say anything... that is how we got here. The Justice Department is nothing but a joke; no one is ever going to jail. You and I both know if we sweep these shysters out of D.C., the next administration will not go back and fry their asses. It won't happen. In the meantime, this whole pile of dung is getting heavier and heavier. It's just too late. If we are going to save anything, just concentrate on those who understand and want to do something about it...otherwise we are just wasting time for nothing.

Governor Snyder responded, Jim, well what the hell do **you** expect outta D.C.?

I tell what I know, Governor Cabbott began. You have a President that has been in over his head from day one. He was probably thinking he could push through a couple of his big time, big deal socialist dream programs, then he could sit back and with a little bit of luck he could coast through it. Play golf every couple of days. And if he got re-elected, he would rinse and repeat.

He's obviously done nothing but piss away fiat and borrowed money and it really seems like he doesn't believe anything bad is coming from it. I think he believes he can do whatever he wants and everyone who kissed his ass will continue to do so. Wall Street's not gonna stop him as long as he keeps the Fed pumping out billions of digital monies at zero percent to them... It's like bringing a tanker of O positive to a vampire convention.

He's never worked a real job long enough to know anything, so for him to figure this out is damned near impossible. He will not listen to anybody who knows what the hell is real. What I think is a mass of the most uninformed voters elected the most ill-prepared and under-qualified executive to the world's largest corporation at the most critical time in its history. What can go wrong? Well, pulling this turd ball out his pocket is a start.

I tell you what I would expect... the opposite of what a reasonable, rational executive would do. I expect he doesn't even have a hint he is coming face to face with the fact that he will be a mile ahead in the race for the most unpopular and lamebrain Presidents to date. I don't think he even cares that the next liberal, eco-loving Dem will only be elected if Santa converts to a Democrat and brings them voters for Christmas. Hell, even if the dollar wasn't gonna tank before this brainiac pulled this stunt, it will begin to Monday when the markets open. And if that wasn't gonna do it, our expected response will. Then after that it will be the point of no return.

I can tell you what D.C. will do...they will make a shit-eating mess of this for us. We just have to be a better chess player and checkmate them before they realize they are done for. Now, let's sit down and start mapping this thing out, because I can tell you this, the President and his dude head bangers are gonna put it to us sideways on Monday. Hell, they're probably yakking it up right now, thinking they got us by the short hairs.

THE CHANCE MEETING

JAMES WAS OUT WALKING JUST AS HE HAD ALL weekend. The early morning that Monday was quite different than the morning before. The traffic and the din of the buses and taxis were in full song. The walkways and sidewalks were showing it was a workday. James thought he would visit the most popular monument and museums and finish up the day back at the hotel's rooftop lounge and take in the famous view of the city in the evening.

On his way back to his hotel room he entered the teeming lobby. The front drive and approach of the hotel was jammed with taxis, shuttle buses to the airports and shiny new tour buses. James glanced at his watch. It was just four-thirty and a little too early to have a drink.

He would head up to his room, take a shower and pack for the trip back tomorrow.

Out of his hotel room's balcony, James could see the Mall and the Capital Building and the Lincoln Monument. He could also see a stream of people heading in and out of the hotel boarding the long line of taxis. Eyeing the crowds, he caught himself watching a middle-aged woman with dark hair pulled back in a bun.

Wow, she looks like... A long pause and he turned around in disgust.

Enough already, enough, he murmured. He lay down and put his feet up, hit the remote and started flipping through the stations. Within ten minutes, he was asleep.

The sound of a backing up bus, beeping at the volume of a fire siren, startled him and he looked around to see what time it was. The darkness out the balcony window at first confused him. Was it time to get up and get ready to go to the airport? Then he realized one of the popular opinion programs was on the television, it was still Monday night.

All right already, let's go down and get something to eat and get your mind right, he said to himself. Tomorrow is the start of cutting and moving on. James figured he had better splash some water on his face and get downstairs. Better get my ass in gear because the kitchen will be closing soon, or it will be hot dogs at the *7-11*. He threw on his blazer and khakis and headed down to the lobby. He was looking in his jacket pocket, checking to make sure he hadn't forgotten his wallet, when the elevator door opened.

There was a second of silence, then ,OH MY GOD! James? James? What are you doing here?

He saw her and didn't believe it. In an instant a flashback of spilled drinks and airport bars flashed through his head.

I see it's you but I'm sure my eyes are playing tricks on me! **Abbey**? Why, What? What are you doing here? He caught his mind racing and **still** didn't believe it **was** her. Well's that's a long story!

Oh James, as she put her arms on her two boys, this is Jeff and Daniel. We were just on our way upstairs.

Oh, of course, James replied, yeah, I guess it's late.

But would you like a drink and get caught up for a few minutes, James added without thinking about what he had offered.

Hmmm, well ,ok, I guess I could be convinced to have a glass of wine, she casually replied.

Let me go upstairs for a couple of minutes and freshen up. Meet you in the lobby say in ten minutes? Abbey offered. That would be great, ten minutes, yeah that would be great.

James was almost stepping on his tongue and now feeling like he had never woken up and this was still a dream. He waited for her in front of the bar, still in the lobby, as if to make sure she didn't change her mind and walk out of the lobby and keep going. After a few minutes he could hear the elevator chime ring just before the doors opened. She stepped out and smiled at him.

For that instant he was back to those summer nights with her. She was like the models from the India Imports catalogs. White muslin top and a jeans skirt and she still had her wood-soled sandals. Her hair was down with the French braids he remembered she would wear occasionally. It was just a hint of salt and pepper in her hair that gave her away as middle-aged.

He met her and gestured to an empty booth just inside the bar.

Okay, who starts first? she said, genuinely interested in a friendly conversation.

James started, Well, Abbey, you seem to have come the farthest, why don't you start?

She began back in her college days. She met her husband at a conference in Boston. He was there to catch up on the latest trends in organic horticulture and she was at the same convention but for environmental impact studies and review updates as per the recent laws and rulings.

Yeah, we dated long distance for about two years and then I just said, okay, enough, and we got married. She tried to cram thirty years into about thirty minutes. When she told him how and why she ended up at the hotel, she told him that the meeting with her congresswoman was a disaster and now she was unsure of anything. At one time she thought the government could do good things, now she just didn't know who to believe. James felt like he was there every step with her.

So, why are **you** here? I've been doing all the talking, she slowed and asked him.

Abbey, do you remember my friends, Russ or Ian, or Jake?

Yes, I think so, I think I remember them.

How about Joe and Tom?

Yes, I remember them too.

They were all here yesterday, he told her.

Really? She was intrigued. Why?

Why? That is the question, Abbey.

Have you followed what has happened in D.C. the last five years?

Not really, I mean I know things aren't getting better, but I've been so tied up with the farm, I just haven't. I just thought it was just me and my world that was turning upside down, she kind of sheepishly answered.

Abbey, this administration is about to tear the country apart. Now with these new executive orders he has announced, he's pushed half the country over the edge.

James tried to impress on her without getting too emotional about it.

I want you to understand what is going on. All of us, Russ, Ian, Jake, and everybody are selling off most of our assets and we are trying to set up a new chapter in our lives.

It sounds radical, but to us, it makes perfect sense.

He stopped to choose his words carefully.

We have, almost stumbled, into a whole new approach to a philosophy to life and making a living.

Abbey's eyes started to glaze over. James explained about New America and how they met Charles in Europe and as much as he could without being too much of a promoter.

I 'm sure you all are doing something you think is best, and I hope you are, but I can't grasp it all. I am just getting used to the idea of selling out to the developers. I have a plan for the time being and I guess I'm going to stay with it, I just can't make so many changes at once, Abbey admitted.

James thought he would most likely never see Abbey again. He wasn't even sure he would be able to come **back** to the States again. It was all too hard to predict what the future would be.

Abbey, do you remember when we used to drive down to the beach that one summer, he asked her. She had kind of a half-smile and quizzically responded, Yes, I can sort of recall.

Let's go for a short walk, what do you say?

He wasn't going to repeat any of the mistakes he made so many years ago, he just wanted to walk and talk to her. Just a casual conversation between friends.

Abbey, this is all too much to cram into one stroll in the park, so I will just say I do hope to see you sometime and under better circumstances. Let's just try and keep in touch.

It's been just too long.

She looked at him differently. It was like a yes, you're right, but without any sense of indifference like in the past. Yeah, let's keep in touch.

They walked back to the hotel and shared a kiss in the lobby, and she disappeared into the elevator.

James walked out of the lobby and into the night air. He thought he handled himself about as well as he could without showing his heart on his sleeve. All the memories of thirty-plus years came flooding back. All this time looking for her and now he knew he most likely would never see her again.

There is going to be a lot of moving on and this was the last one on the list. he said to himself.

This was the last one.

At one a.m. he head back to his room. He would leave in the morning and not look for her.

ARTICLE V

On Tuesday morning in Atlanta, Governor Cabbott addressed the gathered group of 25RTW elected officials along with Governor Miller. It was the congresswoman from the northern Atlanta district, Margaret White, who presented her strategy to counter President Delacorte's executive order. Everyone, please have a seat and we will begin, the governor announced.

Margaret White, our congresswoman from northwest Atlanta district, has come up with what seems to be our best strategy. It is quite simple actually and right in the Constitution, Article V. Basically, if two-thirds of the states decide to amend the Constitution, they can present an amendment and do so without the consent of Congress.

That is thirty-four states. We are already twenty-five. We have two paths to get to thirty-four. It would not be easy but not unreasonable to convince nine states to flip. It would, however, take time. Even if we refused to acquiesce to the executive order, we still cannot escape the calamity when the reality of the debt and the interest payments swamp the ship of state. And on that one, we are really running are out of time.

We can attempt to accomplish the requirements of Article V in this manner and there would be no challenges, constitutionally. Of course, we still must get thirty-eight states or three-fourths to adopt the amendment. That could be a big problem. Of course, the question is, what is the amendment? Under the current conditions and with this administration's targeting of those who remember what this country used to be, there appears to be only one recourse, an equal but separately governed group of states that can operate as the Constitution describes.

In other words, this is proof enough that this euro-centric social engineering LSD trip of the administration of Delacorte is a major league failure and in the process hammering in the last financial nail in the coffin of the country. If this was a one-time administration and a one-time divergence from what we consider normal and reasonable policy, then this would not be needed.

But this is an immutable trend within certain parts of this country. There are too many demographic trends to expect to reverse this course. We who are still able to dig out of what should be a share of the liabilities and responsibility of the nation will do so but will not continue to perpetuate these financial suicidal policies. We are going to separate ourselves from the current laws and conditions that we consider to be contrary to a sound financial future. We will draw up a separate but equal worded amendment to be agreed to and passed by two-thirds of the states and then ratified by three-quarters of the states. I am not hopeful we can make this happen in time to avoid the coming financial disruptions, which now are unavoidable.

So, we have a card up our sleeve. After lengthy conversations with the state legislature of Texas and the governorship, they can divide Texas into five separate states as once was proposed in Texas. This would give us a total of thirty states with just four to go and nine to accomplish this constitutionally. As we move toward equal but separate, we will suspend and ignore the enforcement of the executive orders and laws passed by this administration that are deemed to target and punish us as RTW states.

With this announcement, we need to understand, we will be forcing an issue that this administration may not have predicted, just like every other thing they have done, actions with no forethought to the consequences. Predicting what the next move will be from the President can only take two paths. He begins to face reality and begins a path of cooperation and hard decisions. I do not know why he would do this; it flies in the face of what he seems to represent.

No, it is almost certain he will overreact and no one in his inner circle will have the guts to tell him he is acting like an infantile spoiled child. What we do not know is how many in the White House will just go along to get along and how many will start to lick their chops and go after us hog wild.

It is the wild-eyed radicals that keep feeding him their bullshit that we can't anticipate their effect on his reactions. Personally, I think he will go full tilt nuts, no one has, in effect, literally, slapped him upside the head and said, sit the hell down and shut the hell up. So, hell, I would not be surprised if he doesn't call out the generals and try and nuke us.

We will meet again in thirty minutes to agree on the final wording and make the announcement at noon. God help us after that.

RENO

ABBEY'S BEST FRIEND, MARY JANE COLLINS, from college, always had a gambling bug.

M.J., as she was known, was a whiz at counting cards and would set up the guys from Delta Tau Delta at poker when she needed extra money. When Abbey was still at school and dead broke, M.J. would say, okay, time to play the ponies and head over to the horse track.

M.J. was not your typical image of a soon-to-be professional gambler. She was petite and cute as a button. With her svelte five-foot frame and long, silky, blonde hair, green eyes, and voice like Shirley Temple, she knew how to set up an unsuspecting table of half-drunken college boys with more cash than common sense. M.J. knew Abbey was always short on cash.

One spring morning, M.J. stopped by Abbey's apartment to see her desperately trying to find enough coffee to make a fresh pot of expresso. M.J. instantly used this as an opportunity to head to her most favorite place on earth, Narragansett Raceway.

All right now, M.J. said with a broad smile, time to play the ponies. Here, I'll spot you twenty bucks, let's see if our luck holds up.

They climbed into M.J.'s beat-up VW and in ninety minutes they were in line for the third race. The Racing Form tucked under her arm, M.J. began to school Abbey in the codes and nuances of the form.

All right let's see what we got here. Okay, in the fifth we got Hamptons Hustle, Savannah Pride and Breeze In.

Hampton has finished strong late in the last two races, Breeze started strong and slowed to second in the last three races in the mile and Savannah finished second, third, and second in the last three races.

Okay, girl, I'm feeling good about this race, we'll box this Trifecta and clean up. Gimme your twenty and if I lose, I'll still give you back a ten spot.

Abbey didn't have the first idea what M.J. had said but was willing to go along.

Okay, M.J., let's just do it, and they headed to the ticket line,

M.J. got to the booth. "sixty trifecta, box two, five, seven ,in the fifth" she said as if she had just deposited hundred grand in a bank account.

The grizzled old man in the booth read back, "sixty trifecta, box two, five, seven, fifth race, here ya go...next in line."

Abbey went outside to the grandstand with M.J. She was dismayed by the number of torn up tickets everywhere and the disgusted looks on a good part of the crowd.

It was a cloudless day and couldn't have been more perfect for a racing. It was just starting to warm up noticeably and was now in the seventies. Abbey started to get nervous and tapped M.J. on the shoulder and pointed toward the ladies' room.

M.J was concentrating on the horses warming up and watching as they entered the gates.

Yeah, okay, but hurry up, you don't want to miss this!

From the back of the grandstand Abbey could hear the crowds starting to stir and the volume build. The yells of, *Go... go! Go!* were pouring in from every corner of the stands. Abbey could only think about how many groceries that twenty would buy, but at least she could get coffee, bread and maybe eggs.

As she headed back to the seats, M.J. came sauntering over to meet her, pointing to the lights of the official race results board . Spelled out in lights on the race results were the words and numbers, Race 5 Trifecta Official results" Win #2, Place #5, Show #7.

The race odds went off at 22 to 1. The $60 bet paid just over $800 from the trifecta pool.

M.J handed to Abbey $400 and said, Well, that ought to be enough for some Medaglia d'Oro or whatever than goombah diego coffee you drink is.

Wow, you did it! You did it! You did it!

Abbey couldn't help but scream with joy and disbelief. You're the best, M.J.

All in day's work, girl. All in a day`s work.

M.J let the words just slide from her lips like sweet syrup.

When Abbey graduated, M.J. was there.

Well Abbey, timing is everything, I just got my dream job offer in Reno.

I'm gonna be a dealer at the Peppermill. I love that place.

My Gaud, M.J., that's great! When do you start?

I've got two weeks to get out there, M.J. replied, still excited with the thoughts of going west again.

Damn, I'm gonna miss you. Abbey replied without realizing how true these words would be

I know I will be seeing you before too long.

M.J, now realizing time was short, gave Abbey a hug and said,

I hope so girl, I hope so.

* * * * *

Jeff nudged Abbey and she woke up to a rising sun starting to illuminate the tops of the snow-covered mountain peaks. They had been traveling over eight hours now and it was time to make another pit stop for gas and breakfast.

The end at the farm had come fast. She took the best offer from the developer that had lined up the waiver with the EPA. After paying off all the built-up debts, she had less than a year's expenses available and that was it.

M.J. was surprised to hear from her old friend. She couldn't express how sorry she was that Abbey had suffered so much in the past year. In typical M.J. fashion, she said, well, it's way past time for you to get your skinny butt up here. We'll get you fixed up and get you on your feet. If you guys want to stay for a while, you shouldn't have any trouble finding jobs to tide you over for a while. They're looking for help at the Peppermill, Maybe we can find something for you and the boys right away.

M.J. was right; there were jobs. Not much of a job, but something for the three of them. Abbey was able to find a position in the payroll office. Jeff was being trained behind the bar and Daniel could start as a server. Between the three of them, they were able to find a two-bedroom apartment to rent.

Jeff and Daniel would take turns sleeping on the couch in the small living room, depending on their schedules. Abbey had most weekends off, but the boys would end up working all but one weekend a month and most holidays, because they were the newest hires and lowest on the totem pole.

After a couple of weeks, they had settled into the schedules, and while they saw little of each other during the week, on those weekends that they were together, they would join M.J. and head to the lake and relax.

At least the world made sense for a while.

THE SHARK TANK

AUSTIN HAS AS PART OF THE STATE CAPITAL building a large underground facility known as the Shark Tank. Of the several floors located in this part of the building, there was only one area where there was a large glass dome where cell phones would operate. Here large numbers of lawyers were known to congregate on all levels, circling to get the best reception, hence the name.

Governor Cabbott had suggested that the formal announcement of the RTW states' response to the President's executive order be made from here. Governors from all the states would assemble and make the announcement. The scheduled time was twelve noon on May the seventh.

Just before the gathered state leaders approached the podium, Governor Miller was said to have said he was glad they were in the Shark Tank because that crazy bastard in D.C. would try to nuke them after this bombshell.

"Ladies and gentlemen of the press, Governors, Congressmen and Senators. Thank you for your presence today. I think you will find this occasion to be judged in the future as historic. In response to President Delacorte's Executive Order, E.O. 21876-A, the twenty-five Right to Work States, or as we will be known from this point forward, 25 RTW, have forged a response to said order. We, collectively, are embarking on a permanent solution to this executive action and in addition a solution to the financial crisis that is predicted and unavoidable.

The combination of these two events have forced a decision and action on our collective parts. This action is a pursuit of a Constitutional Amendment to form a separate but equal entity. We endeavor to separate ourselves from the now unavoidable collapse of the currency and financial system as perverted in Washington, D.C. We will pursue the needed approval of thirty-four states to proceed with the amendment and then the thirty-eight states' approval to ratify the amendment. While the amendment works its way through the process, we will continue to send to Washington, D.C., the current amount of revenue in taxes, fees, and duties as of the calendar year ending on May fifteenth of this year. Not a penny more. This will be paid to the federal government daily in three hundred sixty-five equal payments. It is not our goal to impinge on the federal government.

It is our goal to pursue an approach to financial and economic sanity not provided by this administration. It is very unfortunate that the debt level is such that we as the 25 RTW states see no possible manner to maintain a growth path for the country. All trends currently point to a death spiral for the economy. It is the advent of this executive order and the current philosophy of government and administration that has forced this action. Of this we want to be clear. We will pursue no retribution for the executive order; however, we will not acquiesce to it either.

As of today, we are commencing our acceptance of the Constitutional Amendment and further approval and execution if approved. As opposed to this administration, we will adhere to the laws as written and proceed in a fully legal manner. Ladies and gentlemen, there will be no questions at this time. We will again meet at the response of the President and the executive branch. Thank you for your attendance. That is all for now."

The governor closed his notes and left the podium and stage. The historic response was delivered, now it was up to Washington.

THERE WAS A FLOOD

PRESIDENT DELACORTE WAS HEARD SCREAMING. He was livid. He ordered all his aides out of the Oval Office. From behind the closed door, items were heard slamming against the walls. One of the hundred-year-old sailing ship models was thrown at the bulletproof glass of the front window to the office. It lay in a tangled pile at the base of the window.

No one attempted to enter for almost sixty minutes, until the head of the Joint Chiefs of Staff approached the office with news from the NSA and the amount of auto and truck traffic heading into the RTW states, but barely any leaving. The President was at his desk when the general approached the Oval Office door and opened it. The furniture was overturned or askew. Mr. President, we have satellite images you may want to see. Only then did the general notice the crumbled sailing ship and the letter opener stabbed into the President's desk.

He was scribbling on a notepad and did not look up.

Yeah, okay, just leave it here and I'll look at 'em.

Mr. President, I think you will want to look at them right away.

He responded, I **said I'll look at 'em. Thank you, General.** Delacorte was barely holding it together. Yes sir, yes sir, thank you sir, the general replied as he hurried out of the office.

No one approached the office for several hours. At six p.m., the President called his two top advisors into the office.

Okay, here is my response to the so-called RTW assholes.

We are setting up checkpoints and tolls at all state lines from the country to RTW states. The fee to enter a RTW state is two hundred dollars bucks a pop. Enter a union state from a RTW state is five bucks a pop. All airlines, buses, trains, and walkers going into a right to work state...two hundred bucks a pop. Also, I am setting up collection checkpoints on the Wyoming, Nebraska, and South Dakota borders at I-80, 90 and 25.

And I'm doubling the collection points in and out of Montana, Colorado, and New Mexico.

I don't give a damn if they are or aren't RTW. I'm cutting the western RTW states off from the rest of them. I'll break their will and stop this shit cold. Whatta they gonna do?

Write a letter, take a vote? Yeah, that worked so well with single payer HCA.

Hell, I got that through without breaking a sweat and I can do this. I'll fix that high and mighty Jordan, He's gonna know what it like to be cut off. Michigan dared to go RTW.

Well Mr. Jordan, a couple of dozen collection points on I-25 and I-35 ought to make you and Indiana think you're in a Stalingrad siege.

Anybody moving to RTW states must pay a twenty percent surcharge of the value of all goods moved out of a union state. All financial transactions between union state clearing house states and RTW will immediately be charged a two percent surcharge, regardless of volume. I am taking this action under Executive Order, E.O. #21901-A. I am signing tomorrow.

Let's see the bastards squirm now.

Mr. President, pleaded Mallory Barrett, his closest aide, what are you doing?

Do you have any idea this will do to the people and the economy?

Screw 'em, I know what I'm doing! You don't like it...there's the door!

You don't like it, then don't be here in the morning when I make the announcement. And do not bother showing up at your office because the locks will be changed, and I will have accepted your resignation.

Got it.!

She left the oval office wondering where she would be tomorrow at nine a.m.

My God, he's lost it, why didn't I see this before? I think this is an exceptionally good time to review my resume 'and consider this an exit point, she concluded.

THERE ARE TWO AMERICAS

WELL, THAT'S JUST ABOUT WHAT I WOULD EXCEPT from Uber Prez, quipped Governor Miller. The only thing super-duper didn't want was my dirty shorts.

Well, all right, boys, that just about seals it, added Governor Cabbot after listening to the Chief of Staff for Delacorte.

Hell, I don't even want to bother to work out a deal with this uber ego asshole.

Let's just make a clean break of it. We need to schedule a vote on temporary divisions of labor and leadership. Cabbot firmly stated for all to hear, We will respond and begin to separate ourselves. If he wants two hundred bucks a head to leave, well we'll figure a way to make it hurt him as well, but not the folks wanting to come and stay with us.

I guess we can get with the military base commandants and the Navy bases and get that question off the table.

If Delacorte wants the cooperation with the bases, I guess he can come down here and ask us, pretty please, and see how far he gets.

We will need to have an understanding with any of the base commanders up north and west and make sure we are all on the same page.

They'll have to stay up there for now, so we need to work this out first and foremost. We can figure out a working capital after this thing runs its course or if need be, just make one and that will be it and see what happens.

Governor Miller piped in, I tell ya'll, I really don't see there is much we need them for. We can get all we need from South America, Japan, Korea, or Europe. We got most of the oil production, refineries, and ports. Hell, why didn't we do this twenty years ago?

He looked around to see people nodding, but their mood was still somber as they knew what was and most likely would be the end of the country, they grew up in.

Ah, come on, y'all, we are gonna either make something better or kick their asses into shape up there. One way or another, something is going to come of this, and we can maybe make it good for all…maybe, concluded Governor Cabbott. He knew most of that statement was just for the people in the room and to boost the morale.

The days and weeks ahead would be the undoing of the country they had grown up in. It would be hard to remember this would be for salvation of what was still a viable entity.

After a series of votes amongst the governors, senators, and representatives, it was decided Austin would be the capitol, or at least the center of planning and communications and coordinating with the military bases in the RTW states.

The locals who had a liberal bent or transplants from California and New York who had tried to influence the policies in Texas in the past were invited to a meeting in the capital building in Austin. Governor Cabbot explained what was going to happen. The protests were loud and emotionally charged. At that moment Governor Miller stepped to the stage. He was loaded for bear.

Listen, ladies and gentlemen, we understand ya'll are put out, he began. But let me tell ya'll and let's get one thing straight right now, and I **mean right, damn now**. Ya'll voted for this guy, we didn't. We didn't ask for this mess but we're init now. So, here's the deal, if ya'll want to stay, then it will be this group's way. We have **no** room for your old B.S. There is a new sheriff in town and the sheriff ain't taking no shit. So here it is, adjust your attitude or hit the bricks. That's it, there ain't no exceptions. You all voted for this with this guy, you weren't smart enough to see this could happen, so we are telling you the way it's gonna be. If you think you are willing to do it our way, then okay. Otherwise, we don't need any more Delacorte tools here. If it were up to me, I'd give you twenty-four hours to think it over, but it ain't, so I will defer to your governor and you all can work it out. Governor Miller pointed to Governor Cabbott, who moved back to the podium.

Well actually, George, you pretty much took the words out of my mouth. But I will give you seventy-two hours to decide. If you work in the government, you will have to understand, you may have to adjust your thinking because the old ways are done. We have a lot of work and I mean a **lot** of work to do in a truly short time. We have no room for those who are not hundred percent behind this new entity. I suspect if you came here from the north or west, thinking you could influence our way of doing things, well, that ain't happening. You may just want to leave your badges at the desk before you leave this room. There is no sense in dragging this out.

* * * * *

Governor Cabbot was right, there was a lot of work because the understanding was Delacorte was going to react badly, and the reactions would be swift and certain. There would need to be offices set up for the department to establish trade, agriculture, and finance. Many of the social services that had been such an anchor in the past would be up to individual states and counties.

The one thing that had to be communicated and understood was the gravy train of the past was over. The operating philosophy was freedom to be the most productive you could be. The past dictums of spend first and tax to support it was over. The dictum here was: Yes, we will have to tax you, but only enough to support a minimal yet effective government. The number being discussed was no more than ten percent and everybody paid, no getting around it.

Social support was up to the local government to decide on the level available and the tax level, locally, to support it. What used to be a federal program was now all decided at the state and local level. And most important, local solutions for things like education, for example. The best solutions would rise to the top and all could review, copy and/or modify for their needs.

Each governor had his or her work cut out for themselves, because not all the population would want to live under these new but needed rules and laws. It would be tough for some to decide. Not everyone had the desire to be as free as others. Some had already put in their time and were expecting the rest of their lives to be on a glide path. Starting over or with less than they thought just wouldn't work for them. Some would just want things to be the way they remembered it was, regardless of what reality said it was or would be.

Unfortunately, whether they stayed or moved to a more supportive environment or state would be out of their control very soon, and President Delacorte would decide that for them.

On June 1 at midnight, the first of the collection stations was installed on I-95 going into Washington, on I-81 into Maryland, and five other major north-south routes. The major issue and the hot spot that could make this much worse was the forced separation of Wyoming. Collection stations were placed on both sides of the state. All the collection stations were manned by governmental department members and other hand-picked employees.

Delacorte did live up to his promise to separate the western RTW states from the Midwest and Southern tiers. And he cut off Michigan and Indiana by setting up collection points on I-25 and I-35 and all interstate secondary and tertiary roads. Governor Jordan was apoplectic. But short of driving to D.C. and screaming at the President, he knew cooler heads would have to prevail.

By the end of the week, collection points and stations were set up at I-77, I-55, I-70 and I-76, I-40, I-10 and I-90 and I-64 and all secondary roads between states. The reality was sinking in. The mainstream media was only starting to do their jobs and a sense of national crisis was overcoming the whole of the nation. But Delacorte was not deterred; he spent most of his day locked away in the Oval Office devising ways to bend these troublemakers and malcontents to his will.

PEPPERMILL

THE PEPPERMILL RESORT IN RENO WAS ONE OF the finest and most luxurious in the Tahoe/Reno area. Tourists and gamblers flocked to the hotel and rave reviews poured in. That was when the economy was on a roll.

That was years ago. While the resort and the casino were surviving, the high times were over. The turnover at the resort was high because the casino owners knew there were three people applying for every job. And because of that, pay for all new employees was low.

Abbey had been at the payroll office for over six months before she was considered for a small raise. Jeff was doing okay as the four p.m. to midnight bartender on the weekends, but the weekdays were slow, and the tips just weren't there. Jeff and Daniel worked the same shifts but did not see each other at night until closing because they were in two different ends of the resort. The ennui and hopelessness of the situation began to mount on them. While on the weekends they were off, they enjoyed themselves and would go to the lake or just hang out together.

While the boys might have a chance to meet kids their ages anywhere else, the resort didn't offer much of a chance for that. Now that Daniel had graduated and moved away from all his friends, he began to feel isolated and withdrawn and was tired from the working hours most of the time. It didn't take all that long for Abbey to see it in their eyes.

At the end of summer, the boys didn't want to do much of anything, even on their collective weekend off.

One afternoon Abbey got off early and opened the door to the apartment to see Jeff asleep on the floor in the living room and Daniel curled up on the couch. On the coffee table was the remains of a frozen pizza and Diet Coke. The TV was blaring the past week's NFL replays on ESPN. Neither one of the boys stirred when Abbey sat down beside them.

It was the flood of hopelessness that finally overwhelmed her. At first it was just a tear, then sobbing, and then uncontrollable crying. Jeff awoke first and saw his mom, his anchor, in tears. He instinctively wrapped his arms around her, trying to console her, but within seconds he began to sob with her. Daniel slowly began to stir and understand what was happening. He was the one who was able to gather his family together and wrapped his arms around his mom and brother. Together they held each other until the sobbing stopped. Finally, Abbey said that they needed to find a better way. While they were not homeless, they all knew this situation was not working. They would have to find a better future.

THE ROYAL AZURE BAR AND GRILL

James had set up shop in Roseau. After the first couple of months, he was settling into life here. His office was now complete and finished, located in one of the old pastel-colored two-story buildings. It was bordered by a tropical flora-lined boulevard and the slowly meandering river. From the second-floor front balcony he could see the island's lush hillsides meet azure sea.

The scent of jasmine blooms mixed with the soothing sound of the ocean waves and the onshore breezes made the hectic schedule much easier to tolerate. At the end of the frequent twelve-hour days, James would head down to the Royal Azure Bar.

The owner had sold his small chain of specialty high-end pizza restaurants to one of the mega food corporations. Within weeks he had set up his ocean front bar and grill with a spacious veranda lined with bougainvillea and jasmine.

Behind the bar was Ronnie Baer, owner, and proprietor. Ronnie was from New Haven, Connecticut, and had attended the college of hard knocks. Ronnie was a stout fire plug of a man with a voice that was a cross between the sound of sandpaper on glass and a whiskey growl. Along with Ronnie was his long-time partner in the pizza business, Mike Ignacio. Big Mike, as his nickname implied, was a mountain of a man. At six foot eight and a minimum of three hundred fifty pounds, Ronnie rarely had any trouble at any of his establishment with Big Mike around.

Jimmy, how the hell are ya? Hey, it's only five- thirty, what'ya doin' knockin' off early or what, Ronnie bellowed out, about as friendly as he could.

Yeah, early for Friday anyways, Ronnie. Hey, did you get any Peronis in yet?

Yeah, just this morning, lem'me get'ya one.

From the corner of the bar came the now familiar, *How'r ya?*

Big Mike! Hey what's doing, James asked the jovial giant.

In one hand he had a case of Peronis.

I suppose you're looking for this.

Mike lifted the beers up above the bar counter.

That be the one, Mike, that be the one. From the other end of the bar came,

Make that two!

The man walked over to James and extended his hand.

James McBrian? he asked.

Yes, that would be me. James looked curiously at the tall, thin, well-dressed man.

I'm Robert Fuller, he answered. Well, Mister Fuller, good to meet you, what can I do for you?

James answered like he was replying to a sales inquiry.

James, have you been keeping up with the goings on back in the States?

It's a damn shame, Mister Fuller, it's a damn shame.

James' answer relayed the sense of contempt with Delacorte's administration.

But what is a fella down here concerned about the mess up there anyway?

he said without really thinking.

Well, James, I am here to see you, Robert replied. Oh, sure, okay, sure you are! was his retort.

James, have you not been in the import and export business for what, thirty-some years? came the answer.

Well, thirty-five but yeah, me and a couple dozen other guys.

Maybe, but they're not setting up something like you are and we are interested in what you're doing, was the reply.

Really? Who are 'we' exactly? Well, now you're getting down to brass tacks, Mr. McBrian. I am the Deputy Director of Trade for the RTW States.

James put down his beer and turned with a look of extreme interest.

Okay, you got my interest, Bob, can I call you Bob?

Bob is fine. So, here's the deal, James, we gotta get more aggressive with trade opportunities in South America and more in the Islands. And we want to be brought up to speed on your New America progress.

You should understand, what we are doing is not too different from what your entity has begun to do. It is extremely sad, but until somebody corners that murder of crows in D.C. and runs them and the rest of their minions out of town for good, we must preserve what is left of the ideals of the country. We must keep ourselves forging ahead. The dug in and dyed in the wool Dems and henchmen of Delacorte are not going to change.

They can't. Hell ..., why would anyone vote for the Dems if they were told the Dems can't get the money to pay them off anymore. That would go over like a turd in a punchbowl. If the checks stopped, it would be blood in the streets, and they know it. Everybody knows they're running out of money and the thing is about to implode. You should see what is what happening at the borders between states now. Last week there was an incident where some of Delacorte's government goons at a collections station got into a shootout with some returning RTW state guys. This whole situation is a hair away from a scene from the *Killing Fields*.

So, Mr. McBrian, what we need is your help in dialing up our trade relationships in this area and a lot of other countries so we can stand up to the power squeeze from Delacorte and maybe flip the tables on him. James, your title would be Special Assistant to the Director of Trade.

Now that would be an impressive business card to flash at the girls at the bar, wouldn't it?

Now, this would be in conjunction with what we are doing here, not instead of, is that right, Bob?

We can make that happen, James.

Okay, then, so when are you heading back to, Austin, is it?

Day after tomorrow. Do you need a day to think it over?

No, I'll meet you tomorrow, how about noon here, and bring whatever you need me to sign, and we'll go over the details.

James was confident this was the best offer he had for quite a while.

Okay, welcome aboard, James.

Wait until I see the details before we get to that.

Okay tomorrow at noon, it is.

SCORCHED EARTH

THE AIRMAN REVIEWED THE WEATHER IMAGES coming in from the network of satellites over and over. What the hell is going on? He signaled to the lieutenant, a weather specialist sitting right next to him. There are no wildfires over there, it's a thousand miles away from any drought area.

Well from where I'm sitting that looks like smoke trails but that's got to be fifty miles wide! The specialist was flabbergasted.

Airman, run an infrared spectrum analysis. Let's see where these hot spots are.

Sir, yes, sir.

After about ten minutes the airman reported back to the officer.

Sir, it appears most of the ignition points are located inside the bordering states to the right to work states.

He continued, It appears there are, well, neighborhoods and streets that are ablaze.

The lieutenant looked at the airman in amazement.

Damn, I didn't think **this** many people would react like this to spite the President, the airman said under his breath. Easy, airman, you don't know that.

Well maybe, sir, but this isn't the first week of this.

You know this started when the President made that executive order about making those with empty houses paying five thousand dollars if it is empty for more than three months or the Feds would be seizing the property.

Sir, I remember seeing on TV a man throwing a torch on his house and leaving with a truck loaded with his stuff.

Yes, I heard about it, but I doubt this could have anything to do with those people, the lieutenant replied.

Okay, sir, but those are the fires just the same, he responded.

Airman, just put "fire source: unknown" in your report.

Sir, yes sir.

* * * * *

What the lieutenant's order to the airman could not cover up was the now tens of thousands of cars and trucks heading to the border of the RTW states. At some major arteries, the emergency lanes and medians were now choked with abandoned vehicles. Many had taken their off-road and four-wheel-drive cars and trucks off the paved road and attempted to plow through the fields and underbrush. Some had made it, many had not. The fields were littered with furniture and bags of possessions that were dropped and abandoned because the owners just gave up and continued across the borders with just the clothes on their backs. Maybe they would try to recover the goods later, but most just kept walking. Those who had relatives in the RTW states had help reclaiming their things, and many helped others retrieve their possessions they just could not leave behind.

The collection points soon became moot as those leaving union states just learned the back roads or flat fields and paths that were blazed by others. Within the week, auto auctions began to tow away the abandoned cars and trucks with the proceeds going straight to Washington. This action just enraged the escapees from the union states who attempted to retrieve their vehicles days later. Gangs of tradesmen who needed their trucks and trailers to restart in the RTW states broke into the federal government's auto auctions dealers and "reclaimed" their tools of the trade. Some dealers were happy to help the owners, some, where needed, were persuaded by "other" means.

The net result was Delacorte's grand scheme to extract monies from those leaving backfired and people and assets were flowing out of the area of his control like water over Niagara Falls.

Yet not all exits were so easy. The President could nationalize the National Guard, and this was very handy in separating adjoining states. Delacorte had stepped up collections and guards in Wyoming. He was intent on isolating the western states of Idaho, Nevada, Utah, and Arizona. While he was aware Wyoming was a RTW state, he ordered Humvees and Bradley vehicles at the collection points. It was an act of defiance, it was a "screw you, stop me" with his middle finger extend squarely at the RTW states. While the National Guard was required to man these vehicles, they were only parked there at key points by guardsmen. The next day the loyalists to President Delacorte climbed up on the military hardware and acted as though they were there to stop people and collect the fees. He had stepped up patrols and collections in Michigan and Indiana both on the Great Lakes and the highways, secondary and back roads. No one was getting out without paying through the nose. And if you were leaving, Delacorte was getting whatever you left behind.

While the President at first believed he had the support of Canada and Mexico, this didn't last, and after just a few days the Canadians saw through the sheer stupidity of the President's actions. They let those who could get to the border with a passport or just a driver's license travel into whatever province they could enter.

At one point, some overly zealous supporters of the President in Chicago had commandeered a Coast Guard rescue boat and mounted a fifty- caliber machine gun on the bow. One Friday night in late July, one of the heads of one the locals and a half a dozen members brought a couple cases of Miller " kingers" in cans and a couple bottles of Jägermeister on board. He told the impromptu captain to head toward Gary, Indiana, and see who they could scare the hell out of.

Unfortunately, they did find a group of six high school kids who had taken one kid's family boat out for a nighttime cruise. They too had brought alcohol on board. When the local's members caught up to the thirty-two-foot Sea Ray full of teenagers, most of the impromptu sailors were already plastered. Unfortunately, so was the eighteen-year-old boy steering the boat. He responded to the barking orders of the drunken boatswain by telling him to eat a human waste product and die.

Even though the three hundred-pounder landlubber was so drunk he could barely man the fifty-caliber gun on the Coast Guard boat, he did manage to shoot out a chunk of the arm of his buddy coming up from the stern to stop him. He also hit the engines of the Sea Ray, blowing the transom right off the boat. The self-designated captain of the Coast Guard boat panicked and hit the throttles. In the process he rammed the other boat and rode over the remaining teenagers, killing them instantly. The only clue as to who had perpetrated the incident were the two dozen fifty- caliber shells still piled up in the bow of the Coast Guard boat that was partially tied up at the marina near the navy pier and the crushed Miller cans in the stern. No one was ever questioned for the crime.

While the neighbor to the South at first saw this as an opportunity to send more of the masses gathering at the border, they soon found out that the new sheriff in town frowned on this action. They were turned away, facing the pointy end of three-fifty-seven magnums, forty caliber Smith and Wesson and

AR-15s. The greeting was a curt, "We are sorry, but we are not accepting any applications at this time." Within a couple of weeks, the word had gotten out and the flow turned a small trickle until the last of the stragglers had gotten to the border and were turned back.

However, the border guards of the Mexican side had come to learn that some of the new arrivals to the border were gringos sneaking around Delacorte's roadblock and collection stations. The Mexican guards saw this as an opportunity to hit up the gringos for fifty dollars or whatever contribution they could encourage from the desperate escapees. The guards were all for that just so they got money for baby's new shoes.

LT. COMMANDER HIRSCHFIELD

LT. COMMANDER SAMUEL HIRSCHFIELD WAS A
Navy man. His grandfather was a commander during World
War II on the Coast Guard cutter *Campbell*, credited with
sinking and damaging several U-boats during convoy duty in
the early years of the war in the North Atlantic. The sea was
in his family's blood. After being on board Coast Guard cutters in the Gulf of Sidra during the Gulf War, he was assigned
stateside. He was promoted to Lt. Commander for meritorious
service during the war for coordinating the repulsion of a gang
of terrorists in inflatable that were positioning to threaten one
of the Navy's destroyers.

Stationed in Norfolk for the last year, the new Lt. Commander
duty was working with Naval Intelligence coordinating assignments for Coast Guard cutters and Navy destroyers in the
Middle East and the Gulf of Hormuz. Now he was being transferred to a new division in Navy Department. He was to report
to Admiral Merritt, who was the Navy's point man in the planning and coordination of patrols and security of the domestic
coastline.

This was the prelude to the actual divisions of duty once the
25RTW states reached an agreement (or not) with Delacorte
regarding the division or cooperation of the military. What
was throwing a monkey wrench into the process were the incidents in the Great Lakes. The Coast Guard needed to be able to,
forcibly if needed, ensure possession and control of their naval

assets. There could no longer be malcontents stealing rescue boats and wreaking havoc on the Great Lakes.

"Red" Merritt, as he was called, was assigned to establish patrols and enforce laws and protect residences and commerce in Michigan and Indiana traversing the Great Lakes, especially those to and through the Saint Lawrence Seaway.

The Admiral and the Lt. Commander had a friendly and respectful working relationship. It seemed the Admiral's father had served aboard the *Campbell* with Hirschfield during the war.

Sam did your grandfather ever tell you the story about an international incident Sinbad got them into, the Admiral would begin. You know that damn mutt, Sinbad, got snuck on board in New York. Well, all the sailors and your granddaddy took to the mutt, hell they even took the mutt to the bars when they had liberty. So, the damn dog was on board when they left port.

It wasn't long after that on convoy duty they ran smack into that U-boat wolf pack.

I gotta admit, your grandfather could smell those damn subs from twenty miles away. He had his hands full one night and forcing one to come up to the surface. So, your grandpappy gets all pissed off and decides to ram the damn thing. Imagine this scene, all the guns are shooting at this sub and Sinbad is running and barking and hiding under his bunk, barking some more, and making all kinds of noise.

Well, besides sinking that U-boat, your grandfather hits it at a bad angle and managed to slice open the hull of the ship from the five-inch gun to the engine room, and he hits the damn bow plane of the U-boat!

Damn if water didn't flood the boiler room. Lost all power and the ship is a sitting duck. They couldn't radio anybody for help or that wolf pack would be on them like white on rice. So, they're drifting out in the North Atlantic for like a week and if it weren't for Sinbad the sailors all would have gone nuts.

If that destroyer, the Polish navy had in the area didn't by chance, run across them and then come over and save their butts, well, I don't know if you'd be here right now if it wasn't for them. So anyway, the *Campbell* got a hole in her side you could drive a truck through, and she gets towed to port. While they were in port getting repairs, Sinbad goes with the men to the nearest bar one night, I think it was in Portugal. That damn mutt musta got mad when the disgusted bartender started to take his bowl of beer away the sailors got him and bites the bartender. The sailors get all mad and start a fight with the bartender and some of the locals who didn't like the dog being there in the first place. The local cops show up then the SP's and then it turns into some international big deal because of Sinbad. That damn dog kept the sailors on board for the rest of the month before they would let them out on liberty again.

The mutt was on the ship for the rest of the war. The Admiral chuckled and shook his head just in retelling the story.

Anyways, he stopped and motioned the Lt. Commander to sit down. Okay, I got a job for you, he continued. Some damn fools up on Lake Michigan are causing all kinds of crap for the local folks. A couple of the shitheads stole one of our twenty-nine-foot response boats and shot up some kids and their boat. I suspect it's a bunch of Delacorte's old goon buddies but, as usual, no one seems to know anything about anything, big surprises that is.

Here's what I want you to do. Head up there and straighten the place out, knock some heads if you must. Who knows what Delacorte is telling his gorillas to do?

Anyway, kick some ass and see if you can nail who's doing this shit. If you can get a conviction, there may just be a promotion in there for you.

Got it, sailor? the Admiral barked, hiding his smile. Sir, yes sir.

Now this is one more thing we have gotten wind of from one of our insiders, he added, we are getting some rumors that they got something big in the wind, a major disruption. I do not know what the people are capable of, but if it's what we are hearing, it's trouble. The one thing you gotta do is see how far down the rabbit hole this group is connected. These are long-time Chicago goons and it's no telling who's got their grubby paw prints on this thing. I got an idea, and I don't like what my senses are telling me.

Anyway, whatever you find, just make sure you got it nailed down and you've got my support. Whatever you come up with no matter how ... he chose his words carefully, disturbing... report directly to me. That is all, now get to it.

The Admiral patted him on the back and shook his hand as he walked him out of his office.

By the way, the Admiral said to him at the door, you may find out more without the uniform. We've got some people placed in key positions inside one of the union locals.

You may want to apply as a maintenance assistant at the complex there. Here's the details you will need to apply for this job.

You know your way around Chicago, son, don't you?

Sir, I spent a summer there a few years ago.

Good, then you won't have any trouble with finding this office.

The Admiral handed him a printed sheet with a name, a building and an office number.

I'm sure you'll have a better than average chance of getting the job. The Admiral smiled at the officer and finished the conversation. Good luck, son.

THE TRAP IS SET

OK, I TAKE THE ORANGE LINE TO ROOSEVELT STATION. *Then transfer to the green line south to Cermak station. Go through the walkway beside building number one and go to the main entrance to the building four and look for the Maintenance Management offices.*

Sam read the instructions from the Admiral to make sure he knew each step.

As the bell chimed and the light blinked on, the doors of the elevator opened.

Sam stepped out and saw the sign on the wall pointed to " Maintenance Offices."

The offices were small and all business with one receptionist and a half a dozen folding chairs.

The sign on the receptionist desk stated plainly," SIGN IN AND HAVE SEAT."

Sitting at the desk sat a svelte grey -haired woman with her hair pulled back in a neat bun.

The lines and creases on her face gave away her age but she was still quite attractive as the years seemed to be kind to her so far. She was tending to her cup of tea, stirring intently.

The woman looked up and said, good morning, handed Sam a pen to sign in and pointed to the chairs. Have a seat, someone will be with you shortly.

The receptionist reached for her phone, dialed an extension number, and quietly said a few words and nodded as she lowered the receiver.

Within a few minutes, Sam heard a raspy voice announce as she stepped into the waiting area.

Hirschfield, Samuel? Okay, come on in my office.

My name is Joyce Osheffski. So, you wanna work at this complex ,the middle-aged women switched the lipstick-stained cigarette between her fingers with the matching-colored fingernail polish and her overstuffed ashtray on her notepaper-covered desk.

She looked at him with a half-smile, Okay, sign these union forms and you start Monday.

Okay, sure, thank you, ma'am, Sam replied.

Pick up your uniform on the way out, it'll be deducted from your first check, along with your union dues, she added.

Okay, thanks again, Sam said, smiling at her.

Oh, and report to Supervisor George Freeman's office on Monday, he'll be your boss and union shop steward. she said in between drags of a new Marlboro.

* * * * *

Monday morning, Samuel was at the supervisor's office ten minutes early.

You must be the new guy. Mr. Freeman greeted the new employee matter-of-factly and flatly. All right then, give me a couple of minutes and I'll tell you who 'll be showing you the ropes.

The supervisor was in no hurry. He sat down and finished his coffee and after a few minutes picked up his phone to make what seemed like half a dozen calls. After about twenty minutes he emerged from his office.

Okay, head over to Building 2 sub-basement and Frank Slovic will show you what you need to know. Mr. Freeman's voice was relaxed now like he had just solved a nagging problem. Oh, and if Frank isn't there, call Clancy's Bar, he'll probably be having a morning eye opener. The number is in my office on the cork board. And if he's not there, try Mitch's.

He'll be at one or the other. That number is on the board right next to Clancy's

Samuel nodded and replied, Okay, thanks, Mr. Freeman.

Okay, kid, it'll take you a couple of days to get in the swing of it, so don't worry too much if you don't do too much right way, George said to him as he got up to head over to the elevator.

Frank will fix you up, but you gotta work with him a little bit. He needs a break every so often to get himself going, but don't you worry about it. Okay, Mr. Freeman, I'll remember that.

Fine, kid, you be okay, just remember what I'm telling ya, and you'll be okay.

At nine forty-five a.m. Samuel was looking for Frank in his office. He had reported to the sub-basement, but no one was there. He walked over to the receiving dock and asked if anybody knew Frank.

He's at Clancy's; the asshole knows what time it is, came the reply from inside the shipping office. You the new guy? Yes sir, I am, answered Sam, with a little nervous hint in his voice.

Take a left outta the dock on and head down South Archer and it's down a couple three blocks on the left... Call down there first and if he don't show up, go down there, and drag his ass back here!

Out from behind his desk stepped Rodney LaSalle. Rodney was a French Canadian who had moved to Chicago ten years ago. He appeared as though he had just stepped off the Champ d'Lyseille. His five-foot-four stature and pencil-thin moustache only added to his air of European origins.

I told him, I said, hey, one of these times you gonna find your ass up a creek with shit on your paddle, he replied with his thick French accent. If you go up there, tell him I told yous to drag his fat ass back here.

Will do, Mr. LaSalle, will do. Sam was relieved he had run across someone who seemed to care about doing their job. Thirty minutes later, Sam was heading to the bar. After a few minutes he could see the bars signage.

The old metal sign had individual letters with lightbulbs lighting each letter; C-L-A-N. The rest of the lightbulb letters in *Clancy's* were blinking to some out-of-step beat of their own. It was at one time a very fashionable place with its enameled panels in cobalt blue and stainless-steel trim. But now the rust and dirt had dulled the façade and the tiles at the entrance were cracked and broken. The walnut and oak bar had absorbed the dark stains of years of cigarette burns and spilled drinks. The red leatherette on the seats of the row of booths were now split and cracked and the once ornate ceiling tiles had strips of peeling paint and dust and cobwebs hanging from them.

On the last chrome and red leather stool at the bar was Frank. He was slouched over the edge of the bar with a lit Camel in one hand a draft beer in the other. The cigarette was burned down with the ashes bending, ready to fall off at any second. The draft of the day was Schaefer, buy four get one free. There were several empty pilsner glasses still on the bar. In front of another full beer were two empty shot glasses.

Sam didn't have to say a word, as the bartender nudged Frank when he walked in. Frank's body was half bent down over the bar. Like on cue he twisted his head like on a swivel to look up at Sam.

So, you're the new kid, he began to say. Okay, okay, I'll be over in a minute, you head over to there, I'll be there in a couple of ten minutes. What's your name kid? Frank said, moving to stand up. Sam, Sam Hirschfield.

Okay Sam, I'll be over there in ten or fifteen minutes.

At eleven a.m. Frank walked through the opened door to his small office with the one desk that had probably been in the exact same spot for ten years.

Sam had been sitting on a pile of old stacked newspapers with dates going back to five years.

Okay, kid, here's what we'll do today. I'll show you around the boiler room and the electrical closet and the elevator system. There's a phone number for each system. If something goes bad, pick up the phone and call the number. Then you wait for the guy to fix it, you stay with him until its finished or five p.m. After that it's time and a half. For the first couple weeks, if something goes wrong you stick with me, and we'll get it covered. Frank seemed to be comfortable enough with Sam and it seemed like the next week or so would be a breeze.

Do you ever have to figure out how to fix something before anybody else gets here Sam asked?

Naw, most of the time it's against union rules, Frank responded.

The plumber got his union rules, the electrician got his rules, and they get all pissed off if you mess with their jobs.

Frank just knew the way things worked. Okay, kid, why don't you knock off for lunch. If I'm not back by three, I'll see you tomorrow."

Okay Frank, I guess if anything goes wrong, I can find you.
Yeah, kid, just don't look too hard.

SOUTH OF THE BORDER

ABBEY WAS ON HER LUNCH BREAK WITH M.J. A few weeks after her emotional breakdown incident with her boys. She glanced up at M.J. and the tears started welling in the corners of her eyes.

Abbey, what's the matter, was the automatic response when M.J. noticed the tear.

Oh M.J., the boys are so unhappy and I'm so worried about Daniel. He's so withdrawn and sad; I just don't know how long we can stay here. The boys don't tell me, but I know there is just no one their ages for them to socialize and do things.

Listen, Abbey, I don't know if you can pull it off, but I keep on seeing articles online begging for people with agricultural knowledge and experience, but you got to get into Texas and the south. Honestly, I have no idea what it's gonna be like getting through these border collection points they got all set up. I mean it could be tough. I've heard they really expect you to pay them, and I mean real money, M.J. told her.

I don't know, M.J., but I got to do something, I can't keep dealing with the boys being so unhappy, Abbey had to admit. I'll see what I can find out for you, I know a couple of guys who are in New Orleans. Give me a day or so and I'll see what I can find out for you. M.J. didn't want to see her friend leave but couldn't refuse to at least try to help her.

* * * * *

Late Saturday morning the phone rang. Hey girl, what's up, how ya 'doing? It was M.J.

Listen, I heard from my friends in Louisiana. Really, replied Abbey, so what did they tell you?

They said there's all kinds of work and jobs but told me there's no way to get through a collection point without paying somebody real money and they are serious about it. They said they went through Mexico to get into Texas.

Jeez, M.J., I don't know, I just don't know. Well, that's all I know right now, I'll see what else I can find out, okay?

*****

That night Abbey stayed up late for both boys to get home from work. Daniel looked so worn out and tired, she right then and there knew it was time to move on.

Boys, she began, we came here because we had to, but I can see how unhappy you both are.

Jeff broke in, mom, it's not that bad, we can...

No Jeff, it is, she said.

Abbey wouldn't let him try to convince her otherwise. I can see it in your faces, and I want more for us than this. M.J. told me there are better opportunities elsewhere and I think we need to decide we are going to go after them.

Abbey was trying to tell them she had already made up her mind.

Look, for once I am deciding for us. I can't stand to see both of you so unhappy. This place has served its purpose, but it's time for better things and we aren't going to find it here. M.J. told me there are lots and maybe better jobs in Texas and I think we need to find out.

At least we will have something to look forward to and I think we are going to feel like we are moving in the right direction.

Okay, mom, I say let's go. Daniel's tired look and half-closed eyes were all she needed to see.

Jeff, what do you say? Hey, what about the borders and all that stuff, mom, he asked.

M.J. said she's got friends down there now, so I will find out what we need to do.

Mom, okay I'm in. That was all she needed.

She would get the info from M.J. and they would start to plan to make the trip.

HENRICO JOSE DELACORTE JR.

His BIRTH CERTIFICATE SAID HE WAS BORN IN Miami, Florida, to a Cuban mother and Puerto Rican father. Rumors always had it that there were FALN members in the father's extended family. His mother's parents were farmers in western Cuba who escaped during the Marielle boat lift. Many of the others who escaped Cuba with them were just released political prisoners. Many had ties to both Castro supporters and anti-Castro forces.

While growing up in Miami's little Havana district, Henrico's home was always filled with conversation and debate and arguments about politics and revolutions. His father, Henrico Sr., was becoming more militant as time went on. To him the ends justified the means. If it meant violence and breaking laws, he was willing to do whatever it took to further his vision. He was caught robbing a bank, trying to fund a militant Puerto Rican group that demanded a free Puerto Rico. He was sent away for the robbery for twenty years, but the robbery was not tied to the violent militant group.

His mother wanted very much wanted to blend into the fabric of her new life in America and become like her aunts and uncle who had escaped Castro in 1959. That all changed during the Cuban Missile Crisis. His mother, Lena Contessa, had family still in Cuba. They also had nephews and brothers who were killed in the 1962 Bay of Pigs debacle. Years later, Lena still swore it was Kennedy's fault for not supporting the invasion.

After that incident she became more and more angry. She visited Henrico Sr. once a week in prison and as often as she could. He asked her to help in the FALN cause and to do whatever she could to raise money for the group he had started to support.

Lena looked to the drug trade to raise the big money she knew would be needed to further the causes of a free Puerto Rico. Within a year she was dealing 100 kilos a month of cocaine and heroin. She had business all the way up to Jacksonville and as far west as New Orleans. She was sending hundreds of thousands of dollars a month to any pro-independence for Puerto Rico group that asked her for help.

A trip she made to Bogotá to secure more supplies of cocaine changed Henrico Jr.'s world. Lena was to meet her new supplier that afternoon to discuss the logistics of the transaction. The meeting place was a rooftop garden of a restaurant owned by the supplier's family. Lena was aware of the violent past of the group and the bombings of public officials' homes who had tried to stop and arrest the group's key family members.

Before Lena was even comfortable in the wide wicker chair in the plush garden surroundings, shots were heard outside on the street. Then the pinging of bullets ricocheting off the concrete floor and walls began everywhere. The Columbian army was intent on stopping the violence and this was their first target. Before Lena could make her way to the staircase, an army sharpshooter had targeted her. She hit the concrete, dead with a bullet hole now visible behind her ear.

Henrico was twelve years old when that had happened. The incident forced other family members to agree Henrico would only be safe with Lena's parents now in the Brooklyn, N.Y. He would have to leave and leave now. Suez and Salvador Contessa accepted their daughter's son with open arms. They had a stable environment for the boy. Salvador was a retired Spanish teacher.

166

Suez, his wife of thirty-seven years works at the sales office of a well-known premium cigar importer. Suez loved the tobacco business. She still remembered as a child growing the dark, rich tobaccos at their family's small plot of land an hour from Havana and loved the aroma of the broad leaves. And she still fondly recalled when she worked rolling cigars when not at school. She would tell her friends about the factory manager reading from the newspaper to them aloud about the events in Havana and the world. Many of the other factory girls were quite savvy as to the events around them and the coming revolution.

The factory had many of their biggest customers in the United States and most of them were in New York City. When the embargo of Cuban products was imposed on the factory, many of the girls were let go because of lack of work. And her family's small plot with its crop of tobacco was sold at a loss.

Suez never forgot how the policies of the U.S. and Kennedy had affected their lives. She hated Kennedy for not supporting the Bay of Pigs invasion and her family members dying for nothing. The embargo only opened resentments that had been planted before. She felt herself getting angry every time she thought about how much business her bosses were losing because of an embargo that didn't mean much of anything to America but had affected her so deeply.

While she never acted on her resentment and growing hostility toward the government in Washington, her opinions would influence Henrico for the rest of his life.

NOW IS THE TIME

LISTEN LADY IF YOU'RE TAKING THIS RENTAL ONE way to Austin, its five-thousand dollars

What! That's crazy! For a one way! I can't pay that! Abbey was frustrated and furious.

Listen, lady, I'm sorry but it's because I'm never gonna get that rental truck back. I got no guarantee I'm gonna ever see that truck back up here and the rental company will write it off after a year, the owner told her.

So now their policy is five-thousand dollars if it crosses into a RTW state, that's just the way it is. Lady, I'm sorry. I didn't come up with this stupid crap outta D.C., but that's it.

Abbey turned away from the counter, staring out into the parking lot full of small trucks. The answer was the same from the two other rental companies, so Abbey knew she wasn't being conned. She reached in her purse to find some tissues to wipe away the beginnings of tears.

From behind the rental counter the voice of a now concerned kindly man spoke to her. But you know, you didn't ask if I had any trucks for sale, now did ya?

He started his sales pitch. I'm Joseph McDowd, and I do have trucks for sale at rock bottom prices. Okay, young lady, here's what I'm gonna do, what's your name by the way, he asked.

Abbey.

Okay, Abbey where are you planning on heading?

Austin, Texas.

Austin? Oh Jesus, Mary, and Joseph, you`re gonna head down through Nogales, aren't you, he responded, genuinely concerned.

I don't know, I guess we have to, she replied.

Well, I know many folks that left through Nogales. Just make sure you are at the border into Mexico at sunrise, and for God's sake make sure you are crossing from Ciudad Juarez into El Paso before nightfall. Joseph asked, Who's going with you, Abbey?

My two sons.

How old, if you don't mind me asking?

Twenty and twenty-five, she responded with a curious and concerned look on her face.

Well, that's a good start. Can they handle themselves if there's trouble, he asked?

I'm sure they can. Abbey, I hope so.

You cannot under any circumstance get caught with any firearms going into Mexico. If you do, you won't have to worry about getting into Austin, he warned her.

Just go about your business, drive, don't stop unless you have to for gas and then just stick to the main roads.

I think it's just Route 19 in Nogales to Mexico Route 15 to Route 2 and then 45 North to Ciudad Juarez and then into El Paso. Abbey looked at him. You sure seem to know your way around the block, Mr. McDowd.

This ain't my first rodeo, Abbey, so listen ta what I'm tellin' you.

You can make it in one day if you drive all day. You want to be outta Mexico before dark, okay? Okay. They agreed.

So now let's talk trucks.

They walked through the lot. He sold her an eight-year-old van with one hundred-thirty thousand miles on it. It would be good enough to get her where she needed to go.

THE QUIET END TO ROCCO'S AUTO SUPPLY

AFTER A GOOD SIX MONTHS OF PLANNING AND conversations with Uncle G., Stephano walked into Rocky's office and closed the door behind him.

So, here's the deal. We got no more inventory ordered, we got almost everybody paid up that we owe to, so here's what I'm thinkin'.

Man, I'll tell you what, I'm sure am glad Uncle G. had us go through that crap getting Italian passports, I think we are gonna need them pretty damn soon, he said.

I made up a letter to all our good customers we can trust and start to sell off the inventory to them. But I called them to tell them to wire the payment to the bank account at the Banco di LaSpezia and they can take ten percent off the bill.

Did anybody ask any question? Rocky asked.

Yea, the chooch at Montevale wanted to know what about the wire fee, Stephano replied with a hint of disgust.

What did you tell' em? I said take it off the invoice and don't ask no question and I'll send ya back a supersotta. That shut him up.

Rocky chuckled. That augauts, he always looking for somethin'.

I got the counter offer today on the building, so I think we take it. I told the guy for what he wants to offer, I want cash, no terms, so, no bullshitting around, Rocky said to Stephano as they got up to head to the warehouse.

I just hope he doesn't screw us up waiting for the closing. Other than that, we could be outta here in maybe thirty, maybe forty days. Stephano's tone was relaxed and matter of fact.

I'll get ahold of Uncle G. and tell him to send over the passports. If the state or Feds want any more money outta us, it's **afanabola!**

Anyways, we got a lot more crap to dump before we can close up, we gotta grind it out for a couple more weeks, Rocky said, looking at Stephano with sense of dread and regret.

Stephano's comment to his brother before walking out of the warehouse rang clear as a bell.

It's a shame, all that work that Pops and Uncle G. did for all those years getting this thing built up and we gotta bail because of some elected stugauts that couldn't find their ass with either hand. They can't run a merry go round and we gotta pay for it.

Yeah, I know, but at least we can take what we got left before they get their hands on it, Rocky said with more than a bit of contempt.

They both got in their cars and left that afternoon. What they didn't recognize was that they were one of many thousands of other businesses that were just closing, leaving no trace of what it had taken to get this far. Now they knew that they were the generation that would be searching for something to replace what their parents and the generations before them had fought for and now was being pissed away.

Not because they couldn't make it work. They could. They just chose not to fight the battle anymore.

It was the taxes and rules, the lawsuits, and the regulations. It wasn't so much the competition from overseas anymore. They could usually figure out a way to compete. It was a question of keeping what little money was left.

A critical mass had been breached, a turning point reached, a balance shifted. Soon entire towns and villages were void of any business of any kind. Those that stayed were either totally self-sufficient like small farms that had stayed off the grid and were unnoticed. Or those on a government program. Some knew the day might come that the money would run out. Some had already gone before that day happened. The flames and smoke trails of the burning remnants of their possessions were the product of contempt and anger at what had happened.

The Delacorte administration had garnered much of the blame and rightly so. The truth was it had started long before, drip by drip. Years ago, it should have and could have been corrected. But now the gigantic amounts of money needed to keep the system moving were just too massive. All it would take now was just the moment that the fantasy economic system based on trust lost its base of value. That was the belief that the system could sustain itself.

That moment had been reached; it just hadn't caught up to the denial of that fact in Washington. Very soon the check would not be issued or those issued would not be accepted as payment for anything of value. Time was up.

CONNECT THE DOTS

Sam had to walk to Clancy's again on Tuesday. There was a special on Pabst's Blue Ribbon on Tuesday. It appeared that the brewery had sent in an extra delivery truck this morning, judging by the number of empty glasses already littering the bar. Frank Slovic was ensconced at his usual bar stool. Sitting next to him was the brother of his sister-in-law, Stashu Jacyniski. He was also a regular at Clancy's, but usually 5 p.m. until closing were his social hours.

This morning was different. Stashu was chain smoking and downing shots and beers with abandon. The fact that he was expected at work on the loading dock seemed unimportant.

I tell ya, Frank, if anybody finds out about Uncle Mika's arm getting' blasted by me, we're all screwed, Stashu muttered through the haze of several cigarettes lit at once.

Yeah, yeah, I hear you. Hey, you can head to Mississauga and work over at the 7-Eleven that Freeman's brother owns.

Just tell Joyce, she'll hide your timecard until things cool down.

The light from the now opening door swept across the dark corner of the bar.

It was Sam.

Hey Frank, how's it going? asked Sam.

Great kid, great, I'll be over there in ten minutes, and tell the Frenchy, I know what time it is... the asshole.

Don't worry about it, Frank, everything's under control, Sam said to be low key.

Under control, that's good, kid, that's good.

Frank swiveled his head to look up him.

Hey kid, pull up a chair, you got time for a quick one.

Sam thought for a second to himself, *Oh great, breakfast beer...just what I need, what could be worse than that? But I gotta get close to these guys.*

Well okay, Frank, but we can't both be gone for too long so, just one for now, Sam said, thinking what the best way was to handle the situation.

Harry, Frank looked up to the bartender, give the kid a beer.

Frank, who's your friend, Sam asked, looking over to Stashu. Oh yeah, this is Stashu, we're related on the wife's side.

Good to meet you, Stashu.

Just call me Stosh.

Okay, Stosh, good to meet you.

Sam was slowly nursing his beer, when Frank let slip to Stashu,

Don't worry about it, I'll sit down with Joyce, and she'll handle it. I'd give it a couple of weeks and it will blow over, she'll punch your card or you can take vacation time, either way, it will cool down.

All right, Frank, you handle it and I'll see what George says and I'll see you in a coupla weeks.

Stashu lifted his ample and oversized girth up from the bar stool.

Kid, good ta meet ya.

You take it easy on Frank, he said to Sam as he ambled to the exit.

Sam knew if he asked about the conversation, he might just be sticking his nose where it shouldn't go. He could check with the Admiral and see if Joyce was the source on the inside. If so, he would contact her after hours and see what she could tell him.

After work and into the evening, Sam would head over to the Navy pier and the areas around the marinas checking for anything that looked like somebody looking for trouble. The Coast Guard now had armed sailors and MPs at all stations. It would be difficult to pull the same stunt with a rescue boat. But not with the larger fishing and motorboats, who were still causing trouble harassing people on Lake Michigan and the rest of the lakes.

There were still incidents happening with regularity and the incident with the teenagers near Gary was not resolved. If any of these lake pirates and their minions could be caught in a trap and questioned, then maybe they could see where it would lead.

Two days later, Sam called his superior.

Well, Lieutenant, if I told you, yes, she is, that is maybe confidential information, replied Admiral Merritt.

Why don't I just leave it at you could find her to be helpful in your questions.

Thank you, sir, Samuel replied. I will try to be low key in my inquiries, he promised.

On Friday, Sam waited until most of the crews had gone for the weekend to knock on Joyce's office door.

Mrs. Osheffski, are you in? Sam said, rapping on the frosted glass window part of her door.

Yes, yes, come on in, Samuel, what can I do for you?

And hurry it up, if you don't mind, I was just on my way out the door.

Oh, okay, Mrs. Osheffski.

Sam, we're on the same side here, if you know what I mean, and call me Joyce.

Okay, Joyce, well I thought I heard that Stosh wanted to take some time off from the loading dock.

Yeah, I just talked to him about it a couple of hours ago, but how would you know that? On second thought, I don't want to know.

So how does that affect you, Sam?

Well, I could use some extra hours, he replied.

I don't do anything on the weekends, maybe you could find some hours for me helping Frenchy or something, Sam answered her, knowing full well it was his excuse to nose around and see what he could uncover.

Well, nobody else is asking for extra hours around here, yeah, I'll see what I can do. Maybe next Saturday we can get you a half a day or so, she responded.

Then she added, Yeah, a couple of the guys have fishing boats and like to cruise around all weekend, so I guess you might be able to find more than a couple of extra hours of OT.

She nodded and winked as she got up. Okay, I'm outta here.

See you on Monday, Sam.

Yeah, have a good weekend, Joyce.

They both walked down the walkway to the Metra station and went in opposite directions.

THE OFFICE OF TRADE FOR RIGHT TO WORK STATES

JAMES THOUGHT TO HIMSELF AS HE WAS PUTTING the finishing touches on his office, *I'll have this done in a couple of hours and I can head over to the hotel and grab some dinner. Tomorrow it'll be meetings with the trade office people and lunch with Bob Fuller. After that we got numbers and quotas for the year and then head back to Roseau.* He headed toward the door and after opening it, he noticed the new sign attached to it:

JAMES MCBRIAN
DEPUTY DIRECTOR OF TRADE.

Well, I'll be damned, that does look pretty good, he said as he headed out the door. His office was small, but it was on the same hall as the Governor and many of the newly appointed Cabinet officials.

Hey James, come on over here. It was Bob Fuller. Have you met Governor, soon to be President of the RTW states, Jim Cabbott?

No sir, I have not, it's a pleasure to meet you, sir, James replied, beaming ear to ear.

The pleasure is mine, good to meet you, James.

I'm thinking ole Bob is gonna have you run ragged before this year is over for us, he said and laughed, still gripping his hand from the long handshake.

James asked Governor Cabbott, Governor, I didn't know you were to be President.

Well, the deal is it's only two years at a time, and for now we're thinking two years and that's it.

We got plenty of governors and most of us are on the same page, so it's not like we're upsetting the boat or anything.

I'm happy to see you will be first, Governor, James replied.

Thank you, James. Now where are we gonna have lunch?

Bob piped up, Okay, we got the Palms, we got Ruth's Chris, we got Franklin's.

BBQ! said James and the governor at the small time.

Bob and the governor laughed out loud and looked right at James.

Governor, I believe our deputy is going fit right in here.

James looked at both with a quizzical look. Who doesn't love BBQ?

They headed down the hall and to the lobby.

From the lobby of the Shark Tank came a bellowing voice.

Hey where ya'll going? It was Lowell Payne, the Vice-Presidential nominee who was the popular candidate for the job.

His executive experience made him a natural choice and his outgoing personality had just about sealed the deal. The Georgia native always told stories about coming off the farm at seventeen with twenty dollars and his grandma's secret recipe for fried chicken, fried green tomatoes and crackling' cornbread. Ten years later he got twenty restaurants and he was on his way. It was his tax plan that made a name for himself. It was a plan to do away with the IRS and replace it with a combination of a fair tax and a flat tax that had endeared him to so many business and everyday folks.

Where ya'll heading for lunch? Lemme guess, oh hell! I know it's barbeque and it don't matter where!

I hope you know somebody that will go to Franklins and put some brisket on a to-go plate for us, Lowell said.

Dontcha worry, we got it covered, let's go, was the casual reply from the soon-to-be President.

* * * * *

Slowly, the gigantic task of what the insiders were calling "*the cleave*" was being accomplished. They had travelled five miles on a thousand-mile road to complete what was now a solidifying vision of the future. Still, a moment or two of hopefulness did not nullify the months and years of work to stabilize the twenty-five RTW states.

In the coming weeks, now empty offices would begin to fill with employees from RTW states who knew what the plan would be and believed in the vision.

What was not yet known to this group was the undertone that was developing in the western and northeastern states. There was now real concern at all levels of local and state government. Without beginning a rumor mill, some of the dyed-in-the-wool progressive strongholds began to question the wisdom of Washington. There was always the impression that this would be resolved and that all would be forgiven.

Don't worry, this will blow over in a few weeks, the public will be getting ready for the holidays, and this will be a passing memory. That was the talking point coming out of D.C.

But some of the mayors and state legislators in the largest states in the west and northeast began a separate plan in case the President could not pull everything back together. Some states began secret meetings with Canada. Even Mexico made overtures to California, just to see what kind of financial shape they really were in and if the Hispanic citizens and non-citizens thought they could sell a *"Nuevo California"* deal to Governor Sienna, the incoming governor.

Very few of the president's allies knew about the meeting at Camp David the month before. Fewer knew of the outcome.

CAMP DAVID MEETING

JUST A FEW WEEKS AFTER THE MEETINGS IN Greensboro and Atlanta, the RTW governors had attempted one weekend of secret meetings with President Delacourte. The governors never asked for this situation. It was not of their doing. Was this new HCA law the beginning of the end? Yes, most likely. Most of these states never approved of it. But that was long ago and water under the bridge. That was, until President Delacorte pulled this executive order government takeover. There was a sense of one last attempt to find any common ground, no matter how small. At least they could say they would try to reach out to Washington and reverse the disaster.

Catoctin State Park in Thurmont, Maryland, had been known by Presidents and world leaders as Camp David. The woody retreat was best suited to keep out any prying eyes of the media and keep leaks at bay. President Delacorte had flown in on Marine One at midnight with a small circle of advisors and Isabelle, his wife of ten years.

Isabelle was only in her late thirties. Her svelte figure and demur style made her popular among fashion plate and social media types. Her Central American heritage always kept her the subject of conversation with Hispanic and other minority groups. She was stunningly beautiful with her dark mane of carefully coiffed hair and fashion sense. Her penetrating brown eyes could melt even the most chauvinistic male. Ironically, she shunned the fashion magazine requests for photo shoots and interviews. It was her belief that her words and thoughts would be twisted into something she didn't believe or support. While Isabelle was always an active supporter of cases to benefit children and abused animals, she rarely was seen in public with her husband. She was described as extraordinarily independent and pursued her own interests and causes. Her sense of justice and fairness in all matters and on a global scale guided her in her life.

The Laurel Lodge was where the President would meet and greet the governors. They had come to the retreat in small groups throughout the previous days. They were spread out throughout the compound at different cabins and lodges. Governor Cabbott was lodging at Aspen Lodge while others were located at Holly, Sycamore and Red Oak. The wood paneled meeting room in Laurel Lodge made for the best place to discuss the crisis and any possible resolution.

The governors would walk the grounds in small groups to discuss strategy and compromises that might be possible. The President was spending the afternoon before all had arrived at the skeet shooting range and the bowling alley. The barracks on the grounds had it's usual compliment of Secret Service and military personnel manning the compound.

There would be no leaks to the media.

The first meeting was scheduled for Saturday night at seven p.m., right after dinner. At first the meetings and discussion were cordial. It was a rehash of the history that had led up to the current situation. There appeared to be a basic acknowledgement of the other side's position. The President was explaining the way he and his advisors had reached their conclusions and actions… and demands. It was all downhill from there.

Governor Jordan spoke up first.

Mr. President, in all honesty, you realize what these taxes and surcharges will do to my state, and besides, as we just voted to be right to work, we feel like we are getting the screws first. Governor Jordan at that point may have set the stage for the rest of the evening with his next comment.

Look, Mr. President, you gotta have two hundred other places you can cut and end this before it gets out of hand.

The President's look flashed anger, but he caught the glance of Isabelle who was sitting in a Martha Washington chair over near the stone fireplace. Her look transformed from cautious attentiveness to distinct displeasure with his change in demeanor. He regained his composure without lashing out.

Governor, he calmly replied, I know it may seem unfair, but we need to fund these projects and many of them are about to be implemented.

Well, okay, Mr. President, that's fine, but we are still not out of this eighth year of recession, and we don't have income levels in Michigan to support these taxes.

We will fall like a house of cards, and I will not be able to stop it. We'd have to cut the police and fire departments by two-thirds.

Jordan was firm in his statement.

I'd have to raise state income tax to like twenty-five percent. There ain't no freaking way in hell I'm gonna do that.

Well, Jim, you're gonna have to do the best you can, we need the funds,

Delacorte answered, and he intended to leave no room for compromise.

The governor was not going to respond well to being told how it was going be, with no respect and no dignity.

Mr. President, we came here to work on a way out of this situation, interjected George Miller. We are operating on the premise you intend to show good faith and work a solution to this issue. The words were enunciated clearly so there was no mistake what he meant.

Mr. President, and I say that with the respect to the office and the men who held that office before you, but ifin` your mind is already made up, then there is no sense in trying to make a silk purse outta a sow's ear.

Let me tell you, sir, if you have no intention of cutting your damn spending on cockamamie projects and handing out money by the boat load just to keep your party in the green, count us out.

Just wait a minute there, Governor, the President attempted to assert his position into the conversation.

Then the governor responded, No, Mr. President, you have bankrolled these projects with no forethought to the consequences. We are not bailing you out when we are barely holding on now. These executive orders of yours are not to make you king.

The House does the funding, not you. I am sorry that you feel that way, Governor, but seeing as I don't see any House member here, I guess I'm doing the spending. Get it?

No! No, we don't get it! jumped in Jim Jordan. You don't have that power, it is not in the Constitution, it is for the House."

Well, if the House would do something, I wouldn't have to go around them, the President scolded. And besides I got the numbers in the House and the Senate ,they will do what I tell them. A moment's pause was followed by the silence that finalized the evening's attempt to make any compromises.

Okay, boys, let's go, we aren't getting anywhere tonight. Governor Cabbot rose in disgust. We ain't getting' anywhere.

They rose together while the President exited out onto the terrace. Isabelle and Henrico moved to the patio off the side of Laurel Lodge.

Isabelle stared at him, first in pensive analysis of her husband. She asked him, Why did you talk down to them like that, what's wrong with you?

At first, he didn't say anything.

She asked again, Why did you treat them like that?

Aww, shut the hell up, woman! Why did I treat them like that?

Because I felt like it, that's why!

Isabelle sat there silent, but a look of contempt that she had never felt before swept over her face.

They sat there for almost any hour without saying a word. Tomorrow had better turn out better... For all.

THE LONG TRIP THROUGH PERDITION

M.J. HELPED THEM PACK THE LAST OF THE BOXES in the U-Haul trailer attached to Abbey's van.

It was the longest of goodbyes and M.J. hugged Abbey and gave the boys a kiss on the cheek and they were gone.

The trip would be on mostly a lot of state highways and secondary roads and not many interstates. From Reno they would head out to Nevada 80, then to Route 50-A to Route 95 though Hawthorne and Tonopah. They planned on making it to outside of Las Vegas before midnight and stop. The first Motel 6 with a Denny's was as far as they could go.

They had given themselves five days to get to Austin, so they could sleep a little late and be on the road by ten a.m., Abbey figured.

Abbey woke up to a note from Jeff: *mom, there's a pool and we're in it come get us for breakfast.*

She walked out to join them and stuck her feet in the warm, clear water. She let the sun warm her for a few minutes and then headed back to the room to gather their bags.

Okay, boys, enough fun, get dressed and meet me for breakfast.

Around nine-thirty a.m. they stopped to take pictures and were in sheer amazement of the size and grandeur of the Hoover

187

Dam. But sightseeing was not in the cards today. By ten-fifteen a.m. they were in Boulder City and crossed into Arizona.

Mom, Daniel asked as he adjusted his sunglasses, what's next, where do I turn?

It's a right on 93 all the way to Kingman and then Wickenburg.

It would be all day and then outside of Phoenix by eight p.m. Just out of Phoenix and a Holiday Express was enough for the trio. They were dusty and exhausted. The reality of everything they had known in their lives was changing with every passing mile.

Jeff passed the time asking Abbey about some of the summer vacations he remembered when they were small. They winced when they remembered when Daniel had gotten lost at Universal Studios and that night at the emergency room and the twelve stitches in his forehead. Abbey gave a painful look and reminded Jeff about the time his shoulder dislocated in karate class and how everyone called him to make sure he was okay.

Abbey talked about how she moved to California with a dog and a cat in the cab of a small, rented truck. The dog had eaten something bad and threw up on the seat of the truck. She laughed when she told them they had to stop and rent another truck. All the memories kept passing the time but could not remove why they were on this trip. Everything was so different now, every mile behind them took them further away from those happy and breezy times.

Tomorrow it was only as far as Nogales. Abbey remembered what she was warned: be out of Mexico by nightfall.

They arrived late afternoon and found another Holiday Inn Express. Abbey joined the boys lounging in the pool until after seven p.m.

Mom, can we find something other than refried bean burritos tonight? Daniel said while drying off from the pool.

I was thinking the same thing. I saw a sign for an Italian place, let's try that.

Bella Mio in Nogales was a welcoming place and a break from fast food and tacos. Abbey would try to relax, maybe have a couple glasses of Orvieto, her favorite white wine, and get to sleep early.

Boys, tomorrow is going to be tough. She was tired of the road, and just wanted this part of the trip to be over and done.

Listen, we have to be in El Paso by no later than seven p.m.,

We really need to be up and out by five a.m., and I don't want to stop except for gas and the bathroom. I want to get through this, she repeated.

Mom, don't worry, Daniel reassured her.

Yeah, don't worry, we'll just drive and do it, Jeff added reassuringly.

The boys knew it would be tough but nothing like the spring break trip to Panama City Beach, Florida where the two of them blasted to when they were still in school. And Abbey never knew about.

They crossed into Mexico at five-thirty a.m. just as the sun peaked up.

Well, that was easy, Daniel said as they drove through the border station.

The Mexican border guard must have just changed shifts and was drinking from a mug of coffee. He quickly looked at the three of them, glanced at Abbey's passport and license and waved them forward. The road sign now read Mexico 15. According to plan they would drive to Imuris and turn on to Highway 2 most of the way.

The scene from the van was desolate and the highway was barely travelled. The reason they needed to be off the highway was clear. There would be no one to help if something went wrong. There was no way they could have carried anything to protect them. To get caught with weapons here would be beyond serious. They might not ever see the States again.

The bright sun now exposed the colored stucco and adobe cantinas as they rolled past the small villages and towns. The occasion church steeples and the cattle ambling by the roadside made the scenes almost surreal with the mountains and cactus the only thing in between. It would be at least a hundred miles to Imuris. It might as well be a million.

The white and red "PEMEX" sign was the first indication of Imuris. It was almost seven thirty a.m. I'll get some Cokes or something for the road, so we won't have to stop for a while.

The van was not that good on gas, and it took nearly twelve hundred pesos to fill up the large tank. They hoped they would not need to break into the spare gas cans. A quick bathroom break and Jeff took over the driving.

Okay, I see Highway 2 ESTE, Mom, is that it? Yeah, turn here, its 2 East.

Jeez, that sign said 190 kilometers to Cananea and 320 to Agua Prieta.

Jeff read the sign and realized just how much further they had to go.

It's got be another 150 kilometers to Ascension, Then another 150 to Ciudad Juarez. Holy shit, that's another 400 miles.

Well, I suggest you just keep driving, just nice and steady, just keep driving, Abbey responded. , Here's this thing's got a CD player, find something, and put it in, she said. Here's a box of old CDs, she said reaching from behind the seat.

Jeff found an old Firesign Theater CD. What the hell is this? What? she replied, pushing her sun visor up over her eyes. *"Don't crush that dwarf, hand me the pliers"*?

What the hell is this? he said in bewilderment, thinking Abbey had spent time in an asylum.

Oh, you found it, that one's perfect, you'll have to listen to it a dozen times to get half of it, and we'll be in Austin by then, Abbey said, smiling and remembering some of the funniest lines.

Okay, sure, He put it in. It was ten a.m.

THE FAILURE AT CAMP DAVID

Isabelle was up strolling around the grounds Saturday morning. The rustic setting and the crisp mountain air almost removed the toxic atmosphere in Laurel Lodge. The President and the governors were from too different worlds. Worse was the fact that the difference seemed to feed off each other. To her each side was more convinced the other was wrong. While she had sympathies for the governors and their point of view, she had grown up with the ideas and philosophies closer to her husband's. She was acutely aware that her input could help to build a sense of trust. Her husband had always been an emotional man, but she had helped him in his early years in politics to control and react to situations and pointed questions and keep a cool demeanor.

This was different. The country was being torn apart. The basic philosophies and tenets of each party were being put to a real-world test. One would be pitted against the other and the strongest and best would determine the shape of millions of lives for generations.

Isabelle could sense she was going to be thrust into something beyond her ability. She might have to decide if what she was hearing from these great men, these governors, was reasonable and just possibly... correct.

Would she have enough wisdom to know if what her husband and to a certain extent, herself, believed was the only way forward?

The walk around the grounds and down to the pond only made one thing clear to her: she might need to decide what the truth was. She might have to earn her first lady stripes and legacy all in one weekend.

When Jimmy Carter picked Camp David to host the Camp David Accords, he knew the casual and woodsy surroundings would have an innate calming effect. The result was two enemies became friends and worked through seemingly insurmountable issues to do what they each knew was right and just, and a lasting agreement was born from it. Isabelle hoped the same calming effect would take effect here.

The morning meetings started with an upbeat and almost cheery atmosphere. The scent of cinnamon buns and fresh brewing coffee removed any sour feelings between the two groups of men. Isabelle's light and warm greeting invited a sense that the situation wasn't hopeless.

Gentlemen, she began, I know there is common ground amongst us. We should hope to build on those things. We have had differences, yet I know there is a way to work together. Compromise sometimes must mean that small things yield to a larger and more important picture. I hope we all can see the larger picture today.

She was hoping to glance over to see a grateful husband. She did not see that in his eyes.

Okay, that's fine, just fine, Henrico started. We shall see who wants compromise.

Mr. President started George Miller; we may have ended on the wrong note last night. Governor Jordan and I spent most of the night discussing where we may collectively have room to bend and work with you.

All right, George, I'm willing to listen, what are your thoughts? the President offered.

We are willing to contribute to the debt you say we are due to the treasury, Governor Miller began. The amount we feel the Right to Work States should contribute without trashing our budgets is three percent more than our current levels.

We feel, added Jim Jordan, any more than this will spin us down into a financial death spiral. And we have cut our spending, all of us have, to the bone and then some.

There was an uncomfortably long pause, like seeing the flash of lightning and waiting for the sound of the thunder.

Governors, you are proposing three percent additional when I have already told you I need twelve percent, and even that is probably not enough. I can't do anything with three percent, that's a nonstarter.

Then the President turned red in the face and raised his voice to all in the room.

Why did you bother to even be here this morning? I told you what I needed, not these excuses. If you want to talk about a deal, then we start at twelve percent, no less!

All the years that Isabelle had invested in the marriage to her husband and into the hopes she had helped him to be more like a statesman and less of an impulsive hothead were vaporizing right before her eyes.

She spoke up, *Henrico!* What kind of talk is this? You call this negotiating, I call it bullying,

You are the bully I remember you were when I met you!

Ah shut up, *puta*, if I need your opinion, I'll ask for it!

Puta? You called me a puta? she screamed.

You worthless ass, you go ahead and ruin the country because you're a complete fool!

I am done with you! You will never, never see me again ,you worthless ass!

Isabelle slammed the screen door to Laurel Lodge and was screaming as she jumped into one of the waiting limos and commanded the driver to leave.

They were seen leaving through the front gate and sped off. It was believed she was heading back to the White House.

The faces of the governors turned pale as their jaws dropped to the floor.

The President just glared at them and shouted, **Nice going, governors!** *Now why don't you gather up your fat asses **and get the hell out of here!***

He spun around and repeated ,*Go on, get the hell outta here! We aren't doing any more talking!*

He left out the side door and walked out onto the patio and shut the door behind him.

George Miller looked at Jim Jordan, not trying to hide his bewilderment.

I would not have guessed this was the way the country would end... In a hot-headed cat fight.

They looked at each other in shock, shaking their heads and walked down the path past the neatly attended cabins. At Red Oak Lodge, their van was waiting. They both stopped to look around as if it might be their last visit. Then entered the van and left.

* * * * *

Monday morning when the President arrived back to the White House, he found Isabelle's dresser drawers pulled out and emptied. She left no note. She took only a small amount of clothes from her closet and all her jewelry. He knew she wasn't coming back. He would have a press release saying she was going to visit family.

Henrico thought he had gone too far but didn't care. She was always on his back; she became a liability in his mind. He thought he could now concentrate on dealing with these damn governors. He had no idea what she would do and didn't care,

This would be an extraordinarily large mistake.

EL PASO

Abbey knew the last hundred miles would be the most stressful as they raced to get out of Mexico before nightfall. She would let Daniel drive until Ascension. She would take over from there. She figured maybe the Mexican border guards might go easier on a female driver.

From Cananea to Agua Prieta, the road was nearly empty. It wasn't until late afternoon when they reached Ascension and stopped for gas, she noticed the groups of vans and pickup trucks on the side of the road with large group of men mulling around the vehicles.

She thought to herself ,that's got to be trouble waiting to happen.

When they pulled away from the Pemex station, she noticed a black SUV also leave and occasionally, see it in the rearview mirrors.

It was almost seven p.m. when she turned on to route 45N to Ciudad Juarez. As she turned on to the highway, she saw the SUV speed up to seem to catch up to them. The visions of banditos forcing her and the boys out of the truck and leaving them shot on the side of the road began to fill her head.

Mom, slow down! Jeff told her. We only have twenty miles; we'll be out before dark.

She could now see the lights of the city and began to think they would be all right. She started to slow down until the black SUV came racing up behind her. She started to panic. She began

197

to speed up and step on the gas, trying to make the brightly lit truck stop just ahead.

Jeff yelled, *mom, what are you doing?*

The approaching vehicle turned on its blue lights as it sped by Abbey.

It was a Mexican police car and it sped by and disappeared over the hill and around the bend.

Abbey looked at Jeff and Daniel without saying a word.

Within fifteen minutes the lights of the border crossing station came in view. The Mexican border officials had set up a new checkpoint for those leaving Mexico. With the increase of Americans transiting through the country, they knew they could collect an exit fee because the travelers would have no choice but to pay it. She pulled in line and waited behind the few cars now ahead of her.

Good evening, Senorita, may I see your passports and license? The guard signaled to one other border guards to inspect the contents of the van and trailer. He motioned for Jeff to open the back of the van and the trailer. The first few boxes of the trailer contents were searched. The cans of gas were inspected, and they were told to leave them on the side of the trailer. Jeff pulled them off and placed them on the ground. The guards huddled and spoke for a moment away from the van.

Senorita, are you entering the U.S. for purposes of work?

Yes, we hope to find work, she replied.

And your sons as well?

Yes, we are trying to start over, she said without thinking.

I see, senorita. Usually, we charge fifty U.S.dollars per person because of the number of Americans trying to avoid your President's fees and taxes, you see, but my partner and I are low on fuel for our cars so we will keep your gas cans instead. That is, unless you have one hundred and fifty dollars, cash.

No, sir that would be fine, Abbey said with relief.

Well, okay, then please proceed and *buena noches.*

Just ahead was the entrance station into Texas.

Abbey pulled up to the guard.

Good evening ma`am, where are you headed?

Austin, officer,

Are you looking for work and to start right away?

Confused, Abbey, responded, Yes, is it that obvious?

Well, I'll just say that there has been a steady stream of Americans before you and the answers are usually the same, heading to Houston, Dallas, or Austin for work and right away, he responded politely to her.

I see, so you're going to Austin, Okay, here is a list of immediate openings and a brochure of available apartments and houses and the like.

Abbey looked up in sheer amazement.

You're kidding, but how could you have all this already?

Her disbelief broke into a wide smile.

He tipped his hat and said as genuine as he could, We're only glad you made it and you're here. Oh, and here's a coupon book with some discounts on hotels and restaurants."

As he handed it to her, a tear welled up in one eye. Thank you so very much, officer, was all she could muster.

There was the sign for a La Quinta just up off the I-110. It was one of the first discount coupons in the book.

It was the most welcome sign they had seen that day.

FORTY-SIX HATTERAS

SAM CAME TO WORK ON SATURDAY FOR A HALF A day to help change out some old lead water pipe for plastic down off the loading dock. Frenchy was teaching Sam about the nuts and bolts of PVC pipe and basic plumbing. At one o'clock in the afternoon, Frenchy said that was all the overtime the management would allow and that it was time to head over to Clancy's for a shot and a beer and some lunch. Sam was hoping maybe he would see one of Frank Slovic's or Stosh's union connections. He'd keep his ear to the ground and hope to learn something new from these guys.

Hey Frenchy, who's your buddy? the gravel-voiced, rotund man with the White Sox ball cap cawed from across the room.

Giorgio, you dirty S.O.B. where's my beer? Eh? Frenchy replied.

Yeah, yeah, Tommy, get my friend and his buddy a beer. So, who's the kid?

Hey kid, don't you have anyone better to hang with on a Saturday than this old fart? What's your name kid?

Sam, Sam Hirschfield.

Well Sammy, whatcha doing with this piece o'work on a Saturday?

Getting' some OT, while there is some to get," Sam replied, feeling more relaxed.

Dedicated to the job, well, all right then, Tommy, make it a double for my friend.

Giorgio laughed out loud and extended his hand.

Good ta meet ya Sam. I'm Giorgio De Palmeri, I'm the union shop president for local 11. So, you're one of my guys, everybody's been treatin' you good so far?

Great, everything's great, Sam responded.

Good, well make sure Frank and Frenchy don't work yous too hard.

Okay, yeah, okay, thanks, Giorgio, Sam replied with a broad smile.

Good, good, here's to you, kid, and he downed a shot of Calvert's.

Sam followed suit. The jovial mood and the banter continued for most of the afternoon. Sam kept his consumption at a conservative pace. If there was anything to discern, he would have to be sober enough to be aware of it.

Sometime after four p.m., Giorgio had a call come to the bar phone. Tommy immediately gestured to Giorgio and pointed to the extension phone in the back office. The atmosphere of the afternoon frivolity changed in a second. From the back room everyone could hear the gruff union boss explode.

What da' hell do you mean, sniffin 'around? What does that mean?

The din of the room dropped noticeably. Tommy reached for the remote on the television and increased the volume on the Ohio State and Michigan game enough to draw attention from the back room.

Sam watched from his end of the bar as Frank and Frenchy both headed over toward the back while crowding around the tiny office and pulling the door almost closed. From his vantage point he could hear the trio raising their voice and pointing and gesturing with their hands as if to shift the attention from themselves.

The last clear words Sam could hear was, I don't care what you do, just keep 'em off my damn boat, Stosh!

Sam was relieved but confused. He knew he was getting closer to some part of the puzzle, but he couldn't figure out who else was also trailing Giorgio's guys and who did they report to?

Sam knew just enough just to relax and go with the flow for a while. The last thing he needed to do was raise suspicions.

After a few minutes, Frenchy came back to his seat at the bar, looking more than a little irritated and a little nervous. He grabbed the shot of Calvert's and downed it, motioning Tommy for another. Sam seized the moment.

Tommy, next round is on me, he said, raising his glass to Frenchy.

You could see the pencil thin moustache of Frenchy perk up and he broke into a wide smile. Yous all right with me, kid, Frenchy replied. Yous all right!

Tommy, make it a double for my friend, Sam said, and saw his bar mate nod in approval.

By five-thirty the bar had slowly emptied out and Sam had been buzzed and sobered up twice already. He looked at Frenchy and slowly ambled up from the bar.

That's it for me, Sam slowly said to his friend. I gotta go.

Okay, okay, kid, I'm right behind ya' or the missus will never let me hear da end of it.

Well , all right then, which way you going? "Sam asked.

Down to da lake and hang a right for a couple of ten blocks.

I gotta go that same general direction, I guess I'll go that way for a while.

While spending the afternoon in a bar with a roomful of old working buddies wasn't the worst thing he could be doing, Sam knew this wasn't why he was here.

Sooner or later, he would have to start asking questions and nosing around.

And do it very carefully. As they rounded the corner, the lake and the boats tied at their moorings popped into view.

Sam saw his opening. Frenchy, Sam said, looking up and pointing to the lake and no boat in particular, I'm going have me one of those boats someday.

Oh yeah, sure, you know what boat stands for, dontcha? came the reply in his broken French-Canadian accent. No, what?

Bring on another thousand! And I mean dollars, that's what.

Well, it doesn't have to be a forty-foot Hatteras, Sam admitted.

Maybe just a sixteen-footer, something for fishing or just floating around in.

Sixteen-footer? On this lake? I don't think so my friend. One big gust o' wind and that be da end of you and da boat, Frenchy said only partly kidding.

No, yous gotta have a forty-six-foot Hatteras like Giorgio got, then you be okay. My friend, them big waves come upside by each in a little boat and that's it for you!

You might as well be in canoe, Frenchy said with the authority of a seasoned ore carrier captain.

Sam figured just one more question and he'd be closer to the final pieces of the puzzle.

A forty-six-foot Hatteras? I didn't know they make a forty-six.

Oh yeah, Giorgio got one and he does a lot of the union's business on it.

Yeah, that's how he got it, he does the business, and the union pays for it.

I was on it a couple three times but then the union bosses started doing more and more things away from the union hall.

Yeah, now hardly anybody but Giorgio and the big, big bosses use it. He keeps it moored off Lakeshore somewhere, you can't miss it cuz he keeps a huge Local 11 union banner flying from the mast over the bridge.

Every once in a while, when I'd be going with the wife up north, we see it on da lake heading up da lake somewhere.

Well, it must be nice, responded Sam.

Yeah, I'm sure it is, cuz Giorgio likes that boat just so and don't want nobody even near it no more, was the reply.

Good to know, said Sam. Good to know.

ONE SHARE

What used to be the dusty, gravel and broken asphalt road to the tin-roofed airport and control tower had been reinvented. The tropical feel had been blended with imagination, capital, and the will to complete the vision. It was beautiful and functional and efficient. The main road to the terminal was a palm tree and flower-lined boulevard. Lining the new glass and chrome terminal were the flags of every nation that citizen shareholders hailed from. There were close to two dozen flags on display. The deplanements and enplanements had increased over fifty times the volume from before the signing of the New America documents.

On average the volume was approaching six-thousand travelers a day. The expanded facilities now had an intra island service that shuttled airline passengers in brand new luxury buses to the newly expanded cruise ship facilities in Marigot just a few miles south of the airport. From there the buses continued down the windward coast on the new toll road to Berekua, Loubiede, Roseau, Canfield Airfield area, Portsmouth and back to Melville Hall. The loop was fifty-five miles.

The expanded cruise ship and container shipping docks and facilities expanded the Marigot area with new hotels, seaside restaurants and beaches. The town was an idyllic setting of modern glass and stainless-steel trimmed hotels and the pastel-colored tropical stucco beachfront shops lined with palm trees that led to the gentle sloping white sand beach to the bluest waters. Behind the hotels and the coastal highway, the island's mountains surrounded the village. The lush thick green backdrop of the island's mountain tropical forest filled the sky behind the hotels and seemed to divide the town from the rest of the island. This only made it feel more secluded and alluring.

The few condo developments were limited and were only expanded to match actual resident growth. The requirement was to live there and be a citizen shareholder to own property. The island had to maintain its natural interior. Not only to limit growth to what was sustainable for the island, but to ensure that the natural resources were not threatened. In Roseau, the town designed and built a five-million-gallon water cistern fed from the river and rainfall. There were dozens of rivers in Dominica, but that fact did not hinder the efforts to conserve what the island could sustain. Some mistakes of the past could be avoided.

On the southern tip of the island was the village of Berekua. It was the center of fishing for the island. It now had two new hotels that faced the ocean. Centered between the two modern, five-story hotels was the heart of the village with its cafes, restaurants, and bars. From here were the docks that expanded out into the bay to accommodate commercial and sport fishing. Just completed in the past few weeks was the cannery and seafood processing plant. Now fresh and canned seafood was sent up the coastal highway to the fish markets and warehouses, readied for export and distribution to the island's restaurants.

Loubiede on the southwestern tip of the island had developed around its long, gentle beaches, and it attracted divers and scuba from all over the world to its unique underwater pink coral formations. On shore, the walking and hiking paths into the center of the island started here. The unspoiled beauty of the tropical forest island could only be appreciated and accessed from the trails that had been used by the islanders for a hundred years that began and ended there.

Since the documents for New America were authorized, Roseau had expanded its medical university, hospitals, and necessary infrastructure. A water purification system had been added to the cistern system and another five-hundred-thousand-gallon system was planned. The hospital system had been updated and upgrades at the main hospital at Saint Vincent's. This was done by a bond voted on by all citizen shareholders. This was not just to improve the medical system of the island. The bond also paid a compounded interest of five percent for five years. The improvements to the old Dominica and now New America improved the value to all citizens, both directly and indirectly.

The culture of constant improvement and the will to follow through on all proposed and approved plans attracted others of like minds. Soon medical professionals began to appear from all over the world. As did engineering and financial professionals. As did all who could appreciate the philosophies of being able to be fulfill their ability to the best of their ability and to be rewarded for adding and contributing to that idea.

It was a giant benevolent corporation that added to its value by the members who had a like vision. But that vision was only to benefit member citizen shareholders in a positive way. None of the destructive behaviors could be allowed to flourish. None of the financial or social coddling that invited apathy. Pulling your own weight was its own reward. Contribution to the system in any productive way was approved. But contributions were expected. Not just financially. The idea was that labor and intellect could be the means of contribution. The financial reward came from individual effort and was compounded by the contributions of all to a higher value. The sums of the parts were worth more than the individual part. So, it was in this new land. This New America.

James' office in Roseau had expanded to handle the expected load of the growth of Roseau. Two new trainees to assist in the consulting and trade office for the RTW states were starting next week. They would be added to the five full-time employees who were already in that office.

He had now taken over all three floors of the building that faced the Roseau River. The river ran through the heart of the town and the new cobblestone *"River Walk"* lined both sides. The main streets of Roseau all had new layers of asphalt and freshly painted bike lanes for the safety of the increasing volume of workers employed in the township.

It was not like anything the island had ever seen before. The activities and development were occurring all over and in every town. The pace was purposeful but not hectic. The pace was throttled by the limited number of new citizens. Enough to grow steadily but not so much as to overwhelm the system already in place. It had only been a year since the New America documents had been signed. Most of the original Dominicans had earned and saved the amount needed to obtain their first shares of New America. The remaining islanders would have their shares in a few more months. The desire to buy in and own shares was encouraged by the Prime Minister Pierre Boucharde, and he helped guide and reinforce the idea by reviewing the progress and growth of shareholder value with all Dominicans.

He always liked to say, *I can do it, your neighbor and fellow islanders can do it, we all want you to do it, too.* The Prime Minster had on his desk a wooden sign that said: **"One Share."** What it meant was the goal and hard part was to earn one share, and that the value grew with all others and grew all the time.

The sign was also on the desk of Roger Murphy and Charles McGavick.

And on the desk of all of those in James' office. Soon the little wooden sign would appear on the desks of many business and shop owners.

It very soon became the motto for New America.

THE SCENT OF MESQUITE

AUSTIN, 45 MILES. THE SIGNS WERE COMING
more frequent as the trio watched the sun setting to their left.

We'll give it another half an hour and then find a Motel 6
from the coupon book or something.

Abbey was exhausted, but the end of the trip was near. I've
two or three numbers to call on apartments and then we can
start looking for jobs. I hope and pray it will easier than I'm
thinking it will be.

Mom, we'll find something, we always do .Daniel was trying
to be reassuring to her and himself. There's got to be dozens of
places to find a decent job, according to this list.

Abbey nodded and tried to cheer everyone up with the idea
that they had already been through so very much, it would have
to be better.

*****

On Monday morning, Abbey and the boys visited three
apartment complexes. The one they liked the most was not far
from the State Capitol complex. It was larger than anything they
had seen, and the rent seemed more than reasonable. There were
buses to the universities and downtown. And there was always
something going on that was fun in Austin.

Midmorning the scent of mesquite fires and barbeque filled
the air, making lunchtime something to always look forward to.

Wednesday afternoon, Abbey had settled on a three-bedroom apartment that they all agreed would be best for them. Friday evening, they had unloaded the last of the boxes and started to settle into the new surroundings.

It was Daniel that first found a computer programming trainee opening. He was thrilled to find out there were many more jobs available than could be filled. He was to start that next Friday.

Jeff had applied to different bank and financial analysts' openings and had been called back for a second interview with two different positions. He hoped he would have a firm offer from both places; he just had to decide which could offer him the best deal.

Abbey was already breathing easier knowing that the boys were well on their way to a better life. She now could slow down and take her time and zero in on something she could build a new life around.

The first week Abbey went out in the mornings and walked a mile or so to explore the neighborhood. She became familiar with the bus routes and how to get around in Austin. On one of her walks, she stopped for a cup of coffee at a newly opened PJ's coffee shop. In the center of the shop was located a large event calendar and bulletin board. The bulletin board was peppered with info on concerts and lost dogs and job openings.

She couldn't help noticing a printout on job openings for the State of Texas. It was broken down into different departments and the one she kept coming back to was a field assistant to the newly formed Department of Agricultural Export for the Right to Work States. She scribbled down the number. Monday she would call that number and several other job openings. The attitude and the feel were so different than where she had come from. There was confidence, there was hopefulness and there was certainty of being in a better place.

WE HAVE TO FACE REALITY

MR. PRESIDENT, I KNOW YOU HAD SOME TROUBLE
with Isabelle, is everything all right?

Chief of Staff Mallory Barrett asked as sincerely as she could.

She's gone; I don't give a damn if she comes back, the bitch.

I understand, what should we tell the press?

I don't give a shit what you tell 'em, tell 'em anything you
want. Tell 'em she went back to that Honduran hole I found her
in to be with her asshole relatives. I just don't care what you tell
'em, just keep those morons off my back.... got it?

Okay, sure, Mr. President, will do, she dutifully replied.

For a moment, the tension started to subside. Ms. Barrett
then reminded the President of the ten o'clock meeting with the
economic advisors and Treasury Secretary Ralston. The door
to the Oval Office opened and three men slowly took seats on
the couches facing each other in the middle of the office. The
President ignored them for a minute until Ms. Barrett spoke up,

Mr. President, we need to begin if you want to stay on
schedule for this afternoon to make it to White Sulphur Springs
for your two o'clock tee time with Mr. Woods.

Yeah, okay. A look of contempt swept over his face as he
glanced up from his desk.

He rose and walked over to the leather chair and sat down.

Look, gentlemen, you guys got to start finding ways to get
some money in here, he began.

I got a single-payer HCA to get started and you're telling me we don't have the money. What the hell kind of crapola is this?

Secretary Ralston began, sir, we are getting the funds the RTW states said they would contribute, but we cannot keep this pace up with these programs. We are down to under eighty billion in the treasury and that is shrinking fast. You've got to delay some programs, or we are going to start bouncing checks.

We can't keep printing money with inflation at two and a half percent a month. The dollar is worthless as it is."

So, what do you want me to do?

I'm **not** cutting this program; **these are my programs and I want 'em! End of story!** he shouted at the Secretary.

Okay, Ralston, here's what we're gonna do if we will devaluate the dollar twenty percent. That will give me some breathing room," responded the President.

Mr. President, **that will ruin the economy and the people will be ruined overnight, you can't do that,** he warned.

The look on the Secretary's face became worried and severe.

Look, Henrico, we are broke and that is reality. You can't keep this up, you need to stop this spending or there will be riots in the streets! the Secretary shouted.

Ralston had enough. Somebody was going to begin to tell him the way it was and the hell with the consequences.

A look of anger and amazement swept over the President, as he got up and pointed his finger in the chest of the secretary.

Just get me the money, go over to Congress, and raise more taxes on gas and food or something, I don't care what, just get me the damn funds!

There was a stunned silence for a few seconds, and then Mr. Ralston slowly stood up and gestured for the other advisors to leave the office and close the door behind them.

At that point the Secretary's voice lowered and he slowly began, President, you are unfit for this job, consider this my resignation.

I don't know how you managed to bullshit your way into this job, but it is obvious to me, you can't run a god damn merry go round. If you think you are just going to ride roughshod over the country, then do it yourself. He turned around and slammed the door and left.

The President turned around and stared out the window of the Oval Office. The crowds of protesters that had been building for weeks now had started to assemble. He picked up the phone on his desk.

Yeah, send somebody out there and get those assholes out of here, I got a hell of a headache.

A few minutes later, police and security forces slowly marshaled away the crowds. There were incidents of protesters who shouted they had rights, and they could protest if they wanted. The security men pulled out tazers and batons, displaying them for the crowd to see.

Two thirty-something guys in tie-dyed tee shirts, looking like they were still in college, challenged the security officers. They were beaten behind the knees with batons and tazed. As they were carried off, the other security officers challenged others in the crowd and dared them to try any other notions of protesting.

A little six-year-old girl ran over to the security guard and started beating on his knee, pleading for him to stop and why did they hit her daddy? The security officer picked her up and placed her on the step of the police van. In a few minutes, a woman officer swept her up and carried her out of view to her father. The little girl's crying and screaming never made it onto that night's television broadcast; none of the protest did, as the media knew to do so would raise the ire of the White House.

The boiling temperature of the anger sweeping through the country was becoming obvious. The lid was beginning to strain under the pressure. Governors of some of the northern supporting states began to talk amongst themselves and examine their options.

VENUS HAS THE EAR OF THE IRS

Venus Hurlewicz fit right in at the IRS of the Delacourte administration. One of her department's priorities was to level the field in regard to the Supreme Court's decision on the Citizen United case years before. She knew that the administration had always had concerns about matching the election and campaign funds that the corporations were able to contribute to other parties. She knew to change the law would take years. There had to be a way, and the ways and means didn't matter to her. She had a plan, and she would run it by her boss and everyone else she had to.

The head of her audit and collections department was Levin Teacher. He was a long-time bureaucrat who had come to Washington from the Albany, N.Y. office over ten years ago. He was relentless and had several conflicts with small and medium companies over the years. He was involved in an audit and pressured a small trucking company called Red Star Express and its owner, Peter Zambrella, into an overly expensive defense of what was a possible minor infraction. The company appealed and went to court. The fine and taxes due were reduced to five hundred dollars.

Teacher was not at all happy with that and persisted in further reviews and audits for the next three years. The cost of these defenses against the IRS finally bankrupted Zambrella and Red Star. When the employees were told on a Friday afternoon that they were shutting down, they all knew why.

Early Saturday morning, a driver delivering for one of the big internet companies drove by a car in a parking lot with its driver's door wide open and found a man slumped over the steering wheel. When he approached the car, he found Mr. Zambrella with a gun in his hand and a hole through his head. The blood-stained letter found on the dashboard blamed Teacher and his personal vendetta against him.

It wasn't the local IRS office and union that reacted to the discovery; it was the citizens and neighbors in Mr. Zambrella's neighborhood who protested in front of Teacher's apartment for days after a local TV reporter had found out what had really happened and went on the air with the report. Still no official reaction to the report came from Teacher's office.

About one month later, one of Mr. Zambrella's old associates from a Perth Amboy, N.J. trucking company was waiting for Mr. Teacher at his car. He explained that Pete and he had grown up together and had helped him many times and was a life-long friend. He understood that the IRS and the government's union were going to protect him and his job, but they couldn't protect him from what he deserved for what he did to Pete.

He grabbed Teacher by the back of the head and slammed it into the windshield of his car, several times, until blood began to squirt out from his nose and mouth. He then proceeded to slam the car door on his right arm and broke it in two places. He then dragged him to where his car was. He placed his leg at the knee under his car, ran over it and drove away.

Teacher was out of work for six months. When he returned to work, he was notified he was transferred to Washington, D.C., with a promotion. He was now in charge of a new collection and audit division with two-thousand employees under his charge. His new job was to single out groups that raised money for the opposition party and candidates and to *"investigate them for any offenses."*

He thought he had gone to heaven. He could continue to pursue those that he deemed needed to be audited and investigated. His suffering and pain would have been worth it. The ways would justify the means.

When Venus was transferred to his office, it only took a few minutes after meeting Teacher to knew they were the same soldiers in arms, and they would fight the same battle. She knew she would like to be here and would do what she thought was necessary.

She began with scores of groups that were collecting and distributing funds and donations from corporations and well-heeled individuals to what she deemed were organizations with opposing views to the administration. She didn't care if it was legal and done properly; she was going to make their life a hell on earth. After all they deserved to be put through the wringer for daring to be opposed to *her* party.

Venus never had an association with any religion or charities. She just thought of it was an association of losers looking for a purpose. One of the groups brought to her attention was the Brotherhood of a Leap of Faith in America. They were raising funds for several years to purchase a closed public school building. The purpose was to start charter schools for inner city children as an option to failing schools for parents in inner city neighborhoods.

The priest and nuns and laypeople of the church had the idea to raise funds by selling to their followers and friends' hand decorated ornaments with the three wise men and the baby Jesus in the manger or the Stations of the Cross depicted on each one. They were always popular during Christmas and Easter holidays. They had quite a following of collectors because of

219

the care and detail and limited number they would create every year. When one was sold at a charity auction for five-thousand dollars, a local newspaper reported the record sale.

Venus read of the event and stepped in. She immediately ordered an accounting and audit of all pieces going back seven years. She ignored the prior valuation of the pieces and stated that because the one piece had sold for five-thousand dollars therefore all pieces were of a similar value. She determined that the small group of Catholic clergy and laypeople owed the IRS four- hundred thousand dollars, plus interest and penalties. The group itself did not have twenty-thousand dollars in assets.

Venus was nothing but focused and refused to listen to others in her department that this would bring unwanted and undesired ire in the public's opinion of the department. She ignored the advice. She demanded that the Brotherhood provide a list of all individuals who had purchased one of the decorations over the last seven years. They complied within the demand time period. Venus was not concerned so much about the list of people who had developed an affinity for the hand-crafted decoration. She should have.

A member of Congress and the House Oversight Committee had been a big supporter of the Brotherhood of a Leap of Faith.

When he received a call from one of the laypeople and crafters of the decorations as to why his order would not be filled, he calmly told the layperson to not worry, he would investigate.

Trent Gordon was a serious prosecutor from a long line of lawyers. His Charleston, S.C., upbringing, and manners always kept those who had never gone up against him in a court caught off guard. He was brilliant and determined, more than capable of quoting any passage from any legal case book within his large and ample law library. He was proud of the fact that he knew his trade and even the most seasoned trial lawyer hated going up against him in court.

His boyish visage and average build disguised the absolute bulldog attack style in the court room. He had developed a reputation for defending citizens who had been victimized by local governments and municipalities in cases of eminent domain and other overreaches and abuses. He was encouraged to run for Congress when a long-time friend decided to retire. He won in a landslide.

He now was to focus on Venus and others in this department. The subpoenas were being issued faster than they could be served.

This department was now going to be sanitized by the light of day.

The distrust and disappointment with the federal government had already reached an all-time high. Add to this the widening cleaving of the country with the RTW conflict. This investigation would be the match to the tinder.

At first only local talk radio, cable news and C-Span would cover the committee and its findings. As the facts and events were uncovered, the popularity of Representative Gordon was meteoric. He became the symbol of hope to rein in this administration. His bulldog style encouraged others in Congress to regard the public as their reason to be there, not to rubberstamp the President's agenda. A firestorm was building and Venus and her boss, Teacher, were in the epicenter.

Levin Teacher was not a brave man. He began to relive the meeting with the buddy of Pete Zambrella. When he did not show up for questioning at the end of the second week of the investigation, security personnel visited his apartment.

Through a back window they saw a figure moving slowly. When they knocked on the door there was no answer. They broke the dead bolt and entered the apartment to find Levin Teacher hanging from a large light fixture in the center of the room.

The event deflated the full court press of the department. Venus was fired with no pension or retirement benefits. She was told this was her best option because she was getting off easier than if her boss had not ended much of the investigation of the department.

She was stripped of all security ID and escorted to the front gate.

*****

Washington was busy town and many ex-government personnel still lived and worked in D.C. Within a couple of days, Venus was contacted by her one-time campaign employer on the West Coast.

Congresswomen Natalie Mulligan was a veteran senior member of the House. She said she knew she could use some help, and with a few pulled strings she was offering her a job at one of her husband's wine bar and tapas houses.

She told her, listen, it will keep you busy, and the money won't be too bad until all this stuff blows over. Maybe in a couple of years, she could get her back in government.

She accepted the offer. In a few weeks it would be the end of the summer. Venus' daughter would be back from her month with her father, still living on the West Coast. This would give her enough time to get settled into her new role and to get a head start on how she would explain the situation to her now twenty-one-year-old daughter.

Her life was a mess. She thought she was too old to start over, and now as a barmaid or bartender. When she stopped to think how she landed in this position, instead of blaming herself, all she could do was blame Trent Gordon.

And she was furious.

DIRTY LAUNDRY

FOR YEARS AND YEARS, THE PIPEFITTERS UNION always was responsible for repairing and replacing the high-pressure steam piping and systems in the area power plants. They also were responsible for draining the radioactive waters from powered down nuclear power plants for monthly maintenance. The waters were stored in specially lined drums and hauled off by an approved trucking company to a secure and secret facility until it could be shipped to a larger federal facility for long-term storage and handling.

These drums were initially supposed to go to Yucca Flats, but this installation was never opened. Over the years several locations and warehouses ended up with the excess drums. If a few dozen drums disappeared, no one would notice for weeks or months. One of these warehouses was located at 112 Commerce Ave., in Des Plaines, Ill. These drums were stored in a separate and fenced off area but easily accessible to those who worked there. These drums had to be logged in by serial numbers stamped just under the locking band rim at the top of the barrel.

Early one morning, two men, one over six-foot-five, the other six-foot with a shaved head and a bushy mustache, approached the dock in uniforms that had the letters A-E-D in large letters on the front and back of their white one-piece jump suits. They presented official-looking badges that said, "Atomic Energy Department, Research Division."

The two delivered to the shipping office an order from the Washington, D.C., Atomic Energy Department office requesting that twenty-five drums of radioactive waters be loaded onto the waiting truck. The purpose was disposal research of the wastewater, and the delivery was to the University of Chicago's Fermi Lab. There was a number to call to confirm the pickup in the Chicago area.

The suspicious dock supervisor did call the number and when he did the voice answered, Good Morning Fermi Lab at the University of Chicago,

The supervisor spoke with a pleasant voice at the other end and confirmed the pickup number and address. The wary supervisor was slowly convinced the authorization was legit and had the drums loaded. He logged in the incident, the serial numbers on the drums and the time and person he spoke with. He was right to be concerned. The next day a furious manager stormed down to the dock area.

Why the hell didn't you call me on this?

Didn't you check the address? It's bogus! That number doesn't answer, and do you want to know why? It isn't the number to Fermi Lab!

Do you have any idea how much shit we are in if this gets out? I want to know what these bastards looked like; maybe we can use our people to ID these assholes!

Now if you want to save your ass, I'd be contacting anybody you can think of and give me any security tapes you got, and I mean pronto!

The manager decided to wait and not report the missing drums just yet. He thought the drums couldn't go that far, and he and his security team could find the people responsible and return the drums to storage.

He would be partially correct. A letter was delivered a few days later with the address that the drums could be found. And they were filled with wastewater. A check for radioactivity produced just a very slight positive reading but that was enough for the manager. As far as they were concerned the issue was closed.

It was only because the warehouse was owned and operated by a Chicago politician and friend of Giorgio, the incident never was reported or discovered by the press. In a few weeks, the incident was forgotten and never brought up.

However, the news of the incident did make it back through the grapevine to Clancy's. Frenchy casually mentioned the incident while Sam was on the dock with Frank Slovic.

Sam didn't ask about it then.

I'll wait until we are at Clancy's and see what comes out after a couple of beers.

About four-thirty p.m., Frank gestured to Sam and let him know to clock him out when he left. Sam obliged Frank and used it as the excuse to stop at Clancy's.

Hey Frank," Sam announced as he opened the door to the darkened bar. I got you covered.

Okay, you're a good kid, Sam, sit yourself down and have a beer. Jimmy, give the kid a beer.

What ya have, Sam?

Ah, Jimmy, gimme a Bud draft.

Okay, Sam, a Bud on draft. You got it Sam, here ya go.

Sam pulled the red and chrome bar stool toward Frank and took a long chug from the frosty mug. Frank leaned forward and swiveled his body and head as one unit.

And give the kid a shot of Crown, Jimmy.

As he said that, the ashes of the first half a dozen cigarettes marked the trail from the red and black checkered bean bag ashtray to Frank and fell to the floor.

Sam hoisted the shot toward Frank, saluted, and clinked glasses.

Frank, you're the best, Sam said, patting him on the back.

Nah, kid, you're one of the gang.

Yeah, I guess I am, yeah, I guess so. Sam relaxed and waited until he thought he could learn what Frenchy was talking about.

About three shots and beers later, Frank kind of straightened up and laughed just loud enough for Sam to hear.

What's funny, Frank?

That Frenchy, that's what.

What's funny about Frenchy? There was a short pause and Sam added,

Except Frenchy!

Frank laughed out loud. You got that right!

That frog bastard told me how some asshole stole some wastewater from one of the local warehouses and then told 'em where to find them.

What do you mean, and why would they do that it? Sam asked.

I dunno, the water was from one of them nuke plants when they drain the system.

I dunno if it's poison or what? Frank answered him.

Is it like radioactivity or something?

Yeah, yeah, I think he said radioactive somethin'.

Frank didn't seem to care why this was bad and what could happen with this material.

Damn, Frank, that's something else. Yeah, and then the ass-hole tells them where ta get it, makes no sense to me,

Frank added, puzzled but still unaware of the dangerous possibilities of the event.

So, what did the warehouse guys do?

Frenchy said they just went and picked them up where they said to get them and didn't ask no questions.

Huh, well, I guess that's that, Sam replied without letting Frank know how dangerous this was.

I guess so, was all that was said.

At seven p.m., Sam, turned to Frank. I gotta hit it, Frank, I'll see ya tomorrow.

Yeah, okay, I'll see ya tomorrow.

By seven-thirty, Sam had started the encrypting software and emailed Washington. He relayed what he had heard and asked if any of this was being confirmed from other sources.

The reply: *No confirmation of incident, inquire further for details. Do you request assistance?*

Sam thought for a minute. *Will inquire of warehouse detail and address. I will confirm RA or lack of.*

Affirmative, was the reply. *Do you request assistance?*

Negative, at this time, will advise. Sam finished the email.

Sam had an idea that he could maybe find out the location with the help of his insider friend.

* * * * *

Monday morning at work, Sam knocked on the door of Joyce Osheffski.

Hiya, Sam, how's the overtime working out for ya?

Great, great, thanks for the opportunity and hours, he responded.

Well, Sam, what can I do for you? And shut the door behind you.

She had the look of knowing what the situation was and was a step ahead of him.

I, ummm, I heard something kinda disturbing through the grapevine and wondered if…. he began.

Sam, Joyce pulled her fingers to her lips as to motion, *say no more.* She pushed a piece of paper with an address written down on it.

5671 Roosevelt Avenue, Superior Laundry, a little birdie told me something is fishy there, she said to him, not looking up from a report she was finishing up.

I believe you may find this to be helpful. We believe there is a tie-in with the incident, see what you can find out.

She added, There appears to be something unusual about the Geiger counter readings in the area, if you follow my drift.

We have been watching the area and nothing has moved. Maybe you can see if any of the guys knows anything from your side, so we can find out what the hell is up.

He knew he had a friend in Joyce, he didn't know how involved she was, until now. He also knew he would have to do his share of pounding the pavement on the Q.T. He couldn't expose Joyce by being too obvious about their connection. Ok, Joyce … I'll get on it and thanks.

Don't mention it, which was a double meaning response he didn't get until he closed the door and was down the hall back to the walkway.

Sam had an address and a name and an internet connection. He was able to access county records and discovered that Superior Laundry was owned by Gina and Giorgio De Palmeri, the union head he had met at Clancy's. This was going to get interesting and most likely dangerous if he was found nosing around the laundry. He would wait until Sunday because there was a Bears home game and most likely everyone would be watching the game.

The laundry was an old brick and stucco building and quite large, with three floors. The offices seemed to be located on the top of the building because that was the only part that had windows and had a separate staircase leading to it.

Sam parked down the block and opened the trunk and pulled his compact Geiger counter indicator from the car. He walked down one block off Roosevelt to approach the building from the back and the loading docks. As he crossed the side street between Roosevelt and the alley behind the building, he activated the counter. The gauge showed nothing. He noticed two large dumpsters parked in the loading dock areas. This seemed unusual unless a large amount of material was being removed.

Sam first walked to the back of the building looking for security cameras or any type of monitoring devices. The ones he could see were located at the front entrance. There was one aimed at the dock area, but it appeared the dumpsters were obstructing the camera's view. He should be able to nose around without being seen. He had on a large hoodie sweatshirt and large black pants to conceal him in case he was spotted.

Walking around the first dumpster, he noticed a trail of white and grey cement-like power leading from the dock and into the building. He pulled himself up to the top of the first dumpster. He pulled back the blue tarp and looked slowly at the contents. It was filled with empty bags of fertilizer.

What the hell are these guys up to, Sam wondered.

He turned the gauge on again. There was a small indication, but was it the bags or something else? He couldn't tell.

Again, he peered into the other dumpster.

Holy shit, he exclaimed. It's the barrels!

There were at least twenty-some barrels marked with symbol of an atom and skull and crossbones.

What the hell are these assholes gonna do?

The rest of the dumpster was filled with empty cartons marked *"five-gallon containers, safe for motor fuels."*

A look of shock then swept over him.

These bastards are making a dirty bomb! Son of a bitch, I can't believe these assholes are doing this! he said in a louder voice than he intended.

He lowered himself. Staying low and out of sight, he moved toward the trails that led to under the dock doors. He placed the indicator at the crack between the door and the dock and turned it on. It jumped and began to beep. He turned it off.

Realizing if he was noticed, he was in real trouble, he retraced his steps away from the building slowly, back to his car, and headed directly to his apartment.

The email read: *Location found; evidence indicates strong possibility of R.A. toxic device. Device location unknown. Advise rapid response and containment.*

Response was: *Received.*

As the fourth quarter of the game at Soldier's Field began, the address on Roosevelt Avenue was surrounded by Chicago police, HAZMAT teams and FBI agents along with military intelligence. There was no device found, but the components were confirmed, and the area sealed off and evidence was confiscated and documented. The only information and clues that were recovered were serial numbers from the drums and half a shipping address.

The remaining part of the label read," ERCE AVE." and "AINES, ILL." Under the address was stenciled "return for reuse."

Giorgio and Gina DePalmeri were arrested at their home off Lakeshore Drive. When questioned, they said nothing and asked for their individual lawyers.

It was two days before the location of the Hatteras was questioned. It was too late. The Hatteras was located at a small dock in Indiana Harbor ship canal five days later. The Hatteras was swept clean but still had indications of radioactivity below deck.

Of all the people questioned around the docked yacht, only a mid-aged woman whose was working at nearby Marktown remember seeing a large boat tied up to the dock across the canal, There were two large trucks right there next to the boat, she said. It was in the afternoon two days before.

Yes, they were yellow-colored trucks and I believe there were two of them, much as I can remember ,she told the FBI agents sent to follow up on the Hatteras. There must have been four or five of them loading or whatever they were doing, she told the agent.

It was the noise of that lifty thing on the end of the truck that made all that straining noise with those barrels they were loading.

Barrels? Ma'am?

Yes, those damn barrels were clunking and thumping, must have been maybe a couple a dozen of them.

The FBI checked with the main Penske office for any trucks not returned within a day of their agreement. There were seven rentals: two in Connecticut, two in Florida, two in the Chicago area and one in Texas and California.

The Penske trucks in Chicago were rented by a Stoshu Jacyznski. There were two twenty-five-foot box trucks. The trucks were to be returned at the Penske at the junction of I-255 and I -64 just outside of East Saint Louis, Illinois.

The calls were made to Penske to detain the returning parties, but the renters did not return the trucks to that location or any other location.

They were found on a side street in East Saint Louis near a barge loading facility. No one remembered any unloading of the trucks on any barges at any of the docks when the agents interviewed anyone at the nearby loading facilities.

Upriver in Alton Illinois, a towboat had tied up to a wooden piling about twenty feet from the riverbank. During the night, barrels were lifted out of a waiting Boston Whaler with a jury-rigged small crane on the back of the tug. The barrels were transferred to the Whaler while on a trailer on shore and the ramped down to the river. The Whaler was loaded with four barrels at a time from a stake back truck with a small electric crane anchored to the truck in the cargo area. Then the whaler and trailer were ramped down a concrete boat ramp attached to the stake back truck. The entire transfer took under an hour. By six that morning, the tow was heading down river. The towboat destination was known only to the tug captain.

Stoshu left the stake back truck parked in a neighborhood several miles from the river and pulled keys from his pocket for a black Honda and began to drive back to Chicago with two other accomplices. The rest were told to head to Saint Louis and stay there until they got a call to head back to Illinois. None were aware yet that Giorgio had been detained.

The towboat and its captain were heading downriver and would be for another two days maybe three.

THE TRIAL SEPARATION BEGINS

THE GOVERNORS OF THE RTW STATES HAD elected Governor Cabbott as the First Executive of the RTW States of America. Lowell Payne, as expected, was the Deputy to the Executive.

As for all intents and purposes, the RTW States were a totally separate entity, it was decided like fledgling New America, a new currency was going to be established or they would still have the disadvantages of the debt-laden U.S. dollar. For the first two years the RTW dollar would be a set fraction of the benchmark value of the average price of a troy ounce of gold and silver, as of January 1st of every year. After two years, the value could be adjusted more often if it were determined to be beneficial to New America. It would be determined based on the most stable basis.

The RTW States had oil to sell. Oil was also traded for gold for the Treasury of the RTW States. Fort Knox was in Kentucky, which was not yet a RTW state. So, a vault was planned to be installed in the Fort Hood military complex.

The initial surge of people flooding into the RTW states had started to stabilize and had now been reduced to a steady controllable stream. The flow out of the RTW to the Washington, D.C.-controlled states had slowed and was now a trickle. The people who had chosen this course had relatives who could not or would not leave, regardless of conditions. Many just decided they preferred to be with sisters and brothers or parents. Maybe they might change their loved ones' minds, but for now this was the best option.

The "border" now was denoted by a toll plaza and inspection plaza. Coming into the informally called "The United States of the Union," charged a five-dollar toll. Leaving was quite different.

Delacorte had now raised the exiting fee to two -hundred fifty dollar per person, plus a five-hundred-dollar vehicle exit tax. All items had to be declared and itemized and were taxed at twenty percent of their value. Most just sold their possessions and found trails and guides to walk them across the "borders," ironically, similarly like the old days when the southern border was wide open.

The population migration had begun to stabilize. The debt to the Delacorte administration from RTW states was paid as they had planned. The hurdles that had to be finalized were the cooperative use of the military and trade and agricultural cooperation, if any, between the two now.

It was Delacorte's request to the leader of the House and the Senate to recognize only the remaining members of Congress that did not participate in the RTW states activities nor support their narrative. With very few moderates in Washington, there were only shades and versions of the left and the socialist-left Democratic party left in Congress.

With this he had the Congress approve the extension of his term because of the ongoing "crisis" and separation. His term was extended for as many as three more terms of four years each. He could have the job until he was seventy-five if he wanted.

What was now becoming obvious was the financial situation of the Union. While the securities and banking and financial centers of the northeast seemed to be willing to stay where they were, along with traditional centers of higher education., many other Fortune 500 corporations were leaving just skeleton staff and small offices. They had opted to start new name brands or corporations in RTW states. If the Union operations became too costly or heavy with restrictions, they would just close.

With the increased hostilities and a more discernable sense of detriment to their businesses, an agreement between Fox News, Fox Business networks and CNN was reached. The two entities traded business headquarters, with Fox moving to the downtown Atlanta locations and CNN expanding to the midtown Manhattan location that had been Fox. There was an overall sense of relief because many of the news teams and staff were now closer to their original hometowns and family. Both signed off at midnight on December 1 and signed on in their new locations at six a.m. the next day.

At eight a.m. at the corner of Marietta Blvd and International in downtown Atlanta, a crowd began to gather. Then three buses from Georgia State University pulled up and parked alongside Olympic Park. Within a minute, out poured the Georgia State Marching band.

Minutes later, the mayor and other dignitaries lined up in front of the new headquarters. The previous night the familiar "CNN" signage was replaced with an equally impressive "FOX."

The mayor lined up in front of the band, and on cue the band played the song they had worked on all week, *Georgia On My Mind.*

The news that morning on the broadcast was the new arrival …their arrival.

The lobby of the Omni Hotel next door had begun to fill with all the local politicians welcoming, meet and greet style, many of the network staff and officials and celebrities. It was a bright spot in what had been long months of disruption and uncertainty brought on by the slow train wreck of the nation caused by the administration in Washington.

The cleaving of the actual government and all the departments was going much slower and less clearly. What most in the Union government and military hoped would happen could be a truce and separate governing philosophies for both, with maybe a small commerce tax or fee between the two entities.

Of course, cooperation was the key and the military had to come to an agreement as to the "Commander-in-Chief." There could only be one and Delacorte was not most generals' and admirals' choice. It would be **the** most important issue. No one wanted a mutiny or coup d'état.

It was in Delacorte's best interest to work out a sensible agreement. Of course, most in the position to understand the repercussions of a stalemate knew Delacorte was backed into a corner on this issue. It was up to him to compromise because compromise would be his only friend.

Allies from Europe were sending representatives and emissaries to prepare for any major shifts in alliances. Delacorte, while providing a lot of lip service and promises, did not inspire the sense that he really was interested in foreign affairs. Nor cared. Many emissaries and ambassadors would find just the opposite upon their visits to Austin. Their concerns were ameliorated and addressed with in-depth meetings individually with every representative that requested time with the newly elected President and Vice President.

The Allies seemed to sense that the power and the stability in the future was not with Delacorte. This was an event that would seal his future.

THE TOWBOAT *FRANCIS O*

THE *FRANCIS O* WAS A RIVER TOWBOAT BUILT IN the 1980s. She was made to tow as many as twelve barges up and down the major river water systems. Her owner, Global Marine Corporation, used her to transport steel pipe and oil drilling equipment to New Orleans and other Gulf ports from upriver plants and docks. She worked seven days a week, twenty-four hours a day for years. She was on her way to Gulfport, Mississippi to pick up ten barges and move them through the intercoastal waterway to New Orleans Shipping canal and then head upriver.

As she headed to Gulfport, a newly formed hurricane just name Ruth grazed the tip of Florida. As the boat made it just outside of Gulfport, the hurricane turned course and started making a beeline to their exact location. The *Francis O* was tied up, waiting for her barges to be loaded for her to tie up and secure the next day. She never tied up with the barges.

When the giant storm surge of twenty feet had subsided, the *Francis O* was two miles inland down by the stern and her bow just within feet of the I-10 interstate at Gautier. Almost six months later a salvage company refloated and towed her back to the intercoastal water. In Biloxi, she was sold for salvage to the Algiers Tug Company. The twin marine diesels were replaced and within two months she was plying the Mississippi and Tombigbee River systems.

Her Captain, Steven McGuirk, had commanded the *Francis O* for over two years. He was expert on navigating the twists and turns of the Big Muddy and the tributaries. Usually when a company had barges that had to be towed to and from small docks and narrow waterways, Captain McGurik was first on the list. And Captain McGuirk was busy with "off the books" pickups and tows. There was all types of cargoes and illegal goods that some of the operators in the back swamps didn't care to go on the highways. So, they enlisted the good captain to use his off time to make a few runs. He eventually became friends with a few operators upriver, who knew he could be trusted to move dubious cargoes with no questioned asked.

Captain Mc Guirk didn't think anything about the request that came from Giorgio

Depalmeri's call to pick up a load in Alton and drop it off at the wharf at the end of Napoleon and Tchoupitoulas Street in New Orleans. He was to meet two stake back trucks and three men from Giorgio's crew. They would meet him and identify themselves by wearing "*Geaux Tigers*" hoodies in black and gold. He was to assist them with the drum unloading and then head to Pascal Manale's oyster bar and pick up his pay from a crew member in a green and yellow Tulane hoodie. This was the usual procedure, and he was looking forward to a big bowl of barbequed shrimp and several Abita turbo dogs.

The plan had been to unload the barrels and transport them to River Road and Riverbend near the Ochsner Medical Center. There was a double car garage off Deckbar Ave., where the barrels would be unloaded until Giorgio would direct further the operation. This location was important because it was the property of one of the longshoremen officials and the radiation level could be masked by the radioactive medical waste from tests done at Ochsner.

There was a plan to implement, and Giorgio had an idea what was in store but did not make a move until he got his orders from someone high up the food chain. But those orders came from someone much higher. He just didn't know how high. And he really did not want to know.

While Giorgio had known about the plan to use the drums for a disruption, he had no idea what the bigger picture was. He was ordered by a group that had a reputation that was vicious and violent if they were crossed. He had seen some of their handiwork that rivaled that of terrorist groups. Once the details and directions were given, there was no way out but to follow them ...to the letter.

From the detention center in Chicago, the one thing that was always on Giorgio's mind was what would happen to him and Gina if the instructions were not relayed and carried out. Whatever the Feds would throw at him would have no effect because the people who he answered to would get to him, regardless of if he were on the street or in the slammer. Gina didn't know any of the plans but would still be on the wrong end of the stick if the power cabal decided they were a liability.

Giorgio only hoped he would get sprung from the slammer. He only hoped his exit from the detention center wasn't in a pine box.

A NOOSE CLOSES

Stosh drove back to Chicago and arrived in the early hours on Monday. He planned to go to the union hall Monday afternoon and then meet up with Frank and Frenchy after work at the building's loading dock. It wasn't until late that afternoon that anyone got a hint that something was unusual.

He was sure Giorgio would be at Clancy's, so he headed there. He wasn't there.

What's the deal with Giorgio? Stosh muttered, looking at his cell phone.

It's not lika him to not answer the phone. I guess, uh, maybe he's got some big business or witha his ole lady, was all he could come up with.

Gimme a boilermaker, Tommy, he said, leaning over the bar and handing his beer mug to the bartender.

He tried the phone number he had written down on a small piece of paper in his wallet with "*Giorgio, cell*" scribbled on it. No answer.

Ah, hell, what's the story? he said loud enough for Frenchy to hear.

Stoshu, my friend, what's that you so bothered 'bout?

I dunno, it's Giorgio, I've been tryin' to get him ona the phone for an hour, it ain't him to not answer.

Relax, Stosh, maybe he's getting all loved up by the misses. Frenchy knew Gina was easy on the eyes.

He'll call yous when he got the misses all happy and all, I knows it me and I'm tell'ya that's all there is to it. Okay, Frenchy, okay, I'll just wait for him ta call back.

Giorgio didn't call back, but detectives now assembled at the detention center noted the incoming calls and already had a list of several people they were now in the process of following and tracking their incoming and outgoing calls. It was just a matter of pulling in the suspects and connecting the dots. Stoshu Jacyznski was the first dot.

PASS THIS NOTE

GIORGIO DEPALMERI, THAT'S MY NAME AND that's all I'm tellin'yous. It's all I'm gonna tell you guys, I ain't saying a word until I see my lawyer, so stop bustin'my ass. He repeated the same words for an hour.

It wasn't until seven that night that Giorgio saw through the glass room divider his lawyers arrive. He quickly motioned the detectives and other officers to let him speak to his client and exit the room.

Jesus, Giorgio, what the hell is this all about? Those were the first words out of his mouth as he raised his fingers to his mouth, motioning him to not say a word.

Herbert Horowitz was a rotund man with a full, bushy moustache and slicked back graying hair. The Armani suit he wore was his trademark, his image and reputation. He had provided for most of his clients the years of experience he had gained in working the system. Herbert had been the lawyer and consigliere to most of Chicago's most well-known and well-heeled.

Giorgio, don't worry, I'll have you and Gina outta here by morning, he said with the confidence of a big-league pitcher with his curve ball working.

Giorgio nodded and smoothly slipped his lawyer a note with a couple of lines and numbers written on it. The transfer went unnoticed. Herbert told his client not to worry and he would see him in the morning and get him out.

243

Walking out to his car, Herbert looked at the note. All that was written was a number to call with the instructions,

Say exactly this," *deliver load to the riverside location, now.*" The lawyer recognized the area code,"504."

What the hell does this guy got going on in New Orleans?

Herbert put the key in to his jet-black Mercedes, started the engine and drove out of the detention center. The attorney had a prepaid burner cell phone that he kept in case he needed to make untraceable calls.

He dutifully relayed the message, tore up the paper and threw the bits out the window. At the next bridge he crossed over at a waterway, he tossed the phone. In the morning he would visit one of the senior judges in the district and schedule a bond hearing to get Giorgio and Gina out on bond. Then figure out what the story was.

* * * * *

At nine the next morning, Herbert got a call from Judge White, the most senior of the judges.

Herb Horowitz? Yes sir, this is Attorney Horowitz.

Well, you better get your butt down here if you are representing those DePalmeri people.

I don't understand, sir, is there any issue? he asked, now very confused.

Son, there are some high-power people from Washington, D.C., wanting to talk to you.

Uh huh, yes sir, I'll be there in fifteen minutes.

Make it ten and meet me in my chambers.

Yes sir, ten minutes, your chambers.

Ten minutes, he repeated.

* * * * *

Attorney Horowitz?

He was greeted by two men in dark grey suits and a youngish woman dressed just as professionally. I am Special Agent Fredrick Quinn; this is Special Agent DeMay and Lewis.

Herbert shook hands and visibly shaken, asked, well, agents, what is this all about?

We understand you are representing Giorgio and Gina DePalmeri. Is that correct?

Yes, that would be accurate.

We are to escort you to meet an interested party in the case. Can you change your schedule and come with us for a few hours or so?

And really, we aren't asking.

I believe this what they call an offer I can't refuse, Herbert replied, confused.

You would be correct, shall we go? Agent Quinn answered pointing to the main lobby.

Two black Suburbans were outside the courthouse main entrance with the engines running.

Where are we going? the attorney asked. There was no response.

Forty-five minutes later, the SUVs arrived at West Chicago General Aviation Airport. At the end of a row of hangers was a Gulfstream V. As they approached, the stairway to the jet opened and the agents led the attorney to the jet and motioned him up the jetway.

Horowitz made his way up the jet's stairway and was greeted by two very large older gentlemen with dark glasses and even darker suits.

The two men escorted the attorney to a seat and then closed the jets stairway. Seconds later the engines of the jet begin to spool up as if they were being readied for flight.

Looking out the window, the attorney saw the SUVs drive away and exit through a secured gate.

Sir, would you care for a drink? An extraordinarily beautiful female attendant asked before he even knew she was there.

Yes, I think I'd better have one, a Stoly screwdriver, and make it a double. He was still not sure he was absorbing the reality that was unfolding in front of him.

The flight attendant returned in a minute with the drink. Here you are, sir.

Thank you, he paused for a second and asked, Miss, do you have any idea where we are going?

She smiled, acknowledging his question, turned around and walked to the back of the jet and disappeared behind a curtain as she pulled it closed.

A sound of a chime was the next thing the attorney heard as the jet's engines spooled up and the jet began to move toward the runways. Within a few minutes the jet was climbing through the clouds. The attorney could tell they were heading east as he could see the skyline of downtown Chicago and the lake approaching. They were in the air for just over thirty minutes when the cabin door to the flight deck opened and out stepped a casually dressed man in a white polo shirt, blue blazer, and Levi's. He was tall, over six-feet-five with salt and pepper hair. His facial features were roughhewn, with a hardened jutting jaw. He had a swagger of a military man who had seen all the evil in the world and had conquered them at least one time.

Attorney Horowitz?

Ye......yes, I'm Herbert Horowitz. His voice cracked with uncertainty of the situation.

Sir, I am Mac McCracken, I am Special Agent attached to the Attorney General 's Office in Washington, D.C.

Please forgive me for asking Special Agent, but **what the hell is this all about?**

Don't you worry, Herb; can I call you Herb?

Yes. His voice now started to unroll and relax. My friends call me Herb.

Okay, then, Herb, what this is all about is an interest in the situation with the DePalmeri. I can't speak to you about all the details, but Attorney General Holden has an interest in this situation, and we ask that you work with us on this situation and let us take the lead in this case.

Mr. McCracken, you seem like a sincere man. I wish I knew what the hell this is about because I haven't even had a chance to speak to my client in depth about any of whatever you say is this situation.

That would be a very good thing, especially for you at this moment, Attorney Horowitz, the agent responded. I am not at liberty to discuss anything about the situation and so it looks like the less that is known, the better.

Herb, the administration would look very favorably on you if you were to let us refer this case to the D.C. district for further review, very favorably.

All you must do is recommend, because of special circumstances of national interest, this case be referred to the D.C. district. We assure you that Judge White will concur.

Is that proper procedure? Herb asked.

The state and the Federal government will allow it in this case and seeing as there will be no one to challenge the referral, we don't see a problem," Mac replied.

Well, okay by me. Just how favorably will the Feds find this referral?

A million five wired to an account at the Hong Kong Shanghai Bank at the Grand Cayman Island branch under the name of Serling, George Serling. As a matter of fact, here are the proper ID and documents you may need to do whatever you wish with the ...favorable referral.

The attorney scanned the documents and the newly created passport and other IDs.

Yes, this does seem to be in order, Herbert responded.

One question Mac. What if I decide this is not for me and proceed as if we never met?

The agent leaned over and put his hand on Herbert's arm and said firmly,

Herb, the likelihood that you would make it back to Judge White's chambers would be ...doubtful, I'm afraid to say.

Mac, you know that a good attorney never asks a question he doesn't already know the answer to, Herb replied.

Then we have a deal, Attorney Horowitz? Mac asked.

We have a deal.

Good, the funds will be wired before the end of business today.

Mac ended the conversation and headed back to the flight deck and closed the door.

In a minute, the jet was banking and heading back to the western side of Lake Michigan. They would be landing within half an hour. Herb didn't think about the paper or the message or if he should even mention it. The jet landed and taxied back to the exact spot it had been just an hour ago.

Herb walked over to the aviation center and called for a taxi. That afternoon he requested the referral to the D.C. district attorney and walked away. He never saw Giorgio or Gina.

52 DECK BAR AVE.

CAPTAIN MCGUIRK HAD RECEIVED THE MESSAGE with no thoughts of the consequences. He had two stake back trucks to pick up the stored barrels at the Deck Bar Ave. two-car garage of the local longshoremen official. They loaded in the late morning when most all neighbors were at work. By four that afternoon they were already parked across the river in Algiers. Captain McGuirk had known about an auto chop shop back off Highway 90. The chop shop bordered an oil well access canal. His plan was he would deliver the barrels to the chop shop head back into New Orleans and dump the trucks and head to his tug on the big river.

The barrels were haphazardly painted over with any kind of paint they could find for the transport, some of it being plain house paint. The oil-based and enamel paint covered well the toxic warning labels on some of the barrels. However, half were painted with water based latex paint.

To deliver the barrels to the back of the chop shop the captain had to cross a small canal bridge and negotiate and sharp right hand turn to the small loading dock. Captain McGuirk was able to negotiate the bridge and make the turn. However, his brother, the driver of the second truck turned sharply off the bridge. The rear wheels of the truck slid off the corner of the bridge and slid down the muddy bank. All of the dozen barrels tumbled out of the truck and into the canal.

In a panic McGuirk, hurriedly rolled the barrels on his truck off onto the loading dock.

He pulled a tow chain from the cab of his truck ,slid down the muddy bank, attached the chain to the front bumper of the now half stuck second truck.

He shove the gear shift in first gear and slowly pull the other truck back onto the gravel road. They pulled the second truck to the driveway and left it parked next to the dock.

He gathered up his brother and took off.

On the way back to the towboat ,the Captain screamed at his brother they could not meet with their connections to get paid, they needed to get on the towboat and get upriver until this incident had settled down and it would be known what the consequences of the botched delivery would be.

Because several of the barrels, now half submerged had been damaged ,the contents starting to leak into the canal.

The water-based paint some had been painted began to blister and peel away on a few barrels, then wash off after just an hour in the canal.

Later that day, two teenagers looking for crawfish spotted the barrels and the skull and crossbones labels that were now exposed from the washed away paint. One of the barrel's locking rings and plugs were starting to seep out rust-colored liquid. Around the barrels, fish were starting to swim upside down and then just float to the surface.

The teenagers had the presence of mind to call *9-1-1*.

The first to the scene were firemen from their nearby station. They immediately called to the mayor and governor's office when they read the half washed away *"radioactive"* labels. Within thirty minutes the governor had sent a hazmat team to investigate and to proceed with the HAZMAT protocol for decontaminating the affected area at the governor's directions and conference with President Cabbott.

First , determine the extent of the contamination, and contain ,if possible, then investigate who was responsible.

The team had determined that the contamination was limited to the one barrel and that the leakage was less than twenty gallons of radioactive water. The natural action of the water flow would dilute the toxic water spillage, but as a precaution a pump was brought on site and the volume of water of a small swimming pool was captured and stored in tanker trucks until it could be determined the toxicity of the substance.

When the scope of all the still sealed barrels was discovered, a full-scale investigation began. President Cabbot ordered all jurisdictions to be updated to the incident. When alerts and inquires reached the other offices and the military, the Admiral emailed Sam.

The message began: *Missing items may have located in S.E., LA. We have traced serial numbers on barrels to a chemical company in Des Plaines, IL. Can you confirm origin with previous observation? At conclusion, return for debrief.*

Message was returned: , *Acknowledged.*

WITH HOSTILE INTENT

Stosh had returned to the union hall later in the afternoon on Tuesday. When Giorgio was still not there, he began to look nervously around to see if there was any sign or clue or note where he was. Nothing. He then thought maybe he was at his private office at the back of the Hall. It had its own private entrance, and he knew where Giorgio had hidden an extra key.

What Stosh did not know was there was a silent alarm and it had been triggered when he didn't disarm it after twenty seconds. After that, a break-in signal was being sent to the local police precinct. He opened the door to Giorgio's office and looked on the large desk for a note, message, or anything. He walked to the wet bar in the back of the office. Maybe there was a note on a table or bar. Maybe something on the Post-it Note on the fridge under the back bar. Nothing. After ten minutes, he sat down at the large desk. There were doors that hid drawers under the desk. No notes on the doors.

As he was searching through a desk drawer, he noticed the red dot of a laser dancing across the desk and then up and down his chest. One, then another, then another. He was sitting down in Giorgio's chair and begin to understand what was taking place. As the shocked look ran across his face, and he grasped the event before him, a loud voice rang through his head.

Do not move; put your hands in the air and step away from the desk.!

Stosh froze in place; he now understood the reality of the situation.

Again, the voice repeated,

Put your hands in the air and move away from the desk... you are surrounded!

The next instant the front door was filled with police with weapons pointed at Stosh.

All Stosh could muster, as the stain of urine spread across the front of his pants, was to stare blankly at the lead policeman.

Put your hands in the air...now!

By instinct, Stosh did raise his arms in the air, but fell almost into a catatonic state.

Boy, what are you doing here? the closest officer barked at him.

I said, what are you doing in here?

All Stosh could do was stare blankly at the officer.

Boy, what are you, spun up? What's wrong with you?

Ah shit, get this piss ant the hell out of here!

He just continued to stare.

The other two policemen grabbed him by both arms, cuffed him and carried him to the waiting black and white patrol car. He was not brought to the same lockup as Giorgio, but a nearby precinct holding cell. He did not ask for a lawyer or for anyone as he, for the moment, seemed to not understand what was and had happened. He at first just remained silent.

After an hour he began babbling about the missing rental trucks and the barrels and about the incident on Lake Michigan with the teenagers.

At first the other cell mates just ignored him, partly because he was soaked in urine from the arrest and partly because they thought he was just another addict coming off meth or smack. But the cell was under surveillance and being record and taped.

The officers began to understand that Stosh was involved in the APB they received that morning. The precinct sergeant reported to his district captain they had detained a possible suspect in the APB.

A call came in from downtown, Detain suspect and hold for transport to downtown for questioning.

Unknown to any at the other precinct at the time was the fact that Giorgio and Gina DePalmeri were being transferred to federal custody as ordered by Judge White at that moment. They were being escorted onto a jet like the one Attorney Horowitz had been in the previous day. They were not heading to Washington.

Hey, where are you guys taking us? Giorgio insisted on knowing.

Two muscular men in dark glasses, dark expensive suits and the conspicuous bulge of concealed weapons looked at him and smiled but did not say a word.

Hey, come on, where are you taking us? I did what I was supposed to.

There was no reply.

Hey, blurted Giorgio, *I know you,* as he looked one of the men right in the eye.

Where do I know you from? Weren't you one of those pro wrestling guys!

Listen bub! the large man replied, **You sure as hell don't want to know me!**

Giorgio stared at him and was sure he had seen this guy before.

He knew what it was; it was the three-skull tattoo on his forearm that was exposed as he rolled up the sleeve of his white dress shirt. The wrestler looked at Giorgio staring at the tattoo and looked at him with an evil, threatening glance, then turned to the back seat in the jet and sat down. Gina looked at Giorgio, her face filled with fear and a look of dismay. He looked back at her with a look that was supposed to be reassuring but wasn't.

One more time he said loudly, **Hey where are you taking us?**

His desperate attempt to get an answer was drowned out by the noise of the closing cabin door and the spooling up of the jet's engines. In minutes, the jet was above the clouds.

Giorgio didn't have a clue what he and Gina were in for.

GENERAL CHEMICAL CORP.

SAM HAD A LIST OF SERIAL NUMBERS AND P.O numbers from several barrel recovered in the canal. They were from General Chemical Company in Des Plaines. He could call to the office and say he had a half- dozen barrels left at the loading dock of the west building at McCormick Place. There was a stencil on one of the barrels saying to call them if not returned to them.

He called and spoke to one of the shipping clerks who was willing to write down the numbers and look up the consignee on the P.O. What he found left him more confused than any-thing else. These barrels were shipped out over a year ago to Superior Laundry and they did have chlorine bleach in them, but the address was 112 Commerce Ave. in Des Plaines.

Do you have a name of who signed for the barrels? Sam asked.

Yes, but why do you ask? the clerk inquired.

Thinking fast Sam responded,

Well, we get similar barrels here at this complex, maybe someone there may know what the story is .Okay, ah, it looks like a Stashu Jacyniski or something like that.

Stashu, okay got it.

Those were supposed to be returned but never were. We received back twenty-five barrels, but the serial numbers didn't match, not one. We never got them back and they didn't know where they were, the clerk replied.

Sam asked if they wanted the barrels back. The clerk responded that they did, and they would pick them up at any time the loading dock had them ready. Sam thanked him and got his name for the record.

Rashid Lewis, the voice replied.

Thanks, Rashid, you've been a big help.

Any time, my friend, any time.

He had more information to hunt down and a chance to squeeze Stosh without giving away the farm, or so he thought.

First let me get with Austin and the Admiral and see where this goes.

Sam read the numbers of the serial numbers back to a contact in Austin.

His contact was in the Environmental, Agriculture and Land Management Department. Her name was Abbey Quinlan. This was her first big assignment since she had only been in Austin a few months. She and her two sons had just made their way to Austin from Reno.

Sam, those numbers match the barrels we have found so far. We still have three more we haven't found if there is a total of twenty- five. Do you have any leads on how they got there? Abbey asked. I've got something I'm working on up here and I'm close, but I haven't got the noose closed.

Apparently, no one saw anything and there aren't any security cameras near the bayou or canal. We really don't know how many days the barrels were in the water, but it probably wasn't a week or there would have been more leaking, and they didn't get all that far from each other.

I got just a little more checking and nosing around, and I might be able to get this thing figured out, Sam replied to Abbey.

Okay, keep us on the speed dial, was her reply.

You got it, Sam told her and hung up.

MOTHS IN THE WEB

SAM WAS JUST PULLING ON HIS COAT TO HEAD TO Clancy's after his shift at work.

I should catch a couple of the guys, maybe Stosh will show up, he thought.

Before he got out the door, he heard his name from the back stairway.

Hey Sam, you need some OT this weekend!

It was Joyce with a Pall Mall anchored in the corner of her mouth. She caught up to him at the main entrance to West building and stopped him.

Yeah, I got a Saturday if you need some extra cash, she said as she slipped him a note and a paper bag with something folded in it into his hand

If you want the OT, let me know by the end of the week, okay?

she said as she nodded to look at the note, now!

Okay, Joyce thanks.

He walked a few steps and looked at the note.

Stosh is in central lockup. Take him this change of clothes as an excuse to see him, see what you can find out.

Sam made it to Central Police Precinct by five-thirty. He walked up to the duty sergeant and asked if he could see Stoshu Jacysinski.

What'd ya got there, pants? the sergeant asked.

Oh yeah, he laughed, he's the one who pissed himself!

Yeah, okay, you got ten minutes.

Officer, he said, looking over his shoulder. Take this man to our piss-soaked visitor.

He let out a loud, for Christ sake already … pissing in his pants! And he laughed out loud again.

The officer opened the secured area and walked him to the cell with Stoshu and five other arrestees.

Stosh, what happened? Sam said to him, acting as concerned as he could.

Stosh lit up as though he just found a lost puppy.

Sammy? Whada' you doin' here? How'da ya find me?

Stosh, don't worry about it. Here, here are clean clothes.

Sam reached through the cell bars and gave him the khakis.

Aw, thanks, Sam, ah, jeez, what a pal.

Stosh, what the hell happened? Sam was trying to get right to the point.

I dunno, I was look for Giorgio, I ain't heard a word from him since

I got back from St. Louis. What do you mean?

Ah ya know, a job for Giorgio, some big job he had ta do.

What d'ya mean Stosh? I didn't hear about any job.

Nah, it was some big boss and Giorgio, they had some barrels of chemicals or something he had to do, I dunno, I just did what I was told ta do, Stosh blabbed out.

I'm looking for Giorgio at the union hall and the next thing…. I'm all locked up!

You gonna get me outta here, Sam, you getting' me out?

Stosh, lem'me see what I can do, lem'me see, okay?

Yeah, yeah, get me outta here, Sam, hurry, Sam get me outta here!

Okay, Stosh, okay, he said as the officer signaled him to leave.

As Sam was leaving the precinct, he started to piece together the events. But the more he thought, the more his mind started to reel.

What the hell is Giorgio up to and where the hell is he? he asked himself. I got to wrap my head around this thing.

He emailed the Admiral and Abbey his findings. That night he got a response from the Admiral's office.

We have leads on suspects with ties to the administration and their associates. We tracked their activities to an airfield west of Chicago. Suspects are to have been in area for at least two days in last week. We do not have registration numbers of aircraft we suspect was in area. Aircraft was a Gulfstream possibly a V or 550. Can you verify aircraft and involved persons?

Received, will do, was Sam's response.

* * * * *

Saturday morning, Sam drove to West Chicago Airfield, figuring it was the most likely location that the jet could land. First, he would park in the general aviation parking lot and scope out the field. He would make notes of security cameras and entryways. He would check any aircraft that were similar and denote registration numbers. He noted any vehicles that looked like they were government SUVs or sedans.

His plan was to observe the rest of the day. Maybe he would luck into some arrival or an aircraft in a hanger might become visible. He could nose around with people coming and going without looking too suspicious.

Sam started to outline the airfield on a legal pad and filled in the details of hanger location, any aircraft stored inside from his view through the open hanger doors and security, cameras, and personnel.

I got to figure a way to get close to some security people without giving up the farm. Maybe if I can pass myself off as a mechanic or something. I've got to get some credentials made up. I got to get inside the gates and hangers," he said to himself.

Sam spent the rest of the day making notes and watching, but nothing looked out of placc and no sign of a jet like the Gulfstream.

That evening he emailed if he could request an ID that would pass him off as a jet mechanic. The email returned, saying he would get an express package on Monday. It would be delivered to him.

Continue to inquire with incarcerated associate at Central Lockup.

Well, all right, Sam thought.

That night he began to connect dots and the food chain and where it went. He began to draw a flow chart and the last dots to connect were the $64,000 question.

FROM THE OUTSIDE IN

James had been working seven days a week promoting trade and making contacts for President Cabbot and for New America. The simple truth of the matter was what was good for one was good for the other. His deals had taken him to the corporate offices in Canada's largest companies and he was welcomed in the offices of many CEOs. He also was welcomed into the government offices in Ottawa and in all Provinces. He had already been befriended by the mayors in Toronto and Montreal.

He had a day or two to return to Dominica and catch up with the day-to-day events in the office in Roseau. That Sunday afternoon he was returning emails and calls when a new email from the governor of the Maritime Provinces caught his eye.

The governor was Fredrick Princeton. James had meet with him on several occasions over the past months. The governor was a gregarious, tall man with a large barrel chest and an infectious laugh. He was a man who had weathered many winter storms and his face and hands had the toughness to prove it. His email was of extreme interest.

James, we have observed the situation in Delacorte's Union States. We have a proposal that we are to present and would like to consult with you for your opinion prior to presentation.

James replied, *Of course, Governor, when would you require me to meet with you?*

The governor's response was immediate: *We will meet you in Dominica; can you be available one week from this Friday? We would like to meet at noon at Melville Hall Airfield. Lunch will be on us. LOL.*

James immediately replied, *Yes, I will meet you then and look forward to it, Governor.*

Great, see you then. I will be bringing the Lt. Governor and our state treasurer.

* * * * *

James arrived early that Friday and smiled broadly at the sight of neatly manicured grounds at Melville Hall International Airfield. The airfield had been a barely paved strip that could handle only the smallest commercial aircraft before the agreement and the birth of New America. Now aircraft from at least a dozen countries were neatly lined up on the shiny new jetways.

At the far end of the terminal was the area for private jet arrivals. James parked in front of the terminal and went inside to greet his guests. In a few minutes, a Hawker private jet with the outline of a maple leaf on the tail taxied up to the terminal and three well-dressed men departed the aircraft and entered the terminal at a separate doorway.

Governor, welcome to New America, James exclaimed as he reached to shake hands.

Good to see you again, my friend, he responded.

Good to see you. James, please let me introduce you to Lt. Governor Richards and Secretary of the Treasury Richter. James, we meet again, said the Lt. Governor.

James smiled and shook his hand. That's right; we did meet at the Capitol dinner last year.

Pleased to make with your acquaintance, offered the Secretary as he adjusted the angle of his aim while he exhaled a drag on his cigarette. I hope smoke doesn't bother you, but I had to light up after the flight, he said.

James smiled and replied, We don't follow all that P.C. stuff the States went nuts over. What we do here is if someone wants a section for those who don't smoke, we oblige them. We like the idea everyone is responsible for themselves, and we don't assume we know what's best for the individual. Freedom is the main pursuit, but you are responsible for that freedom, James said proudly.

Well, we all respect that notion, Governor Princeton replied with a smile.

James ushered them to his van, and they headed over to the new area of restaurants and hotels near the cruise ship docks. The favorite dining spot of James was up on top of a bluff that looked down on the arriving and departing cruise ship liners with a background of the azure sea and the blue sky. It was beautiful and serene. With the tropical forest and mountain peaks behind them, it was just that, a paradise.

Well, gentlemen, James started as he motioned to toast them.

Here's to days with a bright future. I am extremely glad you are here to see what we are building and that I can share this day with you. Governor Princeton broke into a broad smile and responded, Thank you, my friend, it appears we may have a wealth of your experience to consider drawing from in the future.

He continued, and that neatly segues into our reason for being here.

James, the Canadian government has been approached by several of the union states under Delacorte. They seem to understand that the situation is untenable and possibly immutable.

The course of events is these several states are willing to put to vote the only remedy that seems a viable option. His voice now exposed the seriousness of the consideration. It is to secede from Delacorte and become new province-state aligned with Canada.

James nodded as though he wasn't totally surprised, and his semi-wince expression then became a look of the inevitable acquiescence.

Yes, I admit, I wondered when this type of thing would develop. James' tone was now that of acceptance. Who was the first to approach you?

Well, it was four at once, the governor began. Vermont, Maine, Rhode Island, but this is a curious part, only the northern part of New York, with some vague division above the New York Thruway. The other states are watching. New York City and Albany are adamantly against it, but we are reluctant to begin the process because of the historic effect and repercussions. But on the other hand, if the course is already set, then we need to confer and negotiate, the governor finally admitted.

James sat for a moment, pensive and deep in his own thoughts about how he had made his own decision.

Governor Princeton, my friends, he looked up as though he had experienced an epiphany. I knew I could not reason away what I saw before me. I believe these states and the bulk of their citizens are finally beginning to come to the same conclusion, James said with more confidence. Let's be clear, Delacorte is unfit and unsuitable to govern and lead, but that is water under the bridge. The damage is done, and the numbers are the numbers, they don't lie to those who know what they mean, James said, as though he had reviewed this many times.

I would add, this may end up being a win-win for Canada and those states.

Hell, I'd have 'em up before the end of the week if it were me!

The comment did induce a chuckle, but the seriousness of the thought muted the humor.

James, the Secretary piped in, the numbers are staggering, the transition is still a huge question and then the question of military control and transferring of facility is unknown.

Mr. Secretary, I don't envy you, but it is an opportunity, and it may be best for all. Something's got to give, and this just may be the best option.

The group of friends finished their meeting and took the long way back to the airport. James was beaming as he showed them the progress and the improvements to New America.

The tour ended at sunset and the governor, and his party boarded their waiting plane and were gone.

James watched for quite a long time from the observation deck of Melville Hall as the plane banked to the left into the clouds and disappeared.

His thoughts of the future of his old home were conflicted. Was he part of the cause or the cure to the issue of those states?

He turned and took the escalator down to the shiny arrival hall busy with travelers and strode across the freshly paved roadway. He knew it was out of his hands; all he could do was offer his two cents and gave his input. Where it would go was all that was left to be answered.

LIMBO

THE JARRING LANDING OF THE AIRCRAFT ON THE old airstrip jarred Giorgio and Gina awake. He could tell they were somewhere down south. It was just after sunset and the sun's last rays were silhouetting the tall palms that lined the airfield. He could see off in the distance the glow of a large city and the blinking red lights that would be on the top of a tall tower or building. The jet taxied to the edge of the airfield to the last hanger in a row of old Quonset hut-type buildings.

Beside the last Quonset hut-shaped hanger was a seaplane with its wheels down for landing on asphalt.

All right, you two, end of the line, **get out!** It was the wrestler barking out the orders.

And I mean now! he growled at them.

He pulled them out of the jet and pointed to the seaplane.

Unless you want to be alligator bait, **you better get your asses on that plane!**

He pulled the jetway closed and the jet spooled up, headed to the runway, and was gone.

The pair looked at each other and couldn't decide if they should run for it or wait at the Quonset hanger and try to find a phone or something. That decision was made for them. Within in a few seconds, a light inside the seaplane turned on and the engines started to turn over.

From the stairway of the plane a voice yelled,

Hey, Giorgio and Gina! Over here! It's okay.

They couldn't believe it. It was the old man they used to call Uncle Santos.

Santos! What the hell are you doing here for God's sake, they both said together.

Longa story, my friends, longa story, he said, reassuring them.

Listen, we gotta getta ona the plane, so com'on, I am comin' wit yous.

He hurried them on as the engine of the plane got louder and louder and began to move.

Uncle Santos pulled the stairway up and shut the door as the plane began to taxi to the now lit airfield.

The blue lights that lined the airfield began to blur and the plane lifted off. After a few minutes, the plane leveled out and the noise in the cabin began to diminish.

Uncle Santos, what the hell is going on and where the hell are we going? Gina pleaded.

She reached for his hand, looking for that expression that she knew Santos would give when everything was okay, and she could feel reassured.

Listen, my little niece, it will be okay, it won'ta be too longa and it'll be okay.

She sat back, not sure what to think, but she was reassured because of an old friendly face.

After about thirty minutes, Santos waited until Gina had her head leaning against the window of the plane as though she had fallen asleep. Santos pulled on Giorgio's sleeve and slid over to where he was seating.

Giorgio, here's the story.... the plan witha the barrels went bad.

Your guy in New Orleans didn't do it right and the big boss is pissed.

The big boss promised he could get this done, now he's a very uppaset!

He gotta private island in the Bahamas and we gotta go there so yous can tell him what happened.

The big boss is an old paison of your grandpa's, otherwise he won'ta give you a chance to tell'a your side of the story.

You're lucky, otherwise you'da already be in the river. He looked over at Gina. Both of yous. Just tell him what happened, thatsa all.

He got up and sat in the seat across from him, pushed his hat over his eyes, crossed his arms, slid his legs under the seat in front of him and didn't say another word.

Giorgio stared out the window, thinking, *What is he talking about? How did the plan go bad? How could it? All McQuirk had to do was deliver the damn barrels to the warehouse next to the river, how could he screw that up? And who the hell is this boss making these promises to? What the hell is going on?* He kept on asking himself until the hum of the seaplane's engines droned on and he nodded off again.

* * * * *

Santos tugged on Giorgio's arm.

Hey, we're gonna be there in ten minutes, better get up, both of yous.

The sun was just starting to lighten the horizon and the outline of a small island was appearing below the plane. The plane circled, lined up a guide path and slowed to touch down parallel to a now apparent beach and dock. The first rays of the sun backlit a line of palms and a villa with its walled compound and the stone path to an iron gate. Santos walked them up to the gate and slid a card through a reader and the gate pulled open.

The villa was opulent, with imported Italian marble and stone. The small courtyard was filled with artfully arranged tropical flowering plants and palms around a kidney-shaped swimming pool. Then Santos swiped his card again. The front French doors clicked and opened slightly. He grabbed the large handle and firmly pulled on the oversized door. He stepped inside and extended his arm for them to enter. He pointed to an expensive leather couch and beckoned them to take a seat. Within a minute, an employee from the kitchen staff in a starched white uniform entered with a silver tray with a silver pot of coffee and fresh fruit. For a moment, the atmosphere seemed friendly and welcoming.

From a side door appeared a bent over and ancient man. He was silvered-haired and dressed in a neat white dress shirt, starched white slacks with black and grey suspenders. He slowly shuffled to the center of the room and greeted Santos and his "guests."

Santos returned the greeting by kissing the extended right hand of the old man.

In broken English, the old man addressed Santos.

Tell me Santos, are these the Chicago people?

Yes, Grandfather, they are, he replied.

And has our Capo spoken to them as to the results of our trust in them to perform this task for us?

No, Grandfather, de Capo has not spoken to them.

Giorgio was bewildered as to what has happened.

Gina now looked at the now approaching, slouched over octogenarian.

He addressed her. You are the girl Santos calls his niece, no?

Yes, yes, Grandfather, Santos is like my uncle.

Thatsa nice, very nice, he replied. He then turned to Giorgio.

My son, can you tell me what'a happened that has caused such confusion and that these important men to call me and complain these were not the results they required?

Grandfather, I have no idea what had happened, I gave direction to the towboat captain to deliver the drums to the warehouse near the river.

Yes, Yes, we know all about that, but he did not do the job justa right and now the results are not as the family promised they would be. Trust in our organization to do the job we promised has been broken.

This is very bad; we must explain to these very important people why we failed to live up to our promise.

Grandfather, but I did what I was asked. Yes, you did and that is why you are here to explain what happened.

Now go back to Chicago, I will try to explain to these men and restore their faith in our family. The old man slowly rose and beckoned all to get their feet.

He spoke to Santos for a moment and left to return to his study.

Well, that coulda been worse.

Giorgio sighed a sigh of relief.

I'll say, joined in Gina.

Santos began to joke with them as they walked toward the dock and the waiting seaplane.

They climbed aboard and the seaplane's engines began to turn over and start up with several puffs of exhaust. The plane pulled away slowly and away from the beach as though the plane was taking off in a different direction and out toward the sea.

There were two muffled shots, and the plane slowed, and the bodies were pushed out of the plane.

Then the seaplane then turned ninety degrees and sped up for takeoff, rose off the wave tops and disappeared into the sky.

STOSHU STATABABA

THE ROOM HAD A LARGE TABLE LIKE AT A CHURCH social or a wedding buffet line and four chairs. There were three walls painted a light grey color and a wall that was like a mirror, but everyone knew it was one-way glass. If one stared in one place, one could see the vague images behind the glass. It was the typical good cop/bad cop routine.

Stoshu, may I call you Stosh? I'm Detective Simons.

Look, Stoshu, we know you were looking for something in that office, what was it, the detective asked. And really you might as well tell me because my partner knows you were there for something, and he doesn't have the patience I have.

He added that if Stosh worked with him, he would get off easy, maybe be out by midnight.

But I tell you all I was doing was looking for Giorgio, that's all, Stosh insisted.

Giorgio DePalmeri? he asked him.

Yeah, yeah, Giorgio DePalmeri, what's it to you?

The detective responded, amused, Come on Stosh, everyone know Mr. DePalmeri is a rough customer, he's suspected in a half-dozen missing persons and two suspected killings at his directions that we know of.

Don't tell me you didn't know that.

Giorgio? Stosh was floored. *Oh, I get it, you're tryin' to scare me,*

Stosh said, like he refused to believe it.

273

The room was silent for a second, then the door banged open.

I told you Stoshu, you should have told me everything.

Now Detective O'Malley just doesn't have the time or energy to work with you; he wants his answers, now.

Detective Simons, will you give me a couple of minutes with Stoshu?

I got a couple of question to get to the bottom of this.

The door closed slowly behind the departing Simons.

Okay, Pollock! what the hell were you doing? I want answers and I want them now!

Stoshu melted into the fiberglass chair, stunned, and numb to the reality of what was happening around him.

Nu, nuh, nuh, no, I was looking for Giorgio…that's all there is to it. I was supposed meet Giorgio afta the job, but I couldn'ta find him.

He was supposed ta be back three days ago, I have'a hear nuthin'from him, 'its'a been three days and no nuthin!

He started to repeat himself as though that was all he ever knew.

What, what do you mean three days? The detective now asked in a more reasonable tone.

I dunno, he was doing a job for some guy, this guy, he was a scary kinda guy, Stosh admitted. What do you mean, *scary?* O'Malley asked, now getting extremely interested.

The last time I saw him he was with the big guy with a big tattoo on his arm, he told him. It had'a three really big laughing skulls on his arm and somethin' written under it," Stosh added. It was somethin' like FLAN or FALN or somethin' like that.

Uh huh, FALN you say, O'Malley inquired.

Stoshu, are you hungry?

Do you wanna eat some dinner and look through some pictures?

The detective started to soften up .I think we can work something out with you in a couple of days if you can help us with some things.

Well, okay, yeah sure, I'd lik'a some dinner; can I get a couple of cheeseburgers?

Stoshu, you can get whatever you want. Okay, I'll look'a at sum pictures.

An hour later Stoshu was thumbing through a series of photos.

Na, Na, Na, Wait this guy look'a like him, but maybe about ten years ago, he look'a older, maybe bigger but thats'a looks like him, Stosh said, reassured he was right.

Are you sure, Stosh? Are you very sure? Simons asked again.

Yeah, I'm sure, thats'a him, who's this Garcia guy anyways?

Stosh, he a very bad guy we'd had an eye on.

Well, good, he was a scary man, what's he done?

Stosh, we think he killed six or seven people in a bombing several years ago and we never could touch him.

Oh, holy mother of God, I had no idea! Stosh was stunned.

Take your time with your dinner, Stosh, I've gotta confer with my partner, O'Malley told him.

They left the room and walked down the hall to an empty conference room.

Listen, Rick, that's the bastard who bombed that bank in New York. He's that guy we suspect killed those bank employees in that robbery ten years ago. If we had more evidence to tie that bastard, we may have nailed his ass.

Hey, it gets even better; there's been a sighting of this guy in D.C. I'm tellin' you we've been hearing this SOB is an old family friend to Delacorte, how you like them apples?

Ah shit Dave, this thing stinks. I know one thing, we better keep an eye on old Stosh there or he may just disappear, if you catch my drift. Well, we can't really hold him forever and if Giorgio doesn't come to clear or claim him, we gotta decide what to charge him with or let him go. Yeah, well let's talk to him and tell him to button his lip about the picture and maybe he'll live another couple of weeks.

Okay, Dave, I'll talk to him, and we'll let him go.

Yeah, but we better put a tail on him, or he may just end up sleeping with the fishes.

The detectives walked back to the investigation room, approached the subject, and cautioned him not to repeat to anyone that he talked to them and released him.

The detectives walked over to the captain's office and closed the door and explained what they had just ascertained from Stoshu. The captain contacted an old friend, Ken Markham. They went through the police academy together and he had just been promoted to captain in one of the D.C. precincts. He told him about Garcia and the missing DePalmeri couple.

He issued a BOLO on Garcia and put out feelers to try to track him for a while.

Listen, Ken, this Garcia is tricky sonofabitch. He eluded everyone for years. Then the bastard turns into a bundler for Delacorte and gets off. Now I hear some of his lieutenants are go-betweens with Delacorte.

The rotten apple don't fall far from the tree, Captain Ken Lewis grumbled.

Yeah, shit, don't I know it, we been watching a couple of Garcia henchmen, but we don't have a thing on them yet.... I mean what'd we do, arrest for jaywalking, for Christ sake?

I hear you, Mike, but sooner or later someone's gonna screw up, somebody's gonna show their ass and then you can pull somebody in.

We'll keep plugging, Ken, something's gotta break.

Yeah, damn I hope so, we 'll just keep our ear to the ground.

THE LAST DOTS

The "N" in Clancy's neon sign over the deteriorated remains of the oaken doorway was blinking on and off. The blue flickering light lit up the sidewalk and the broken bricks of the walkway in front of the bar as the evening came early. The sheets of silver film on the street side windows, to block out the noon sun, were now wrinkled and pulled down from the top corners of the windows. Inside, the trails of cigarette smoke swirled and disappeared behind the row of regular patrons. Then the huge back bar of oak and maple and its mirrored back would cast the blue hue of the blinking neon light on the barflies slouched over the bar.

One of them was Stashu Jacyniski. A jumble of shot glasses and beer bottles were before him like so many pickup sticks. When Sam opened the oaken door, Stosh's face broke into a broad smile.

Sammy, my friend, Sammy, am I glad to see ya!

Stosh, I went by the lockup to get you out and the sergeant told me they let you out! What happened?

I dunno, these two cops were asking questions, then the next thing I know I'm looking through a book of pictures of a bunch of guys while I'm eating cheeseburgers. Then they let me out and said don't talk to nobody about Giorgio and dis other guy Garci, Garco, or sumthin' like that.

Geez, Sam, I wasn't supposed to talk about Giorgio missing and all.

Stosh then winced and looked down at the bar, shaking his head.

Ah jeez, Sam furget it, I 'm supposed to keep my mouth *s-h-u-t!*

Don't worry about it, Stoshu, my lips are sealed.

What'a pal, Sam, whata pal. Stosh downed the rest of the beer in the bottle in front of him.

Sam signaled the bartender to bring another round. Stosh looked at Sam and raised his shot glass and downed it.

Sam, I knows I ain't supposed to say nothing, but this is sumthing else.

I needs to know what's going on, now wit Giorgio not showing up, I got ta talk to somebody.

After a moment Stosh started retelling the events of the last few days.

I get back from the job from St. Louis for Giorgio and no Giorgio.

Stosh slurred some words but clear enough for Sam to get the gist of it.

So Stosh, what d'you think happened to Giorgio?

Sam asked, trying to fish for more info.

I ain't got no idea what's happened or where he is.

Stosh wanted to talk about what the cops had warned him.

Reaching for his beer mug, he continued. And I ain't got no damn idea who this Garcia guy is the cops were talking about.

I tell ya, Sam, the cops were hot about the Garcia guy, and they really wanted to talk about this guy!

Stosh kept talking. Yep, bad news, this guy is. They sat there for a minute, Sam trying to piece the events together.

Stosh got up from the bar stool, looked at Sam, swayed from left to right like he barely could keep his balance, and said right at Sam,

It's this guy the cops asked me about, I dunno what Giorgio was doin' wit this guy but sumthin' gone wrong and I ain't got a good feelin' bout this.

He turned and stumbled toward the men's room. After about ten minutes, Stosh didn't return to his bar stool. Sam began to get curious and got up to find him.

He was slumped over the table in a booth, snoring and passed out. Sam signaled the bartender and left twenty dollars for cab fare to get him home.

After the cab pulled in front of the bar and the driver was given his address, Sam left and walked home. There was work to do tonight.

With the weekend coming, he would use his credentials and nose around the West Chicago airfield. Maybe there were still some stones unturned there.

That night he contacted the Admiral: *Who is Garcia? My contact here implied connection between the events in N.O. La. and DePalmeri. I will observe any movement of any suspect at W. Chicago airfield and make report.*

THE SLIDE INTO THE OCEAN

Hold for the Congresswoman, Mister Mayor, the voice of the aid to Natalie Mulligan said pleasantly.

Mister Mayor, thank you for returning my call, she was cheerful, yet there was a sense of concern in her voice.

Franco, we are calling for a meeting of mayors and congress people in the state for this Friday evening, but not in Sacramento, she explained.

We would like to keep this as private as possible with no media coverage and definitely not open to the public, she added. And really, she continued, the only two mayors are you and Henry Liu, and Henry is speaking for most of Northern California. Sounds serious, Natalie.

We think so, Franco, she replied. Eight p.m. on Friday, then? Yes, most certainly, I will be there, was all he said.

* * * * *

The meeting was arranged to be at the private residence of Congresswoman Mulligan. With the eight-foot-high privacy fences and the wrought iron gate, the invitees were able to arrive, unnoticed, and in small groups until all were present.

"Let me begin by saying I am very happy you all were able to attend with such short notice, the congresswoman began. I have requested we gather to discuss what could be the future of our great state. As most all of you know, President Delacorte has severely reduced or totally eliminated any federal money to aid in the cost of support to the political refugees and undocumented persons we all have allowed to stay in the country and in our state. And the cost of the additional mandated program he has installed has crippled our economy. This with the exodus of commerce and business to the RTW states or just closing shop has rendered us bankrupt, she added.

These facts will now come face-to-face with reality in two weeks when we will no longer be able to send any aid to citizens on state aid. In another four weeks, we will not be able to issue payroll checks to state employees. While many in the state legislature are in denial, when they can't cash their payroll check, the fact will have hit home.

Now, is there a way out of this crisis we have brought on to ourselves? Well, yes, there is but I am afraid the only solution in sight may be hard to accept.

She took a deep breath and began.

It is the opinion of the assembled congressmen and women here, along with most of the state legislatures and the governor, that we begin talks and negotiations with British Columbia and Ottawa. They have offered to fund our liabilities for the next ten years. **But,** and this very big but, in exchange we must agree to be absorbed by Canada.

We have conversed with the governors, Congress people and legislature in Oregon and Washington State, she continued. It appears that the numbers are grim at best. With no aid from the Feds, our obligations are over two hundred billion dollars a year and we estimate we might have one and a half billion if we don't lose any more of our tax base. The other states are quickly getting as bad, and they know time is almost up. So, we are here to decide how we are to survive and to set a timetable to start negotiations and announcements of the decisions. We should all plan to meet at this same location tomorrow, ten a.m."

All in favor vote aye.

The ayes carried the vote. Tomorrow would be the beginning of the end of the West Coast of the United States, union states or not.

SATURDAY, WEST CHICAGO AIRFIELD

WHAT CAN I HELP YOU WITH, SIR, ASKED THE UNI-
formed guard at the counter of the general aviation main
building.

Yeah, hi, my name is Sam Hirschfield, here's my credentials
and ID. I'm supposed to install an upgrade to a Cessna Citation
owned by this guy, DePalmeri, Sam said confidently.

Let's see, the guard said. DePalmeri, yeah, that'd be Hanger
212 west. The guard pulled out a map of the airfield with the
hanger locations and names of the companies or owners inked in.

Yeah, take your vehicle through the west gate and its up on
the second row of hangers halfway down.

Sam looked at him for a second, looking at the map, moving
it from side to side and looking confused.

Tell you what, can you make me a copy? I don't know my
way around the place. I'll give it back to you on my way out if
you need it back, Sam said, looking up from the counter.

Yeah, I'll make a copy, but I will need it back. The code for
the gate is today's date, six numbers.

He turned and slipped the map into the copier under the
counter and hit the copy button. The light of the machine
glowed from underneath and in a second Sam had a ticket to
what he needed to stake out the comings and goings of aircraft.

Sam pulled his truck out, drove to the gate, entered the code, and drove onto the access road and then onto the tarmac in between hangers and parked. He made notes on the hangers and the companies and individuals renting the hangers. There were two that caught his attention. Depalmeri's at 212, but right next door was 214, leased to the Department of Labor of the Union States. Next to it were some notations and aircraft registration numbers: Gulfstream V, REGS # NV605.

Well, looks like someone did all my work for me, Sam thought. *I'll scope out the field and give it a couple of hours to see what goes on. Maybe I'll get lucky.*

Saturday at the airfield was hectic. Aircraft of all types were moving across the tarmac to line up for takeoff. The morning brought out the avid hobbyists and businessmen flying home for the weekend. The parade of restored aircraft and individuals working on their pilot's license kept the field buzzing all morning.

The line of trainers from the war was impressive. There was a yellow Boeing-Stearman model 75 biplane and AT-6 Texans. The one that caught Sam's eye was the silver and red Ryan trainer from the late 30s. Off to the end of the row of hangers were two DC-3s. One was just starting to turn over and start its engines. The silver and royal blue paint scheme looked like an airline retirees' group had just about finished a long restoration project.

Sam was in heaven just walking around and taking in all the mornings' activities.

He headed to the hanger with the Cessna and started to make notes of the aircraft and its contents. In the center console were hand-scribbled notes. But one caught his attention. It was eye-opening.

The note was in a plain white envelope marked "for Garcia" was plainly written as if the author had no fear of being read by anyone. It stunned Sam.

For Tomaso Garcia
Upon Completion Of Agreement
HSBC HOUSE
68 WEST BAY
GEORGE TOWN, G.C. KY-1102
Acct 022000020-1148940

He scanned the rest of the cockpit for any other notes or scribbles by Giorgio. He found some photos of Giorgio and Gina with some of the D.C. elites and presidential aides. One struck him as very strange.

The photo was of Giorgio and large man with salt and pepper hair and a wide bushy moustache and President Delacorte. What was strange was they had their forearms laid side by side on a fancy dining room table. On their forearms was the same tattoo of three laughing skulls. He grabbed the photo, laid it out flat and took a picture of it from his cell phone along with the note address to Tomaso Garcia.

Sam relaxed for a few minutes, thinking he might have enough to send to Admiral Merritt and the RTW agencies to squeeze Delacorte and make a connection to the New Orleans incident.

His thoughts were abruptly interrupted.

Hey, you, what the hell are you doing here!?

At first, Sam could not make out the figure yelling at him.

Then he could not but recognize the face, it was the mustached figure in the picture.

I said, what the hell are you doing here? he repeated.

Sam gathered his composure.

Hey man, I'm supposed to be upgrading the avionics on this Cessna.

Here are the work orders and my credentials, he said with authority.

Lemme see those! He grabbed the made-up work order.

I don't know anything about any work on this aircraft!

He menacingly approached Sam, *I mean it now, get it?*

Listen, I don't know who you are, but I don't know nothing about this, so, you better leave, and I mean right now!

Sam began to gather his duffel bags and said, okay, man, I get it, and I'll wait until my shop tells me what to do.

I'll have them clear this up and they will call you back on the work, Sam replied.

Yeah, you do that! answered back the mustached man.

Sam headed out the door and got in his truck and headed through the gate.

I gotta get a picture of this guy and send it to the Admiral, he thought.

He headed over to the general aviation parking lot and parked. After a few minutes he grabbed his camera and telescopic lens to head back to the hanger.

Sam walked the length of the perimeter fence and positioned himself across from the hanger and the Cessna. To his surprise, down the tarmac was a shiny new Gulfstream V, tail number NV 605. Heading toward the jet and the extended stairway was the salt-and-pepper-haired mustached man who had confronted Sam. He got about a dozen photos and left.

In an hour he had the photos sent to the Admiral and to the RTW agencies with the notes:

This guy tied to Delacorte and DePalmeri. There was a confrontation at DePalmeri Cessna hanger, my cover has been compromised. Awaiting your advisement.

The return message was: *Agreed. Return to D.C for final report and debrief. 09/05 18:00, Report to Mitchell Airfield MAC C-17.*

* * * * *

The next morning Sam packed and got ready to drive up to Mitchell Field. His phone buzzed and he checked for a text. The message in the text was clear.

Photos ID: Garcia. Link with Delacorte established.

THE CONFRONTATION

In the office of President Cabbott, a large group had gathered, heads from most all departments and military attachés from the Department of the Navy and Army. The mood was all business and seriousness because of the recently uncovered malicious intent of Delacorte to disrupt and harm the New Orleans area and by extension cripple commerce throughout the Mississippi River basin.

You all know what seems to have been the intent of the incident in Algiers, he began.

It appears Delacorte is rotten sonofbitch and he and his asshole henchmen tried to make one of our major cities partly uninhabitable and suspend commerce and business activities through the waterway. I have no plans of negotiating or making nice with this shit for brains.

Abbott then moved to a large flat screen on the edge of the large conference room table and dimmed the lights.

Here's what I am proposing. A total and final statement of separation and we are not leaving D.C. until we force the issue. This is not a negotiation per se, it is a document of screw you, you and your numb nuts way, you are on your own. His tone was even and controlled.

We are to present a final division of military assets and states borders. All departments will finalize with their counterpart departments, but we will command and direct the conversation.

His tone a little more pronounced. I have notified Delacorte that we intend to meet with all departments and finalize the cleaving, and that we are most serious.

We don't believe he understands we have connected him directly to the incident.

That will be our ace in the hole, he continued ,but he's fixing to find out.

Naturally, Delacorte has not responded but I have set aside the week of September 19-25 to accomplish this end, with or without Delacorte. I'll let you all clear your schedules and get with Vice President Payne and make final arrangements with your counterparts.

Cabbott then moved away from the podium and let the Vice President take over the meeting.

All right everybody, Payne began, these are the department heads and assistants we will see this week. He began with the military attachés and staffs, then one by one all departments. Treasury, Commerce, Trade, Agriculture, and Interior would all be represented.

Payne then added, I'll see Ag and Interior last because some staff are still in New Orleans with the final toxicity and damage report. We'll have them fly directly to D.C. and meet them there. The Vice President then listed in order the departments. Okay, Admiral Merritt and General White and respective staff, tomorrow nine hundred hours.

Tuesday, Treasury, nine A.M., Wednesday, Commerce, nine A.M.

Thursday, Trade nine A.M.

Friday, we will finish up with all departments and review. Lowell Payne's voice was like God, thunderous and low. His voice and attitude were that of authority but at the same time reassuring.

Paine turned to his secretary. Molly make sure all who aren't here are brought up top speed and know their butts better be here on time, no, exceptions.

Yes sir, Mr. Vice President, she replied briskly and as a seasoned professional.

We still need to get Trade in here from New America and a few others' assistants.

Well, get 'em in here and let's get moving.

Sir, yes sir. She turned and left the meeting to start to contact the absentees.

The Austin complex was exceptionally large, and though some departments had been in place for many months, not everyone knew or met the staffs of all departments. A few departments were not in the same building, some were even blocks away from each other. Some meetings of staff would be for the first time in D.C.

AN UNPLEASANT REALITY

MOM, WHAT DO YOU MEAN YOU ARE WORKING IN a tapas bar? Venus' daughter was floored.

I thought you were way up the ladder with the IRS!

Look, Sarah, it happened, and it wasn't my fault, she explained. I was doing my job for my boss, but he did something years ago, there was trouble and an investigation.

She continued, I don't know what he did but he, he just snapped and hung himself! Those bastards who were after him couldn't get him, so they fired me, boom, gone, on the street with nothing!

Sarah was a strong minded idealistic young woman. She had grown up in the liberal strongholds of San Francisco. And with a serious influence of liberal politics, she had in her mind who were her friends and who were not. She had been a social justice activist. Along with taking care of others, she also took care of herself and kept herself in shape from a regime of kickboxing and yoga. And contrary to many others she knew, she had a concealed carry permit. While this would represent no issue in some states, it was an issue in D.C. This would come quickly into play with her arrival, living back with her mom.

What do you mean, mom? Sarah asked repeatedly.

You mean some redneck lawyer accused you of something that your boss may or may not have done and he hung himself and **you're** in the street?

Is that about it, mom?

So now at your age, you're a waitress at a bar and grill because of some asshole hotshot lawyer congressman, that's what it comes down to?

Is that accurate? And on top of it you got no pension or anything because they took that back?

Venus swallowed hard and spoke up. Look, Sarah, it happened, there's nothing I can do about it, but Congresswoman Mulligan says she can get me back in the system after a couple of years, then I can start again when this blows over. The time will go quickly, it's already been two months and I'm doing okay. It's not all that bad, Venus tried to reassure her.

In a couple of years, you'll be sixty!

What if you can't get back into the system?

You want to be a waitress at a bar filled with Washington assholes? she retorted.

I'm sorry you feel that way, I gotta stick it out for now, was all she could muster.

Sarah was not going to settle for what her mom had accepted. The very worst trait that Venus had at one time was a vengeful nature. It was much worse in Sarah. She would get even, and she didn't care who got in the way.

For the first week, things with Venus and Sarah seemed to improve, or so Venus thought. What she didn't see was Sarah becoming slowly more enraged at the thought of her mom leaving six days a week at noon and coming home at midnight. She believed her mom was supposed to do great things. She after all singlehandedly got Congresswoman Mulligan reelected.

She worked at the FCC and the IRS. *She deserved better than this.*

She damn well deserved better than this!

Sarah seethed with anger. She began to plan to extract her revenge. She studied the incident with Levin Teacher and how her mom had been involved in the case. Of course, she didn't care about any accusations of wrongdoing or abuse. She began to research the prosecutors and zeroed in on those involved. With her laptop she began to build a notebook about the case. And a plan.

Sarah began to search through Army-Navy surplus store and Goodwill. She was looking for something. She knew she would find it. And then she could proceed.

SEPTEMBER 18TH
HOTEL WASHINGTON

THE HOTEL THAT JAMES AND HIS FRIENDS HAD
met in all those months ago was once again the epicenter for
the RTW states. This just inflamed Delacorte, having the bane
of his existence just a short walk from the White House. At first
Delacorte had planned to meet with Cabbott, but he decided
he would blow them off and attempt to forge a deal, personally, with China to sell bonds at a more favorable rate.... for
the Chinese.

Delacorte was planning on pitching a twelve percent, five-
year bond because the Union States were almost out of options,
unable to move any more payments around. Soon benefits and
payroll checks would have to be exchanged for script or IOUs.
The Treasury Secretary had warned him repeatedly the rest of
the world was planning on replacing the dollar as the reserve
currency if the dollar dropped further in value. Many of the
developed countries were in fact using cryptocurrency as a
workaround to the dollar.

Delacorte's back was against the wall. The dollar was almost
worthless now after the massive devaluation. If he could not
sell treasury notes to somebody, Delacorte would not be able
to stop the waves of the population demanding Delacorte and
his administration's heads.

When the rumors began to ring true and the first waves of IOUs were mailed to government suppliers and vendors, the news spread like wildfire. The demonstrations began slowly, first only small but vocal groups, but as the days went on the crowds grew with each passing day that week.

It was September 16th, a Saturday. The following week had demonstrations scheduled all over the city. But the biggest assembled on the National Mall and the surrounding area leading up to the White House. So far, the demonstrators had been vocal but peaceful.

The delegations from Austin were not surprised by the demonstrations and the crowds, but they were unaware the scope of the crowds that had planned to pour into the city in the next few days now that the rumors of no benefits checks, or IOUs were to be issued in their place.

They were going to be in the very center of the match head and the flame. It was to take only the appearance of one man, one congressman to strike the match. That would happen sooner than anyone had believed.

* * * * *

Sunday morning came with a clear sky and the scent of fresh cut grass from the Mall and the area around the Washington monument. Many of the RTW elected officials and their aides and assistants had already arrived and checked in to the hotel. Some would arrive late Sunday morning, but all needed to be there by noon for the first of the departmental meetings and review of the agenda and final statement. This would signify the official cleaving and separation.

One by one the individual department took their turns, and all signed an official statement to validate the separation. At the conclusion of the department meetings, President Cabbot addressed the signees and participants.

President Cabbott began to speak in a firm and resolute tone.

"We are at a point where none of us could ever think we would be willing participants in a modern-day version of the bombardment of Fort Sumter. We never would have believed that rampant incompetence and malicious contempt for its citizen would lead to this clash of ideals and philosophies and a dissolving of the melting pot that this country was built upon. It is more than just an agenda that is foisted upon citizens, it is when a portion of the citizenry, willingly and actively submits to the tyranny, soft or not, that others who genuinely love freedom and sovereignty must decide and react to this agenda, that is so reviled.

It is not as the Jesuits teach, to convince the inconvincible, to sway the unswayable. To use logic and common sense to make those who are blind to see a righteous way again. Those who have evolved to believe they are free to live off the governmental largess and the sweat of the brows of others, have only two choices, make a way for yourself or be a slave to the imaginary security you believe you have found. But the truth be told, freedom and security do not and will not be etched in stone for anyone. These two concepts are fought for and must be defended every day and from many different types of threats to its existence. Those who ultimately understand, know freedom and security do not exist in harmony. The concepts are at odds with each other and that only an unsteady truce exists between them.

Sadly, for decades that truce and understanding that had existed in what was America, has now vaporized. It is gone because those who once fought daily to maintain a balance of these ideas have no longer the strength of numbers to sustain a unified continuation of their beliefs. They see what used to be a land of opportunity. They find themselves in an environment that sees them as enemies. These individuals no longer want to live within a system where so many prefer to be an anchor to their efforts and to punish and vilify them for the desire to be a success or rise above the average and mediocre. This evolved because the philosophies of individual responsibilities have grown to be an inconvenience for too many.

This is anthemia to all we believe and cherish.

He continued with a sigh,

So, we will forge our own way and finalize a new beginning and it may be that our success and example will be a shining star for others to learn by and follow."

One by one, the attendees and participants signed the documents that clearly stated that from the point of this presentation of documents to President Delacourte or his representatives, the separation would be complete. The last to sign were President Cabbot and Vice President Payne.

There was no toast to the event. There was only the clinking of coffee cups being filled and refilled. This was not an event of celebration, only sadness.

Sadness because this should have been unnecessary and avoided by the insistence of just a few more men of like minds to adhere to tried-and-true principles. Yet when self-control and discipline were the only tools needed, they were thrown away like a broken toy.

September 18th would mark the end date on the gravestone for what used to be the United States of America. The gathering began to break up into small groups and mill around and make plans for the evening and dinner.

James had sent his deputy in his place because he was afraid his flight would not get him back in time for the beginning of the signings. He was flying back from Sao Paulo, Brazil, after meeting with the Minister for Trade in the Americas. He had to finalize on a trade relationship with both New America and the RTW states on raw sugar, lumber, and native hardwoods. The agreement had already been tentatively approved but needed a final review and sign off.

The flight back had run into violent thunderstorms that surround the equator in the summer and fall. The flight arrived five hours late after a stop in Brasilia to let the storms pass. At almost six p.m., he checked in at the hotel. James was exhausted and decided to go straight up to his room and maybe rest for a couple of hours or so, and then come down to the coffee shop or dining room or whatever was open.

There wasn't much for him to participate in as the official documents were signed and were to be presented tomorrow. He would accompany President Cabbott and officials, but it would be back to South America by the end of the week to work out a similar deal with Chile.

It wasn't until after eight p.m. that James awoke. The drapes that hung in front of the sliding glass door and balcony were gently swaying in the cool evening breeze. He walked out onto his balcony, and it struck him he was in almost the same room the last time he was here.

There had been so many massive changes and thousands of miles since the last time he was here. He thought about Abbey and knew she had moved to Reno. He had emailed her before the holidays, hoping to hear from her. But never did. As the months passed, he decided he had the few memories he had of her and that would be it. He couldn't continue with the stubborn fantasy that he would be able to recreate something that never existed in the first place.

He had spent so much energy hoping that there was some slight chance of this that he now realized he had just wasted his time on a fool's errand.

He tried to remember what got him to this point and what a wild ride it was. It was time to count his blessing and be grateful.

*****

President Cabbott and the heads of the Departments were met by a private security detail at nine a.m. in the lobby of the hotel. The plan was to take three SUVs to 1600 Pennsylvania Avenue and the White House. There was a sense of apprehension and uncertainty as to how they would be received. They knew by news reports that Delacorte was on his way to China. There was no surprise amongst the members, they would have expected this.

No, it was to whom would they deliver the proclamation and statement of separation?

Cabbott expected the Vice President would be the most likely candidate for this job. This was not the case. As they entered through the Portico, Joseph Walesa, the current press secretary greeted them.

President Cabbott was cordial but when it became apparent that the press secretary **was** the one to receive the documents, the mood changed from apprehension to reaction to an insult. Cabbott and Payne stood in stunned silence when told there was no one else to meet them.

Look Joe, I know you didn't know what the story here was, but we expected at least someone from the Executive Branch to be here, Lowell Payne began.

I'm sure your boss is busy selling his soul to the Chinese for another thirty pieces of silver, thought that was more important, but we did come here as equals and were willing to negotiate in the spirit of cooperation. But quite frankly, this is beyond the pale, so why don't you assholes go screw yourselves and tell your boss to kiss our ass.

He turned around and raised his arm over his head and gave the press secretary half of the peace symbol.

President Cabbott turned to Joe and extended his hand to shake hands, and said, couldn't have said it better myself.

The group turned and left. It was in fact now over...and there was no love lost.

The rest of the day there were emails and texts sent to Austin to inform all how the meeting went and the events so far. There was a text to all to plan to meet in the private conference room behind the main dining room at three p.m.

The text was from President Cabbott.

The meeting was to the point and a recap of the conversation with Delacorte's press secretary. The group could tell he was still visibly angry with the disrespect shown to him and the group.

I want to tell you all that with an event this important, one would expect a modicum of respect, he began. Well, we didn't get it and to tell you the truth, with this administration, I'm sure this is how they view everyone else, as insignificant peons. I believe that our results will speak for us from now on. I see no reason why we, as a group of like-minded individuals with the beliefs we are committed to, cannot rise above any circumstances that may be obstacles. We have come a long way, but we have many, many miles before we can begin to look over the land we are creating, hand in hand and begin to smile. But that day will come, this I promise you. Good night, and I will see y'all back in Austin.

President Cabbott and Vice President Payne left that night. The rest of the group were to leave throughout the next day.

James' flight wasn't until early in the evening tomorrow. He had expected some negotiations, but once again he had time to think and walk around some. He was all that aware of the demonstrations and how they were building by the hour here in D.C., but he had seen only a few smaller groups today. The large groups that had begun to surround the city did not descend into the city yet, but they would be and soon.

*****

James was an early riser. At about six-thirty, he decided to grab some coffee in the hotel coffee shop. After that he could take his time and walk around the Mall and try to relax a bit before his flight that evening. He was sitting at the counter with his back to the lobby, oblivious to the comings and goings of some of his associates from Austin. A half-folded newspaper was on the counter; he picked it up and thumbed through the sports section.

The tap on his shoulder didn't register at first, and then a gentle nudge caught his attention. It was Frank Sullivan from the Agriculture and Interior Department.

James had met Frank when he was just setting up his office in Austin.

Hey, Jim, how the hell are you?

I don't see you much when I get over to the Shark Tank, he said. You're the one travelling all over hell's half acre, Frank joked.

James began to turn from his newspaper. Oh, and Jim, have you met Abbey from the AG Department?

There was a stunned silence and wide-eyed expression from both.

James! OK, this crazy!

Her expression was more ,what are the odds and amazement!

How? What are you doing here?

She was starting to show the expression of genuine happy surprise.

Me? I'm the Deputy to the Secretary of Trade, James exclaimed.

Abbey! Come on, what are *you* doing here!?

He was still absorbing the fact she was standing there.

I wrote you Christmas in Reno but never heard anything, how did you get here?

I came to Texas through Mexico over six months ago. I've been in Austin at Ag. and Interior for five months.

How did I keep missing you?

Ah hell, your office is on the other side of the grounds, I guess, that's how, but still I can't believe I never saw you. This is incredible! Frank, why didn't you tell me Abbey was working with you? James asked still stunned.

Well hell, Jim, you never asked!

The three of them sat for an hour. They agreed to meet again for lunch and catch up.

NOON SUNDAY SEPTEMBER 18TH

THE TRIO MET UP AT THE CAFÉ ON THE PATIO OF the hotel. From there they had a wide view of the National Mall, the Washington Monument, and the back of the White House. It was a beautiful morning with a gentle breeze and the scent from the neatly trimmed rose bushes in a row along a wrought iron divider that bordered the sidewalk.

James was comfortable with Abbey. The atmosphere was light. The emotional cascade that had been James' weakness with her was nearly removed. It wasn't that she wasn't still the most beautiful woman he had ever seen, still, but it was more a sense that he had given it his best shot and it was over. In his mind he had acquiesced. It was the uncoupling from an emotional hook that took years and years to wear out and dissolve away. He could pull away and life did still go on.

He did have one of those mnemonic short circuits in his mind with her. Long ago on that one summer night when he fell for her so deeply, she had worn a sleek yellow dress and that memory was seared forever in his mind. He couldn't tell if she had saved the same dress all these years, but she was as beautiful an image of a woman as there ever was in it. Abbey never really had to do much to herself. Her hair was a full mane of silk, raven-colored, and longer than shoulder-length. As the sun did shine through it, just the slightest hint of henna and the few strands that had grayed were detected. She was the svelte girl who had grown into a woman, and she did it gracefully. James would feel the twinge and knots in his guts but now he knew how to look away and break the spell she would cast upon him like a modern-day Medusa.

Frank was a great buffer. He had kept the conversation focused on the events of the previous day and what he expected would happen to Delacorte and D.C. for that matter.

At twelve-thirty, Frank looked at his cell phone and announced he needed to get going as he had a two-thirty flight. He smiled at Abbey, shook James' hand, dropped a twenty on the café table for his share of lunch, turned and was gone.

For a second there was pregnant pause and then they both exclaimed, *hey, let's take a walk.* And both broke into laughter.

James smiled at her and replied, okay, let's meet back down here in ten minutes and we'll walk the Mall and wherever we want to.

Abbey nodded and they both headed to the elevator. See you back in ten, she said to him.

James waited for her to go up first. He caught himself almost reaching to kiss her on the top of the head and fill his senses with the scent of the young girl perfume that she had always worn. While he knew it was just garden variety drug store perfume, it might as well have been a thousand dollars an ounce and from Paris.

The scene outside the hotel was not so light. The mass of people who had stayed out of the city last night began to descend upon the Mall and the monuments and the museums. As the morning turned to the afternoon, the crowd had started to build ever larger in front of a stage that had been erected that morning. There was to be a series of speeches to address the events that had cratered the dollar and what to expect from the Delacorte's administration in handling the crisis.

In a few minutes, Abbey and James walked out of the lobby of the hotel, only to be swept up in a current of people slowly but forcefully flowing to the front of the stage. Abbey and James were swept alongside the stage's stairwell and were able to find a place to carve out without the pressure of the ever-growing mass of people. One of the speeches was to be given by Trent Gordon. He was one person the crowd felt would tell them the truth.

Abbey was intent on hearing the congressman. While he was no longer in Delacorte's Congress but with the RTW, most of those still in the Union States respected Gordon to be straight with the people no matter where they or he was.

Abbey wasn't the only one who was hoping to see the congressman. Many from the Austin group were slowly making their way to the stage area, caught up in the flow. At first it was a slow parade of local officials and the mayor promising that services would improve, and things would get better.

The mood of the crowd went from patient to restless to perturbed with the passing of every speech. Finally, the congressman walked from behind the stage and climbed the stairs in front of Abbey. In the best of times, this might have been another matter-of-fact speech for the congressman. This was not that.

As the congressman approached the podium, the crowd pushed even closer to the stage. Some people skirted the push and pressure of the crowd and slid under the stage and appeared right in front of the speakers. From their perch, Abbey was right in the line of sight to see the people slide under and popping up in the front row. Congressman Gordon began to speak, *My friends, we are all living in times I never in my wildest dreams ever expected to experience. Just a few months ago I would never have expected to be addressing this crowd and consider myself an outsider.*

From the crowd hecklers began, You're damn right you're an outsider, what are you doing here?

He responded quickly, *Hey, I'm here because we are trying to talk sense into President Delacorte, but he decided it wasn't important. That you weren't important!*

How would you know what's important? You bailed out on us.

Then one person began the chant, and then another, then another began,

How would you know what's important?

Why should we believe you? Why should we believe you? Why should we believe you?

Louder from the front of the crowd to the middle to the sides to the back as far as the eye could see.

Why should we believe you?

A graying lady began to berate the congressman. She became irate and her son came to her side to steady and console her. The congressman looked to exit the stage and for a clear path to do so.

The crowd slowed just enough for Abbey to see an opening to try to escort the congressman off the stage. She beckoned him to follow her to the side stairs. As she stepped to the first step, the congressman's eyes opened wide and grimaced.

No one had heard what a girl in a military-looking uniform had yelled as she pulled out her 9mm and fired the first shots. James had seen her pull her gun from under her jacket and raise it up. More shots were fired. He reached for Abbey, tearing her yellow dress down the side. She turned to see what happened and fell up the steps. As she did, another shot rang out, hitting Abbey in the back as she fell toward the congressman. The girl in the military uniform was screaming as she slid back under the stage.

You bastard, you ruined me and my mom, die you sonofabitch!

She made it to the far end of the stage and slid under it.

She emerged from under the other side of the stage where those who had seen what had happened couldn't get to her.

Stop her stop, that girl! someone yelled out.

She ran off and around the corner. She made it out to the entrance of the Smithsonian and was caught on camera as she stuffed her gun back under her blue double-breasted jacket and ran down the block and out of sight.

Abbey had fallen forward into the stage drape behind the podium, taking it down with her. It wrapped itself around her as she fell. Congressman Gordon was hit twice. He was motionless and, on his back, however, because he had the good sense to listen to his security guards, he had a bulletproof vest on under his jacket. The bullets impacted directly in the solar plexus and were stopped by the vest. The impact knocked the wind out of the congressman. In a few seconds he coughed and began to move.

He said loud enough for those in the front row to hear,

Son of a bitch, she shot me! I don't believe it!

James rushed to Abbey. He dug her out of the drapes and hurled them to the side. He picked her up and ran down the stairs, carrying her in his outstretched arms. He could feel the blood from her now running down his arms as he fought his way to the hotel through the crowds screaming at the top of his lungs, **Clear out, make a path, she been shot!**

James got her to the lobby of the hotel and screamed,

Call 9-1-1, for God's sake, call 9-1-1!

He held her as the blood continued to run down his arms and into a small pool where he was with her on the marble floor of the hotel lobby.

Somebody gets some towels, I've got to stop this bleeding, hurry, get some towels!

She began to moan and then went limp. He held her and kept whispering in her ear so only she could hear. Within a minute man in military fatigues came running over.

Who's been shot? Where are they?

He told James to lay her down on the towels.

Listen ,I've got some medical training from the army ,let me look at her until someone gets here. He began to exam her and from where the blood was oozing. He slowly slid his hand under her back and felt the blood. He saw an entrance and exit wound.

What's your name, son?

James.

I'm Nick, he replied.

I think the bullet hit her shoulder, shattered, and exited in several places, there's one out her neck, but I can't tell what other damage was done. The bleeding is not spurting so it may not have pierced anything major, or she would still be pouring out blood.

I can't say for sure, so keep this towel compressed on the wounds. His voice was reassuring but firm.

The EMS should be here in any minute, just hang tight and we'll get her the closest hospital.

The crowds had not been stopped but proceeded past the Mall and the ellipse to the White House. The chaos continued and built further, erupting into further volume until it reached the White House gates.

James could only hear the shouting and chanting in the background, like a muffled explosion far away from the hotel, but paid no attention to the events. Even when someone said they thought they heard more shots outside, he ignored it and continued stroking Abbey's now blood-soaked hair. He kept whispering in her ear, hoping she would hear him, but she didn't move.

The EMS pulled up to the front of the lobby of the hotel and two men in white uniforms ran to Abbey. The first EMS looked at James and Nick, and asked, *what happened here?*

She was shot in the back, Nick replied, looks like multiple exit wounds and there's one near her neck that could be bad. Nick looked at James, and said ,Hey they got this, I'll just be the way.

You stick with them, and they'll take care of her.

James, nodded as Nick disappear into the crowd now formed in the lobby around Abbey.

The senior of the two EMS personnel asked, Who brought her in here?

James piped up ,I did!

Ok, we'll take it from here but stick around, I may need your help.

Think you can do that?

Yeah, just tell me what I can do, James replied focusing on Abbey.

What's your name, the EMS asked?

James, he responded knelling next the Abbey.

Ok James, I'm Carl, my partner is Sanjeev.

They immediately began to treat her. The EMS attention shifted to his partner

Ok. get her heart rate and BP, check her airway, he began like he was checking off the boxes in his head.

Abbey began moaning,

Oh God, it hurts, it's burning!

Oh my God it hurts!

Carl began to cut away the blood-soaked part of Abbeys yellow dress.

He revealed a large wound that extended from her right shoulder blade up her shoulder and exited in front of her collar bone. There also was a wound at the base of her neck.

Abbey's blood was oozing from three places.

Heart rate 112, BP, 84 over 58 was the reply from Sanjeev less than a minute later.

Start an IV with 100 milligrams of TXA in 200 cc's of saline, Carl called out,

Ok James, I may need you help me stop some of this bleeding ,he calmly said.

It looks like her collarbone maybe broken from the bullet and I am concerned about this neck wound. She got some dark blood oozing from her shoulder and there maybe a vein damaged.

We got this thing called a quick clot bandage made for this sort of thing, Carl explained to James. I need you to hold one over her shoulder blade and one on her neck wound with just enough pressure to stop the bleeding.

Hold them in one place, if it gets soaked, here's some more, just place it on top of the other one. Sanjeev and I will get her on the gurney and get her to the ambulance.

The wheeled gurney was unfolded, and she was very carefully lifted on it and wheeled to the waiting ambulance.

Carl asked James if she had any next of kin. James replied she did, but none were here in town. He asked James if he wanted to go with her to the hospital. He nodded yes and they loaded her in and sped away.

* * * * * * *

Down the street and around the block, a girl sat on the curb, sobbing, and mumbling and swearing to herself. It was Sarah. She had on a navy blazer, double-breasted, and white skirt like a female junior officer in the Navy might wear. Next to her was a 9mm Glock with four rounds still in it. No one noticed her with all the chaos and confusion.

The sound of police cars and their wailing sirens blasted past her. She stirred as if coming out of a daze, then threw the gun down a sewer drain. The navy jacket was discarded into a recycling barrel, like the kind for plastic bottles. She kicked off the patent leather heels, threw the Navy-style cap into a row of bushes, and walked off. She didn't know how many people were hurt or worse. She didn't care. She did what she had to do for her mom. She didn't even care if she got caught. And chances were she wouldn't even say anything to her mom.

She had imagined she would feel relieved. She felt nothing.

The sirens and the sounds of the chaos grew louder all around her.

Police lights and sirens blared. She kept walking.

THE AFTERMATH

THE NEXT MORNING PRESIDENT DELACORTE, JUST back from an unsuccessful sales trip to China, ran into a buzz saw with the White House press corps. While the scene and the events the day before with the protesters killed in front of the White House were nearly blacked out and swept under the rug, the President swore from that point on, not another word would he speak to the press. If the press secretary wanted to deal with them, fine. He was done with them.

A meeting was scheduled in the oval office, with Delacorte's closest advisors.

Mallory Barrett arrived early and began to speak to the President while they were alone.

Mr. President, I really think this press corps blowup is not going to work to your favor.

Then you want to be the press secretary too? Go ahead, I'm not talking to those sniveling little bastards again, end of story!

Well, what about the documents the Right to Work States left when you opted to go to China instead of meeting with them?

What? I don't give a damn about those assholes.

They're only lucky that numb nuts screwed up that New Orleans job or they'd be kissing my ass for help right about now.

What are you talking about, Mr. President? What New Orleans job?

Ah, don't worry about it, it was just some side deal I was working...don't worry about it.

Okay, sure. Mr. President, she replied. I'll just forget about it.

She thought to herself, *Like hell I will*.

The door opened and the rest of the advisors entered the Oval Office. Not another word was spoken about the incident. Secretary of the Treasury Ralston and Deputy Secretary Sam Edleson entered the Oval Office. A minute later, Commerce Secretary Bogdan.

All right, Delacorte began. You guys asked for the meeting, what is so damned important?

Mr. President, we are out of money, we don't dare create more, because as you found out, the rest of the world thinks this place is doomed and so does Congress, that's why they won't lift the debt ceiling and I don't blame them!

Ralston told him straight-faced and deadly serious.

Mr. President, you have got to stop these inane programs and rein in the spending, he said, his voice getting more emphatic. Tomorrow, we are out of cash, tomorrow we start handing out IOUs and script, tomorrow we tell the SSI retirees their checks are delayed, and **zero** money is wired to these people.

His voice was firm. What are **you** going to do about it, sir?

I've told you over and over what to do but you chose to ignore my advice and all the others who agree with me. The secretary now had a hint of desperation in his voice.

Mr. President, if you thought this past weekend wasn't the shape of things to come, just wait until no social security payments are sent.

Then the fireworks start. You'll be lucky to get outta town in an Abrams tank, **and I mean it!**

I am your Treasury Secretary, and I am telling you, we are bankrupt!

Delacorte shifted in his chair and pulled a cigar out of his suit jacket inside pocket. With a smooth motion he picked up the cigar cutter and clipped the tip of one end. He took a small box of wooden matches out of his pants pocket and struck the match and began to rotate and light the cigar.

Immediately Mallory Barrett spoke up,

Mr. President I believe there is no smoking in the White House.

He took a long slow, draw on the large cigar. He watched the smoke swirl and rise into the air and spread out around the room. He then let the smoke slowly pour out of the side of his mouth as he raised his chin in the air and exhaled the thick smoke off his palette.

Mallory repeated herself. Mr. President, there is no smoking in the White House!

The President looked longingly at the cigar.

Nothing beats a Cuban, now that's a smoke.

Once again Barrett interrupted him. Mr. President!

He erupted. **Shut the hell up, bitch, can't you see I'm enjoying myself?**

He then turned to Ralston. Okay, I'll authorize enough to pay half of the social security payments, keep the rest.

Ralston looked at him, stunned. *What do you mean, half? What half? Who the hell am I supposed to pay and not pay? This is insane!*

Delacorte looked at him, slowly took another slow draw on the cigar, and replied,

Listen, I don't give a damn what you do, that's it, that's all you get.

Ralston and all the others got up, stunned, and started to leave.

Then Delacorte continued, Oh, and by the way, you're all fired, leave your resignations on my desk tomorrow, no better yet …do it now.

Ralston stopped and looked at him with a half-smile, half-smirk. He opened his briefcase, took out a legal pad and pen and scribbled on the top page.

Mr. President,
You are a sick son of a bitch.
I quit your sick ass administration.
Effective, right f $#king now
Screw you
Signed
T. RALSTON

He threw it on his desk and left.

Mallory broke into tears, now understanding that the man she so admired either had turned into a ruthless dictator or was insane. Either way, she was out in the cold. She would have to do what she could do to take care of herself. Maybe this New Orleans thing might buy her some time or influence and leverage.

She closed the door behind her with tears streaming down both cheeks, walked down the hall, down the stairs, and out the side entrance.

Mallory asked her driver to drop her off down the block from her Georgetown townhouse. She knew she had to find out what this incident in New Orleans was. She had no information about it. There had to be someone she could contact. Maybe someone at the EPA?

No, chances were they would call Delacorte.

No, there was only one way. She needed to email someone in the RTW offices. The only person she knew she could contact was an old college roommate who had moved to the Dallas metro area right after college, Gail Clemens.

Mallory had bumped into Gail last year at the Athens Diner. Gail told her she was planning on taking a new job in Austin. She was hoping to start as a communications liaison with the governor's office. Mallory searched for her number and email address. She knew she kept it; she just had to find it.

That night Mallory found her number slipped into a pocket in her purse. She thought about what she needed to say to her old friend. How could she subtly ask about some incident in New Orleans but still not let on she was fishing for information ?

*Okay. Good to hear from you, hope you can get
down here, I'll see what I can find out for you!
Gail.*

The response was all she needed to see. The rest of the day and into the evening Mallory tried to figure out how she could slip into the RTW without leaving to much of a trail. Mallory thought long about her old contacts and only one name came to mind, Senator Silsbee. He had been a mentor to her when she was still in law school.

Even though he, too, had now cut contacts in D.C and sold his residence, she knew how to get his email address and cell phone number, her mom.

Hey, Mom, how are you and Dad doing? she asked from her cell phone.

Are you guys gonna be around this afternoon? I'd like to swing by.

Sure, honey, come on by. What's up? Is everything okay?

Yeah, I'm okay, what time is good? Mallory asked.

Any time, we're home now. Great, I'll be over this afternoon.

Sure, honey, I'll make some coffee.

Mallory got in her VW beetle, folded the top down and headed toward Gaithersburg, Maryland, where her folks lived.

After only a few miles she noticed a grey sedan, typical of a government-issued vehicle. After a few more miles, she decided to find out if she was imagining it or if she **was** being followed. There was a Texaco station ahead. She decided she would pull in and throw in ten dollars' worth, wait a few minutes, maybe gets some gas station coffee, and see if the sedan was still there.

After ten minutes, she pulled out and headed west on the interstate. Within a few miles she saw the sedan in her rearview mirror, hiding behind a large box truck. The truck would slow down going up a hill and the sedan would pop out into the fast lane and then slid back behind another car just behind her. This went on for miles, long enough to know Delacorte **was** having her trailed.

She felt madder and angrier than scared. She knew she hadn't said anything over her cell phone that would let on to what she was doing. But it just further confirmed in her mind than Delacorte was not to be trusted.

She decided as she pulled off the interstate for Gaithersburg to park a couple of blocks from her folks' house, just to see what her tail would do. She would park a couple blocks down and a couple blocks over so she could take the little path between streets to see how intent they were to follow or scare her or even stop her. One way or another, she would know.

As she took the exit ramp, she noticed the sedan fall back and disappear.

Well, maybe they are just keeping tabs and don't really care what I do, she thought.

She kept to her plan of two streets over and two blocks down. She pulled the convertible top up, locked it in place, locked her doors, and headed to the little path to her parents' house. As she turned to walk up to the last block, she could see through a row of pine trees the grey sedan parked just a few houses down.

Those bastards, she thought. *Well, they couldn't have seen me yet; I'll sneak back and come in through the back door.* She was still mad but not scared.

A few minutes later she opened the back door to the glassed-in back breezeway and walked in.

Mom, Dad! Mallory called out.

We're in the den, dear, and guess who's here, some friends from college!

Who, as she rounded the corner. She could see the two men sitting in the upholstered chairs. She immediately recognized them from Delacorte's security detail. She wasn't afraid; she figured they were told to follow her and that they were doing their job.

Well, hey guys, what brings you to these parts?

Yeah, hey, it's good to see you, Mallory. Bob and I were in town, and we thought we'd just stop by to see if you were still in D.C.

Yeah, the other one said. We figured your mom had your number. Well, that's sweet of you guys. Tell you what, give me a couple of minutes with my mom and I'll get caught up with you guys How about this, if you guys will wait in front, I'll be out in a second.

They looked at each other, shrugged and got up and waited outside by the front steps.

Mom, do you still have that card from our old friend, Senator Silsbee?

I'm sure I do, why do you need it? Well, he has a number I don't have, and I wanted to say hello to him. You know he's getting up there in age.

Don't I know it. Give me a minute and I'll find the card. She emerged a few minutes later with the card. Here, here it is, do you want it?

No, you keep it. I'll just write down the numbers I need, she said while copying his cell phone number, new office number, and personal email address. Thanks, mom, you're the best. Tell you what, let me get with my friends for a little bit and I'll swing by before I head back, she told her.

Okay, fine, honey. She gave her a peck on the cheek. I'll see you later.

Mallory stuffed the paper into her purse and walked out the front door.

The two security men were still waiting for her. She slipped her arm into their arms one at a time, linking the three of them together and walked down the walkway in front of the house and out to the sidewalk.

Okay, you two bastards, what the hell do you want? She was firm but not threatening.

Take it easy, Mallory, we were told to follow you, so we are following you! the one called Roberto replied.

Who told you to?

Come on, Mallory, who do you think?

Delacorte, she replied, disgusted.

Duh, they both responded. He gone crazy, the son of a bitch, she responded instantly.

You don't know the half of it, Roberto offered.

You should see some of the shit we've seen. He goes into the theater room and stay in there for twenty-four hours at a time, watching old film clips from the Cuban invasion.

He'll start screaming about something or other or start swearing at his wife, even though nobody's seen her in weeks.

Christ, I didn't think he was that far gone, she said, aghast.

So, what are you two assholes gonna report back to him? she had to ask.

We'll tell him you went for a long ride, got some gas and coffee, and headed back to Georgetown, he said. Isn't that accurate, Mallory?

Sounds good to me!

Well, alrighty then! We'll see you when we see you. The trio shook hands and the two security men headed to their car and left.

Mallory walked back to her folks' house and joined her mom for a quick cup of coffee. After a half an hour, she got up, kissed her on the cheek, told her she would see her soon and left.

On the way back, she called the senator and retold him about the New Orleans reference and what had transpired in the past few days.

Mallory, where are you, he asked. I'm on I-270, near I-495 just outside D.C., she replied.

Turn around, head back to Gaithersburg, head over to the general aviation center and I'll have someone pick you up when you get there.

Mallory was stunned. Are you sure, Senator?

Mallory, you stumbled into something we need you to talk to us about. Just make sure you can get back to the airport, he told her. *And I mean it!*

Within a couple of hours, she was being led to a hanger and a Cessna Citation. Ten minutes later she was watching the trees and hills of Maryland disappear beneath a layer of clouds.

She asked her escort and aid of the senator where they were going.

Moisant Field, he replied. The senator will meet you there. Where's Moisant Field, she asked?

Well, it's called Louis Armstrong International now, but we all know it from the original designation of MSY ,it's in New Orleans ,ma'am.

She relaxed for a moment and thought,

Wow, what the hell is this about? She would find out soon.

SAINT ELIZABETH'S HOSPITAL

ABBEY WOKE UP FROM SURGERY SOMETIME AFTER midnight. Her right side and part of her neck were bandaged, and her shoulder and arm were in a cast. The monitors beeped to a clock-like rhythm above her head and to her side. She had a clear plastic oxygen tube under her nose and IV needle inserted into the other arm.

Ohhhh, oh, my God, oh my God it hurts, she moaned, loud enough to wake James who had fallen asleep in a chair pulled up to the hospital bed with his hand just touching her free hand.

Abbey don't move, James cautioned her.

What..., what happened, she was barely able to ask.

You've got an IV in your arm and bandages on your neck and back.

She weakly asked, James, what happened to me?

I don't... what happened? Someone shot the congressman and hit you too.

You got the worst of it. She looked at him with a painful wince and tears started to pour down her cheeks. He reached for her hand again and held it gently.

Abbey, the doctors said you were lucky because the bullet hit your shoulder blade but then it broke apart and a big piece broke your collar bone, and a piece was lodged in the side of your neck.

Oh no! she whispered. He leaned over to her, stroking her hand.

The doctors think they removed all the fragments and say you should be up in a couple of days, but for now you need to lay still and rest.

In a couple of days, they're gonna double check to make sure they got all the fragments, then after that, maybe you can go home. She looked at him as though a haze was lifting.

Owww! She winced again. For a minute she tried to focus on the room and James.

For a minute she seemed as though she was aware, and her mind started to clear.

James, she whispered to him.

He slid closer to her.

I heard what you kept saying in my ear.

Oh, you did, he whispered back.

Yes, yes, I did.

She glanced at him for a second. And a little smile started to emerge, then she closed her eyes and the look of pain swept across her face.

Ooow, it hurts, she whispered and grimaced.

Abbey, just lay still, he consoled her. He held her hand, stroking it softly for several minutes.

She closed her eyes. In a minute, the pain medicine helped her slip off to sleep.

THE GARDEN ROOM

Miss, follow me, the maître d' led the pair up to the Garden Room.

Senator Silsbee turned to Mallory. Ms. Barrett, you mean you've **never** been to the Garden Room at Commander's Palace?

No, Senator, I've haven't, she replied. I've never been to Commander's at all.

Oh, Missy, you are in for a treat!

They were led through the kitchen with all the hustle and bustle of a crowd at Grand Central Station, to a small out-of-the-way staircase. The top of the stairs emerged to a spacious glass-lined room surrounded by a huge live oak. The branches two foot thick seemed to wrap around the dining room and barely let the light of the patio down below shine in.

My God, Senator, this is lovely. Mallory let a wide smile sweep across her face.

Ahh, this is nawthin', wait till you try the oysters and the redfish.

The Senator reviewed the wine list and asked his guest,

My dear, do you prefer Pouilly Fusse' or a Vouvray?

Senator, you choose, I'm still taking in this beautiful room. The waiter stepped right in, and the Senator chose for them.

And the Oysters Bienville to start, the Senators added.

I hope you like my favorite starters. I highly recommend any gulf seafood, you just can't go wrong here, he said with the authority of the most demanding food critic.

After the wine was brought to the table, the sommelier gently removed the cork and offered it to the Senator to inspect. He rolled the cork with his forefinger and thumb while checking for its integrity.

After a nod of approval the wine was poured, first to the Senator to taste. With the approving nod, the selection was poured to the guest.

Mallory, you know you have our attention and cooperation, the Senator offered as politely as possible.

I know, Senator Silsbee, that is why I knew I could call you, then she added, and trust you.

Please, you can call me Tom if you wish. Miss Mallory, please tell me why you reached out to us and what has you so concerned?

She looked around from the corner table where they were sitting as though she needed to throttle the volume of her voice.

Oh, don't worry, we can talk here, you are amongst friends here, the Senator whispered, leaning over to her.

Senator, quite frankly, I am concerned, and afraid President Delacorte is no longer able to hold that office. I have seen him act very irrationally, and reports from security people say they think he has gone over the edge. I never believed in what he was doing to force the issue with you and the Right to Work States, she sadly admitted.

But we all believed he knew what he was doing. I have to believe there is something very wrong with him, she continued.

Then he let slip some issue about a job here in New Orleans that went wrong. I don't know what it was, but after I saw how he reacted to Secretary Ralston, she paused for a second, and me, I knew he was extremely sick.

The Senator had a look that someone would have if they just found the missing piece to a difficult picture puzzle.

Mallory, we know what the job was.

He paused for a moment and sipped from his wine glass.

The job was intended to be most harmful to this city and to disrupt the RTW states in general. It is our assessment he meant to make New Orleans barely inhabitable, poisoning the waterways and the city with an extremely powerful truck bomb. It was to be radioactive bomb filled with waste waters from nuclear power plants. Had he succeeded, we most likely would not be able to be here having dinner.

We suspect the people he hired were in too much of a hurry or didn't get it right or something. In any case, we were able to contain it and recovered nearly every gallon that leaked, which luckily wasn't much, he told her.

We have some undercover people who gave us a heads up and we have most of the proof in place, but we didn't have you to confirm what we suspected.

He looked at her and pulled a blown-up photo of an image from Clive's video tape. And on top of that I have an image of someone who shot congressman Gordon, and an aide of ours who works in Austin.

We don't have any idea how to connect this to Delacorte, but we assume he or his henchmen are in there somewhere, sure as God made little green apples.

She paused for a second nearly floored. *Jeezus Christ, how crazy is he?*

What happened …are they okay?

Well, I'll tell you what, if'n the congressman didn't have the vest on his security crew told him to wear, he'd be a dead man. The poor aide got shot in the back.

The poor girl got through the surgery but she's gonna be out for quite a while, I'm afraid to say.

Mallory was stunned. Oh my God, *now what,* Senator?

Now what? Well, that is a good question.

First, we have got to figure out how we are going to handle this mess. I'm hoping we can find some solution. Of course, the answers will open another can of worms.

What do you mean, she asked him.

Delacorte had what, over six years to let this thing fall apart, it's only, as you know, gotten infinitely worse. The problems that were ignored for years before are not going away, the debt, the devaluation of the dollar, all these expensive programs with no regard for who the hell is paying for it.

He didn't start it but he sure as hell made it a hell of a lot worse. You know, once you start to give away money to the majority of the people, it is impossible to stop.

He couldn't help but show how the extremely difficult issue had influenced him.

Mallory, it may be better just to let it play out and let the people learn firsthand this kind of free-for-all cannot exist. It may be better to let the fire burn itself out and restart Washington after the ashes of this administration are washed away. The years of a free lunch and the politicians that handed them out for everything they could think of are in for a mass awakening that lunch nowadays is paid for in full.

We had to separate ourselves from the disregard for sound policy. We are making sensible policies and great progress.

We don't want to fight those old fights, he told her, as if he was dreading even thinking about the recent past.

Honestly, I think your only play is to confront Delacorte with the evidence and either he steps down or the Congress or people from the administration have him removed for mental inabilities and being unfit to do the job.

Listen, I am so glad you stepped forward to offer what you saw and experienced. It may be the straw that breaks his back. It may be that history will remember you very fondly for your part in whatever the outcome becomes. The Senator was extremely serious, and Mallory could sense it.

She paused, Senator, I am no longer in the employment of the President, neither is Secretary Ralston or his staff.

At the last meeting on Friday, Secretary Paulson told him the checks would start bouncing or not be issued at all, tomorrow, she admitted. That's when the President just seemed to clearly detach and fired all of us, like he just didn't care what happened anymore.

I don't know what he is capable of doing or what kind of deals he's got going on in that sick head of his. He's got to be desperate, she admitted.

She paused and took a long sip of her wine. Long enough that the waiter filled her glass and signaled the Senator to ask if he desired another bottle, to which he nodded with approval.

I think the only person he would ever listen to was Isabelle, she replied.

The problem is they had a huge fight when a few of the Governors from RTW states were last at Camp David, and no one has seen her in months.

Hmmm, what if I told you, we know where she is, he shyly told her.

Of course, that would be a start, Mallory answered, but where has she been?

Honduras, he whispered.

Well, that does make sense, she is from down there.

What has she been doing, she asked him.

That is a disconcerting issue. We have been watching her and she has been associating with some very unsavory characters. We don't know exactly who they are, but we know they are not boy scouts. But we know how to contact her. We can run it up the flagpole and see what she says, he offered to her.

I could speak to her; we were on fairly good terms. I know she loves antiques and I think she is somewhat familiar with New Orleans.

Maybe I can tell her we could spend the days around Decatur and Royal Street. We could take the streetcar out to St. Charles and walk over to Magazine Street.

Maybe go to the casino for a couple of hours, the Senator suggested.

Well, I can ask, anyways, I'll need to tell her in advance what we want to do.

I don't want her to think we aren't being up front with her.

Okay, sounds like a plan, Senator Silsbee replied.

Just then the waiters presented the Redfish Grieg.

This looks wonderful, Senator.

I hope you like it, my dear, it's my favorite, he said, smiling.

* * * * *

That night the Senator had made arrangement for her to stay in the French Quarter.

Here we are, Mallory, we like this little hotel very much. It's nice and quiet and you can walk down to Bourbon Street if you like and see some sights.

Oh, it's very pretty, she remarked. "Maison Dupuy", I think I will like this very much, Senator.

We hope so, I'll pick you up at nine a.m. sharp and don't worry, we 've already taken care of everything.

Okay, Senator, thank you so much!

Well, Mallory, we've got a lot of work ahead of us and tomorrow may be a very long day.

THE RELUCTANT RETURN OF THE FIRST LADY

You want me to come back to the U.S., is that right? To New Orleans?

She was listening intently pressing her cell phone to her ear against the sound of the waves of the Gulf of Mexico from her villa.

I don't know, Senator, I like it here in La Ceiba. Well, Isabelle, it might be exceptionally good for all of us if you would be willing to help us, the Senator told her.

I...I don't know, I ...am done with him, I...I just don't know if I am willing to do this.

Look, Isabelle, you may be helping the whole country and we could make it worth it to you, he added.

No, no, I don't want your money!

She paused for a second and quietly asked, tell me how I could be helping other people?

Mallory spoke up. I think you can help more people than you can imagine. I think there are millions of people who are suffering and will suffer much more if we don't try to help the President, Mallory told her as sincerely as she could.

Isabelle, we believe the job may be too much for him and his ability to cope with it ...well it may have made him sick.

Oh, he is very sick!

She paused and thought for a second. He's too emotional, too much of a hot head. When he thinks he is right, no one can convince him is not!

That is his problem. I know he was elected again but I don't think anyone ever knew who he really was and that he does not care about anyone but himself.

I cannot stand the very sight of him! I despise what he has become!

Please, I don't know what I would do if I saw him again. I think he is an evil man, that's what he has become is an evil crazy man!

I should tell you to hell with Henrico, he is your problem.

I am not going to be part of what he has done and what he has caused, no!

She paused, after what seemed like a minute, she sighed and the expression of her emotions and frustrations became apparent.

She said, softly, I am back here with people who I care about very much.

People who I feel I am very much like. I believe what they believe.

I do not want a life with Henrico. I want him out of my new life!

I am happy for the first time in a very long time.

No, I should tell you no.

She sighed like a someone beginning to walk up their last steps to the gallows.

But... I can't, she finally admitted to herself.

There were so many people who were so very nice to me.

There were so many people who seemed to care about me being happy in the White House.

She started to soften her voice.

And you Mallory, I know you went out of your way to make me feel welcomed.

I cannot turn my back to you.

Isabelle paused again.

It was as if she had resolved the issue in her mind.

She softly responded; I think I know what I can do.

Yes, I think I know how to help.

Yes, I will help you.

You were the people who I thought genuinely wanted the best for the me and your country, too.

Our country? Mallory asked her.

Yes, I do not think I would be happy in Washington anymore. I am sorry but this is what I feel.

I don't care what happens to Henrico, but I think I can help you, she said to Mallory and the Senator.

Isabelle, thank you, we do not know what else to say but thank you, the Senator replied.

I can have a car meet you, say nine a.m., in La Ceiba and our jet pick you up in San Pedro Sula to New Orleans. We could arrange this for say tomorrow morning, continued the Senator.

Yes Senator, I can do this, she replied.

I will be ready to do this, her voice expressed a sense of commitment and clarity.

The arrangements had gone off without a hitch.

Mallory met Isabelle Friday morning at New Orleans Airport.

They did spend the afternoon together and enjoyed each other company, walking and talking and enjoying the sights of the city.

They boarded the St. Charles streetcar and got off in front of the Columns Hotel.

The white wooden veranda was wide and inviting. The large Doric style white columns that gave the hotel its name transports one to a time when white linen suits and debutantes in flowing gowns were the norm. One can view the panorama of the canopy of tall live oaks and ancient magnolias lining the Boulevard and the scent of their blooms is intoxicating. The carefree and laid-back atmosphere that the city induces is magnified at the Columns.

At four o'clock they met the Senator on the veranda. Isabelle was genuinely happy and at ease with Mallory and the Senator.

After a few minutes, Isabelle made a request and hoped she wasn't expecting too much.

She asked a little shyly, I have heard that Saturday night at the Plimsol Club is fantastic, can you do this for me.

Isabella, why we already made the reservations, the Senator laughed!

A Plimsol is a safe level marking on the side of a cargo ship that denotes how high or low a ship rides in the water and that is where the club derives its name.

The Plimsol Club is at the end of Canal Street and in the Westin Hotel that overlooks the Mississippi River and the city.

The view of illuminated ships that ply the river and the whole cityscape at night is spectacular. And the Saturday night buffet matches the view.

Is it all you were expecting, my dear? the Senator ask politely.

Oh, Senator, Thank you so very much, it is more than I hoped it would be, as she was finishing her crème de brule`e.

Thank you again Senator but now where are we staying? I am very tired.

We have you right next to me, it's a lovely hotel right off Toulouse St., you will love it, Mallory told her excitedly.

Okay, fine, but no Bourbon Street, I'm too old for all that noise, Isabelle confided in Mallory.

Hey, sleep is our friend, I'm bushed too, was all Mallory had to say.

A RENDEZVOUS

As Ralston said, who exactly am I supposed to pay and who doesn't get paid?

As it turned out, he didn't pay anybody. No monies were transferred to the Social Security Department. No wires were made, no checks were mailed. Others who hadn't been affected by the first rounds of script or IOUs were shocked to find them in payment envelopes now. Within hours the crowds started to ring the Capitol Building and then the White House.

By the end of the week, over five-hundred thousand people had descended onto the city. Most had camped out on the National Mall, or other national sites. No amount of police or troopers were able to move them. A handful of protesters had been arrested by the police and guards, but they didn't attempt any more for fear of lighting the fuse to the immense power keg. By the weekend, the numbers had doubled. The National Mall had protesters completely filling all areas around the museums and the Ellipse. The crowds now wrapped around the White House.

The staff in the White House had hunkered down and were staying to protect the residence. They would be the last line of defense from an angry mob intent on destruction because of frustration. The President had left days ago through the maze of tunnels under the White House and exited through Blair House. The few staff who still served at the pleasure of the President insisted that he relocate to Camp David. One of the staffers still at the White House was the aid to the Vice President. His name was Jeremy Rand. He accompanied him to Andrews and escorted him on the helicopter.

Mr. President, I'm glad to accompany you and we will get to Camp David shortly. The Vice President will join us and then we can schedule meetings with the economic advisors and work our way out of the situation.

Jeremy's words were the kind of encouragement that Delacorte appreciated. It was easy to see why Jeremy was a lifelong friend to Vice President Roffle.

He was a staffer when the Vice President was a congressman from New York. The staffer was a tall young man with a wide smile always at the ready, and his mannerism made all who met him feel at ease. He was extraordinarily loyal to the Vice President and his family.

The grounds of Camp David were not the President's most favorite retreat. The memories of the disasters with the RTW states governors and with Isabelle had made him on edge and irritable. He entered the Aspen Lodge and announced that he would like to get some sleep and meet with everyone in the morning. He hoped to meet again at nine a.m.

The night was not kind to the President. Sleep eluded him. He would sleep for no more than an hour and be up for two. The events that had happened here made it impossible to relax. He swore he would have been better off if he had stayed in the White House. Despite his anger toward Isabelle, he missed her. She kept him on track and never let him retreat in a state where he was either too angry or too depressed.

The morning meetings with advisors and staff went poorly.

Mr. President, the best recourse is to suspend payments to any foreign country for aid. We need to cut the amount of federal aid and social programs in half, immediately. And we need to increase all taxes across the board by 15 percent, the deputy advisor to the Secretary of the Treasury said.

We can then pay benefits of Social Security to most recipients, but only if we cut the payments by 20 percent and means test anyone making any more than $60,000 a year. These people will scream but they are better off than most, it will be tough for them but that's the best we can do at the moment. And that would be immediately. If we institute these changes now, we may be able to announce by tomorrow that payments have been restored and that you, Mr. President, have resolved the crisis.

Delacorte looked up from his seat at the head of the conference table and yawned. He then announced,

Yeah, okay, I don't care, just go with it. I'll make a little speech and tell the people we got a plan, and they'll get their damn checks and then I can get the hell outta here and go back to DC.

Well. Mr. President, that's not exactly what we had in mind but if that's what you want....

Yeah, that's exactly what I want, so set it up with the damn networks! he barked.

Yes sir, we will do that, he replied.

Okay, do it! he said to the staff. Now I'm gonna take a break, he growled at the gathered staff.

We'll work on this after lunch. He got up and walked off to his room.

He lay down and slept for about an hour when the phone in the Aspen Lodge rang.

Jeremy answered it. *Isabelle!* how are you!

Fine, I'm okay, Jeremy, is Henrico available?

I'll get him for you! He nudged the door open and slowly walked into the room, turning on the end table lamp.

Mr. President. Jeremy tugged on his shoulder.

Whaaat, what is it, Jeremy?

It's Isabelle, she's on the phone!

Oh! okay! well bring it here.

Isabelle!

Is it you!

Yes, Henrico, how long will you be at Camp David? she said softly.

I think most all week, why?

Well, I think I've been away enough. I would like to come and see you up there.

Yes! Yes! I would like that very much. When do you want to come?

I think this weekend, would that be, okay?

As she asked, she could hear him melt into the phone.

Yes, that would be wonderful. He almost jumped out of his skin. *I can't wait to see you,* he told her.

Listen, Henrico, I will come to Maryland, but on one condition.

She told him to consider what she was going to ask.

I will come up to Maryland, but I ask you to meet with Mister Cabbott and the Mister Payne. You know they want just to have an understanding with you and asked me if you will see them, maybe just for a day.

He thought about it for a second. *You will come if I agree?*

But I want you to come the day before they do," he said to her.

I know you would ask this , Henrico; I knew you would, she replied.

But if I do this, I will be there for dinner on Friday night and I will ask them to arrive on Saturday.

I will stay until Sunday if you try to work with them and control your temper.

I promise, I will, he pledged.

All right, I will come Friday night.

She hung up.

After lunch was a different story. He was excited and rejuvenated. He signed the orders to make all the changes that were suggested. He may have had some second thoughts, but at the time his thoughts were only about having Isabelle to himself.

That night on the major media networks, he announced the changes to Social Security and that most would get money wired to their accounts or checks, He told them that those he considered to be "well off" would be means tested, but they should be happy to help those not as lucky. He then said that these changes would take effect immediately.

The reaction was **not** what Delacorte's administration and advisors had expected.

The next day instead of the crowds dispersing, they intensified. The crowds were insulted that some were "*considered worthy*" and some were not. The mobs centered around the Capitol Building and the White House.

From the safety of Camp David, the President, Vice President, and the assembled aides watched as the crowds grew. By Thursday, the aides decided they needed to gather any family in the capitol and remove them from any danger. This left the President and the Vice President and a staff that manned Camp David.

The President called out the National Guard, Capital Police and Park Police to protect the Capitol Building, White House and all monuments and members of Congress who had not already fled D.C.

For several days, the protests continued. Only those who had altercations with the police were arrested. This was to keep the lit match from the already smoldering power kegs all around the city.

Other protesters and mobs gathered in New York and Chicago and had rallies calling for Delacorte's immediate resignation. Effigies of Delacorte were hanging and set on fire all around the capitol. For all intents and purposes, the Capitol was shut down.

It was a temporary standoff between the immense mobs and the authorities. Riots were only a thrown bottle away from erupting and encompassing the city.

Delacorte didn't seem to care; he was only waiting for Friday evening and Isabelle.

THE CLOISTERS

OVER THE BLUFFS OF THE HUDSON RIVER, JUST north of Manhattan in New Jersey, were the Cloisters. Lining the ridge were mansions that dated from the 1800s and 1900s. One of these prominent locations had been chosen as a quiet meeting place for several members of the Delacorte cabinet. Not everyone was aware of the sudden forced resignation of Secretary Ralston, who had in fact called the meeting.

Gentlemen, I am compelled to announce that I have resigned from the administration of President Delacorte on Sunday, he stated, as though he was reading the death sentence to a prisoner. My associates, my friends, I am in extreme fear for the continued existence of the U.S. in any form. I am not even addressing the separation attempt by the Southern and Midwest states over the President's foolish attempt to extort funds and payments for his exorbitant and quixotic programs.

Gentlemen, the President is unfit for the office. It is my belief that he is in the middle of some psychotic break from reality, the Secretary continued.

Jesus, Tom! what is it you are telling us? John LaPointe, the Secretary of Agriculture asked in near horror.

I'm telling you that when I told him that the country was bankrupt, he blew it off.

I told him he had to stop pissing away money because we couldn't make S.S.I payments. He said pay half of them and piss on the others.

I asked who am I supposed to pay and not pay, and he said he didn't care. Then imagine this, the bastard lights up a big stogie and ignores Barrett when she tells him there's no smoking, which was a big mistake in any case. So, he starts screaming at her and fires everyone in the room and there were five of us, *boom, gone*, he told them as the room grew deadly silent.

So, gentlemen, I called this meeting because I am convinced, we must take steps to remove him...and I really don't care how.

So, Tom, why are we here? asked Hugh McDonald. the Secretary of Commerce.

Well, I will tell you, gentlemen, I am six-foot-five-inches and 310 pounds.

He looked at all in the room intently. I am planning, with or without your help, to enter the Oval Office and explain to him that he must resign, and I mean before the end of the day.

If he gives me any shit, I am gonna tell him it is a long fall out of the window behind him. If he starts to threaten me, I'll deck the little bastard; I doubt any of the White House personnel will want to stop me.

It might look a little more professional if you all were there as well, Ralston explained. Not that I think he will give a fiddler's shit.

Gentlemen, I felt compelled to update and include you in my decision, but if you choose not to, I understand, but that does not change the fact this country may have no more than a week, maybe only hours before the lids blows off. We certainly don't have past the first of next month. That's when the next S.S.I payments go out.

After that, all bets are off. I'd take bets the White House gets severely damaged, maybe totally destroyed.

He was as straightforward and to the point as possible. Yep, nothing like a horde of young angry activists with nothing to do but loot the White House and any place else they can get some loot from. Yes sirree, nothing like it!

His look was just matter of fact, with little sense of humor.

Jesus Christ, Tom! LaPointe bemoaned. You **are** going to do this, aren't you?

John, this asshole put a turd in the punch bowl. Somebody's got to dig it out, it might as well be me. Ralston just looked at him and shrugged. If you want to hand me a pair of gloves before I dig it out, that would be helpful.

Just one thing, Tom, I want to help throw the bastard out the front window. LaPointe smiled and shook his hand.

Ralston opened a bottle of twelve-year-old scotch and poured a round to everyone. They didn't leave until it was finished.

FRIDAY NIGHT

THE GOVERNMENT LIMOUSINE PULLED UP TO Aspen Lodge and the driver quickly opened the door for the First Lady. He popped the switch for the trunk and reached into it to help her with the three bags she had brought with her. She insisted on carrying one of the bags herself when the driver reached for it.

Even though Henrico was ready to jump out of his skin in excitement, he tried to be coy and matter of fact with her.

Isabelle, dear, how was your trip? he asked her, as he reached for her and kissed her on the cheek.

She looked at him and smiled, knowing he really wanted her there.

Oh Henrico, no need to be smooth, I know you're glad I'm here.

Yes, yes, my dear, you know me too well, he admitted to her.

Please, let me have your bags, he said to her,

She signaled the driver to let the President tend to her things. She kept for herself her small travel bag. After a few minutes of small talk, he poured her a glass of wine and they headed to the patio. Henrico felt like there was no lost time and that she had not been gone for all these weeks. He was extremely glad she had come back.

Henrico, I'm starved, can we have dinner soon? she announced.

Dinner is all ready for you, and I had the chief prepare your favorite, *osso bucco*.

Oh, you are so sweet, she looked at him and gave him a half smile.

Her look was that of a woman who had been by his side for years.

Their dinner conversation was light and there was no sign of lingering animosity from their vicious fight. They drank wine, shared the occasional laugh, and finished the night out on the patio of Laurel Lodge under the star-filled night. The walk back to Aspen Lodge was just a few minutes away. They took in the brisk air and the clarity of the night.

Henrico opened the cottage door for her, and she smiled as she entered the lodge. He took her by the hand after a few quiet minutes and led her to the bedroom.

Henrico, I have a surprise for you. Let me freshen up and I have something special I brought for you tonight, let me slip into.

He lit up in excitement and replied,

Of course, that would be wonderful, my dearest.

She reached for the small suitcase she brought with her and headed to the bathroom and shut the door.

In a few minutes she emerged in a silky black nighty with a small handbag. She gently pulled back the quilted cover on the bed and sat on the now exposed sheets.

Henrico, you look so very tired and tense, I have a surprise that will make you feel better. She reached for his hand and rubbed it.

Why don't you let me rub your back, and after that I know how to make you very happy.

Isabelle, I'm just so very happy that you are here, he said, rolling over on his stomach.

I know you are, my love, she replied.

She reached over to her bag like she was reaching for a lotion.

Henrico, let me start here.

She pulled out of her bag a silvery, ten-inch-long ice pick. In one motion she thrust it into him right between the spine and the skull. She jammed it in all the way to the handle, swirled it around a few turns, pulled it out, and threw it back in her bag.

She rolled him over and looked into his eyes as the life in him faded. From her bag she took a switch blade knife, pushed the silver button on the handle and the blade swung out. In one motion sliced open his throat.

The only noise heard was the soft gurgling from him as he was dying in front of her.

She looked at him and smiled.

You are not the only one who has anger, she whispered into his ear now filling with his own blood.

In an act of sheer vengeance, she slapped him across the face and slammed his head back into the pillow.

She packed up the weapons, covered him up with the covers, took her time washing off the blood and changed her clothes.

After a few minutes she slipped on a dark outfit like a woman in the naval support base there on the grounds would wear on duty and walked out the front door. She stopped at the elevator that would take her down to the bunker entrance at ground level. She pulled out the key to power the elevator.

She turned the key and pushed the button for the ground level exit. For a few seconds she looked around and slowly walked down the path past the three golf tees and on toward the fence surrounding the compound. She continued through the thicket for another one hundred feet. Pulling out a pair of wire cutters, she snipped several wires and slipped under it.

She hurried her pace and emerged onto Manahan Road and walked the planned few hundred feet where a waiting Jeep met her. The driver was not anyone from the RTW states or from the White House staff or security. They would take the back roads out of Maryland for just 20 minutes to a small private airfield just outside Carroll Valley, Pennsylvania. From there a small twin-engine plane met the pair. Within minutes the aircraft was heading north toward Lake Erie and a small airfield just on the other side of the lake.

From there she would disappear.

CALIFORNIA NO MORE

THE MEETING AT THE AUBERGE DU SOLEIL DID not go well.

It was not because of the environment. Napa Valley's beauty and serenity could temporarily remove concerns and stress from most people's daily lives.

The inviting view from the restaurant's patios and open decks encompassed the wide valley and the vineyards below. It should have been a place to iron out differences. It was not.

We are not going to be railroaded into a decision and then have it forced down our throats. We have a totally different approach to our future, and it is not what your people in San Francisco want, Congressman Issacs told the assembled group of invited mayors, congressmen and their aides and staff.

There are several other congress members in Southern districts that will not under any circumstances go along with Sacramento's plan to go it alone with this "nation- state" talk.

You are aware of the fact the northernmost counties in California have been talking once again about the proposal of Greater Idaho and leaving the state.

Most of the military bases and the officials at the ports of Long Beach and Los Angeles do not want to go along with the plan.

Most of the remaining counties are pushing for a vote.

The consensus seems to be to go with the RTW States. The decision to approach the RTW was the option that made sense.

Mayor Vargas, you are in Los Angeles, why do you not want to approach President Morales in Mexico? All Hispanics would feel more at home with our heritage in Latin America. This would make this an extremely easy transition, said Maria Muniz an aide with Congresswoman Mulligan. I know many of the congressional districts in the Bay area have voiced the same opinion, added Congresswoman Mulligan.

I have had a long and serious conversation with all the details involved in the proposal with Congressman Issacs about Mexico, he responded.

The military base commanders in El Toro, San Diego and at Vandenberg, said they won't go for it. They said they refused. It was RTW or no deal.

I have spoken with the elected officials in a dozen counties, and they oppose Sacramento's plan.

To tell you the truth, this is a no brainer, he quipped. We couldn't possibly believe we won't turn into another drug addled war zone if we let the Mexican cartel drug lords get an even bigger presences in California.

At least the guys in Austin won't be storing cocaine in L.A. City Hall and in the State Capital Building, Mayor Vargas answered.

And we can throw out those stupid ass laws the morons in Sacramento crammed down our throats all these years and get some fricking water to the farmers again, he added with a sense of relief.

And I'll personally deliver to Sacramento a bucket full of their precious snail dater fresh out of the fryolator, and they can have a goddamn fish fry with the rest of them for all I care!

He paused for a moment and shook his head.

I don't know what Governor Lopez in New Mexico is gonna do.

Why is that Mayor? the Miss Muniz asked.

Because his butt is gonna be surrounded by RTW, he needs to do something or it's gonna be the Island of New Mexico.

As it stands now, we need to finalize with the counties that are going to stay with Southern California. We don't know how far up the San Joaquin Valley before the split, but it's likely all of it will want to go RTW. And we really need to get a handle on how far north up I-5 this is gonna go. For all we know this thing could be drawn at the I-10. I'm thinking everything around I-15 would go RTW for quite a while. The rest of the northern counties sounds like they decided it's Greater Idaho, he replied.

I really don't care at this point what you people in the Bay Area do but it sure is sounding like you made you bed now you're gonna sleep in it, Congressman Issacs said to Mrs. Mulligan.

She glared at him with the look of contempt and beginning to understand how deep the impact of their Sacramento plan will be. It will not be a new Nation-State, it will in fact, dissolve away.

The parts of Oregon and Washington west of the Cascades are talking about going with Canada. Eastern Washington and Oregon have pledged to merge into Greater Idaho. And as I said some of the northern most California counties are going with them, Issacs reminded Mulligan.

I don't know what they will finally decide but they are going to do something, it'll be sooner rather than later, Congressman Issacs said.

The Mayors, the Congressmen and others involved in the decision who would decide to form the Southern State of California, prepared the documents of enjoinment with the RTW states. They believed within hours they would feel the ire of President Delacorte.

It was not to come.

SATURDAY

In the morning, as expected President Cabbott and Vice President Payne prepared to fly to Maryland and then make the drive the last few miles to Camp David. As the sun began to shine through the hills and illuminate the grounds of Camp David, the staff began to prepare the morning's breakfast and prepare the other lodges for the soon to arrive guests from the RTW states.

The ground keepers kept the area finely trimmed and impeccable, and the blooms of the flower beds made for a pulchritudinous, serene backdrop for the planned meetings. The aroma of freshly brewed coffee mixed with the scent of freshly mown lawns. The scent of mountain laurel and the pines floated in the air. Mist from the hilltops started to lift.

At eight a.m., Jeremy Rand entered Aspen Lodge and heard the soft *beep, beep, beep* of an alarm clock. From outside the door he asked, Mr. President, Mrs. First Lady, is everything all right?

Not a sound.

He asked again, Mr. President, Mrs. First Lady? and again, no sound was heard.

Mr. President?

Jeremy reached for the doorknob and the door swung open.

He said again Mr. President, Mrs. First Lady?

Jeremy slowly approached the bed and saw there was someone under the pulled-up covers.

Mr. President? He nudged the shape under the covers. He saw something dripping from the edge of the quilt and onto the floor with a dark pool just under the bed.

Mr. President! Are you alright?

He pushed on the shape under the blanket with no response.

His foot slid on the partially hidden pooled blood. He began to understand what happened.

Jeremy lifted the edge of the quilt and saw the blood-soaked covers and Delacorte as Isabelle had left him.

He gagged and ran out the door, screaming,

Oh my God! Oh my God!

He ran down the hill to the security barracks and screamed,

He's dead! She's gone! Someone please, help! Oh my God! He's dead!

As he ran screaming, the other buildings' personnel ran out into the main pathway and began to grasp the gravity of the situation.

In the confusion, one of the female employees asked, where is the First Lady!?

It quickly morphed into, *Oh, no, she's gone, someone has kidnapped her*, then into,

Oh, no someone has kidnapped the First Lady!

Within seconds, it became a series of employees screaming,

The First Lady been kidnapped!

Guards from all post started to run by instinct to the sounds of the screams.

Within minutes, guards from Laurel, Hickory, Oak, Magnolia and other lodges converged on Aspen and surrounded it by security details as the grounds were being searched for any signs of the First Lady or any evidence and clues to the tragedy.

President Cabbott and Vice President Payne and their aides were just minutes away. In the confusion, the front gate was monitored by just one guard who was told over his radio to search the immediate area for the First Lady or any evidence of any trace of her.

The guard saw a strip of cloth and bushes pushed aside and branches broken, the cut wires and a set of tire tracks alongside the road in the soft ground.

The guard believed this was evidence that someone had kidnapped the First Lady and only concentrated on what was before him.

The commanding officer of security, Captain Dwyer, a twenty-year veteran of the Navy, ordered a communication blackout and a lockdown of the grounds.

However, the RTW motorcade drove up to the front gate, and seeing the gate open, drove through and pulled up toward the assembled hysteria in front of Laurel Lodge.

Two uniformed guards approached the motorcade who told them to stay in their vehicles.

What do you mean, stay in the vehicle? the driver asked.

Yes, what do you mean? President Cabbott asked as he rolled down the rear window and addressed the guard.

I'm sorry sir, but there's been an incident, the guard responded.

As they were still responding to the guards' questions, Captain Dwyer stepped up to the lead SUV.

I'm sorry, President Cabbott, but there has been a terrible incident and we are still investigating what has happened.

Captain, I appreciate your concern, but certainly you can share your initial assessment of the situation, Cabbott asked with all due respect shown to the officer.

President Cabbott, I sorry to report that President Delacorte is dead, and the First Lady is missing.

What!? How is that possible, what happened!?

Cabbott replied in total shock. He opened the door and stepped out of the SUV.

As he engaged the captain, Vice President Payne also exited the vehicle just behind them and joined the President.

Cabbott turns to the Vice President, *Hank, Delacorte is dead, and the First Lady is missing.*

Oh, my sweet Jesus!!, no! what could have happened!? Payne turned away in disbelief. *What about Isabelle?*

Sir, that's all I can tell you at this moment, the officer responded as professionally as he could muster.

Sir, I believe your visit here is now a moot point. We have an investigation to undertake, and I believe your presence here will only hinder things, he explained.

Would you consider leaving me a number where the staff can update you as things unfold?

I believe you should be aware of the situation as it develops.

Captain Dwyer held Cabbott in high esteem and was more than willing to keep him informed as the incident became clearer and questions were answered.

Thank you, Captain Dwyer. Cabbott handed him the contact information.

The group from the RTW huddled around each other for a few moments in shock. At the request of the captain, they reentered their SUVs and one by one left the compound.

One more thing, President Cabbott, the captain requested, let us release the news to the public.

Please keep this amongst yourselves until the Vice President addresses the country, tonight, would be my request.

You have my promise, Captain, Cabbott responded with all due respect.

Before the morning was over, the Vice President had been sworn in by the Chief Justice of the Supreme Court who was flown in on a Marine helicopter.

A critical assessment to the agenda of Delacorte and the situation of the past years would now begin, but to most people it was too little and way too late. The dismantling had begun, the crushing debt too much to overcome. The animosity and apathy were overwhelming.

An historic dilemma was before the Vice President, even before he was sworn in and decisions he made would have ramifications more far reaching than the Civil War.

The investigation had only begun. The next twenty-four hours were the summation of every crisis the country had dealt with in the last three centuries, all rolled into one.

SATURDAY AFTERNOON

VICE PRESIDENT GEORGE ROFFLE WAS A NEW Yorker. He understood the mentality of New Yorkers. They were not to be anything but the center of American finance, business, and culture. It was inconceivable that the northeast would not be American. He heard about the unrest in some of the New England states and understood their frustrations, but he would not bend to their desire to leave the Union of the States.

He interceded in the discussions with Canada. Any talk of dissolution from the States would be short circuited if he had any say in the matter. His threats to the now recalcitrant governors of the northern states had the desired effect and they relented and backed down from their secession plans.

But this calamity was thrust upon him now with the death of Delacorte. He was prepared to end any crisis and begin a working relationship with the Right to Work States for the moment.

Roffle was a smallish man in stature but not in purpose. His balding head, bushy moustache and a rough, weathered complexion were all business. His resume as a crime-fighting district attorney for the state gave him an aura of a larger-than-life authoritarian. When Roffle considered an issue, he guided it to its conclusion. Words meant things and he always meant what he said. His natural position was law and order followed with a dose of common sense. His followers were many and his many enemies feared but respected him. Many began to wonder why he wasn't president instead of Delacorte.

He was now going to use these skills and attempt to undo the chaos that Delacorte had wrought on the country. His first act as President was to address the country and inform them as to the events of the past hours.

The media had been kept away from Camp David and were unaware of the events of the past few hours. They were given a pre-address summary only moments before the national address. The Right to Work States carried the address as well as a sign of respect to the new President.

But the changes now couldn't undo the damage to the country's psyche and trust of the system. The populations had already shifted. Lives were restarted. The mobs still surrounded Washington, and no speech would ameliorate and undo that fact.

The immutable facts were that a financial crash was well underway everywhere. The virus had spread from an epidemic to a pandemic. Businesses of all sizes and types were shuttering by the thousands every day.

Now the National Mall was lined with tents and cardboard shelters. Many, indeed, most of the people came to D.C. as a final act of desperation. They were hoping something would change. The fact that these masses had become dependent on the government was a moot point. Yet this was the very origin of their problems.

They had become accustomed to the programs and support for years from a government that was more interested in the elected governmental officials' wants, wishes and most of all, the power, not the people they were elected to serve.

The vicious cycle of the pandering and promises of benefits for votes evanesced the sense of self-satisfaction of accomplishment and the pride of earning them.

The manifestation of these decades of omnibus budgets and reconciliation to jam through gigantic spending excesses now had run its course. The hand that was feeding was now gone. The country would now grind to a halt. There was no check in the mail, there was no monthly social security wire transfer. Those with any savings or means found that the daily inflation killing them a nickel and a dime at a time was now out of control. There barely were any banks, gas stations, offices, grocery stores or schools operating normally. It was like a nation experiencing the first oil embargo, except it was **all** businesses along with the gas stations. There were scenes of masses crowding around town halls and police stations, even though no one there knew what to do.

The few who had farms or lived near fishing lakes or hunted knew what to do to get by. Some had shelters that were stocked with emergency supplies in anticipation of severe weather calamities. A few groups trained in survival techniques started to hold meetings to teach others how to live off the land.

But those in the cities lined up at firehouses and schools for the basics like canned goods and bottled water. There was soon no cash available at any bank. They would soon close for a banking holiday of three days or more. Most could sense it would be weeks or months before any sense of a civilized society would begin to reemerge.

To Roffle, it was inconceivable that the country would now be less than one-half the size it was when he was sworn in. But this was the legacy of Delacorte, not him. He was a supporter of Delacorte in the beginning, but he soon became disenchanted and that grew to disgust.

He knew his first address to all the States would set a tone of rational common sense, and that of a no-nonsense administrator.

He would tell the public what they already knew, the Union States could barely afford any more chaos and they could barely afford the bills. Big changes were coming but common-sense changes. He would not write a draft or a finished and polished speech. He would tell them the way it was...no more, no less. His speech to the nation and for all intents and purpose, the world, was to be, not from the Oval Office, but Camp David.

He was not nervous; the weight of the events had already sunk in, and he would do first things first. It would be reality and the crisis at hand. It would be from the heart, and it **would** be the **truth.**

At noon on Saturday, he would address the now divided nations.

The hastily assembled staging was in front of the fireplace in Laurel Lodge with him seated at the large conference table. At exactly twelve noon he began.

"My fellow countrymen, I address you at a time of intense chaos and tragedy. I sadly and regretfully must tell you President Delacorte is dead. He was killed in a manner we yet do not understand. I must also report that to you that the First Lady is missing. We do not know yet of her location or situation. I can tell you all available agents, detectives and police are investigating.

I must address you now as the President and I must be clear and truthful in my intent of this address. It is my intention to speak from the heart because I do not need to write down what is my heartfelt belief. So, I will start with the truth.

We do not yet know happened in the death of the President or the location of the First Lady, but we cannot allow ourselves to be paralyzed by the events. We will mourn for our President;

we will mourn and then we will begin to heal. We will heal and then we will move on and address our most pressing issues.

Sunday, President Delacorte will lie in state in the rotunda of the Capitol. I will declare three days of national mourning. We will announce the viewing times and the services this evening at six p.m. All other services will be announced tomorrow at noon.

I cannot express my sorrow, but I can honor our President by taking the reins of government and attempt to carry on as he would wish we would. I will address the nation as soon as we know more of this horrible incident, and I promise to keep you as informed as possible. Please help us heal, and those of you already in Washington, please allow the next few days to proceed with respect for our fallen President.

God bless you and God bless America in our hour of sorrow."

The weekend did proceed peacefully, the nation did show a modicum of respect and the burial service was sorrowful and honorable as Delacorte was laid to rest at Arlington.

President Roffle addressed the nation on Sunday to say there were no definite clues as to the First Lady's situation, but all available evidence was being investigated and they hoped a breakthrough could be announced soon. Roffle also said he would begin to outline his plan to deal with the problems and crisis facing the nation.

He was to speak again Monday evening at seven p.m.

It will be to address the severe financial crisis we are mired in and my plan to deal with it, he said with the authority of a Puritan preacher and confident leader.

Again, the national address was carried by all networks and into the RTW states as well. He began exactly at seven.

"My fellow citizens, we must now face a crisis like we have never seen before. This crisis is already affecting everyone, and it is all around us. You have already experienced disruption at banks, grocery stores and gas stations; every facet of our lives is affected. These are the facts: we are in financial trouble, very deep trouble.

My first act as President is to declare a bank holiday, which I have ordered at six p.m. today, so the banks are now closed and will be for three business days to analyze and take inventory of their assets. After that time, the banks will open, and the value of the dollar will be deflated to reflect its truer value.

This will be difficult adjustment at first. You can expect prices of goods and services to rise. But at the same time know this: for every adjustment, it is a sign of the true road to financial stability. The dollar as a currency has been abused and rendered nearly worthless. It will take a tremendous effort on the part of the citizens of this nation to bring it back in line and have a semblance of its value of just a few years ago.

The division of the country which was precipitated by a deep misunderstanding of the needs of the individual states has cast us into a nation tearing itself apart. This is now a moot point with the official separation of many the Right to Work states. I can stand here before you and say I don't blame them, I, too, thought these states were singled out, unfairly. But this is a separate matter, and it too will be addressed, and a conclusion will be reached. The outcome, however, is unclear.

I am not speaking to you to say we will be in good shape, and everything will be fine shortly. We won't. But you can now believe we **are** on a tried-and-true path to healing and addressing the most pressing issues that face us. We as a nation will begin to feel again the self-worth and confidence that comes from addressing our problems head-on.

362

I will address you, often at first, so you can be assured that you, as participants in this process, will be informed and you will know where we stand in our recovery.

So that's it. I can't paint a pretty picture of the events and situation, but now you are truthfully informed, and I hope a seed of trust in this new government will begin to grow. I believe a population that has faith in its government and trusts its decisions will only accelerate its sense of wellbeing, build a sustainable recovery and we can step back from the edge of disaster.

I will address you tomorrow and as events warrant it. But rest assured, my thoughts are with those who are suffering and may have lost everything in the past days, weeks, months, or years.

I will close with this thought by a French man named De Tocqueville who had come to America in the 1800s to observe what made America different than any other nation. He said, America is not great because of its strengths but because of its ability to address its faults.

I believe we will now begin to address our faults.

Thank you, my fellow citizens, and good night, may God once again bless America."

President Roffle rose from the table once the camera and lights were turned off and sat outside on the patio where Delacorte had been just a few days ago and began to hope he had started on the right foot. He called the governors of the Union States to have their National Guard on the ready for the next few days and until the banks reopened. He would leave for the White House tonight and begin assembling a team of advisors and aides to hit the road running.

There was no time to waste. Mob anger had to be defused and they needed to be convinced to return to the homes. These were only the first steps to a return to what everyone remembered America used to be.

RETURN TO AUSTIN

ABBEY WATCHED THE SETTING SUN FROM THE rehabilitation center's second floor sunroom. She had only been in Austin a few days after leaving Saint Elizabeth's Hospital to recover from her wounds. She was fortunate that there was no further damage to her neck or any other vital areas. Her shoulder and side still ached, and with her shoulder in a cast she knew it would be several weeks before she would be cleared to return to work. James's apartment was not far away, and until she could get the cast off, he and her two boys would help her get through the next few weeks.

Abbey, I got your favorite, black walnut ice cream, James announced as he walked into her room. And I got two spoons for sharing.

Well, it's not really sharing because you still have to spoon it out for me, she laughed.

Yeah, so you better be nice to me. He gave her a peck on the cheek and sat down next to her, opening the lid of the pint of frozen treat.

She was propped up in bed and he sat on her side with no cast, so she didn't have to move. He slowly dug out a small spoonful and she smiled as she savored each little bit.

Slowly, Abbey, you don't want an ice cream headache on top of it.

She made a pouty face that gave way as she enjoyed the small pleasure.

They were a million miles away from the reality that had brought them here. It was a bubble in time, insulated from the world around them. Abbey was weeks away from trying to begin work again. James had turned the operations in New America and the trading company over to the staff in Roseau. He would check in with the office in the morning and they would on occasion text him for advice and direction, but in general, things were under control. The trade office in Austin was busy with international agreements and conferences but was well-manned with top-notch and experienced people. James knew there was several on staff who could handle any basic negotiations and report in if there were sticking points.

Abbey's sons visited every day, and they became fast friends with James.

Jeff and Daniel had heard of New America but had no idea what it was like and how fast it had grown in just a few short years.

James and the boys sat for hours as he told them of Dominica and Roseau and how it became New America. Abbey smiled as the boys' eyes lit up when James told them of the new cruise ship facility or the fishing or the crystal-clear water.

Abbey smiled because she knew it wouldn't be too long before they would get to see it firsthand. She smiled and the pain slowly ebbed away, along with her fear of the future.

NOT MUCH OF A COUNTRY

Please stand by for the President, the pleasant voice on the phone was one of the White House communication secretaries.

In mere seconds the voice on the phone firmly began,

Is this President Cabbot to whom I am speaking? This is George Roffle.

Mr. President ,yes, this is Jim Cabbott.

Jim! How are you and the fellows doing down in Austin?

Very well sir, and how are you sir?

As you can imagine, I have a handful at the moment.

Well, what can I do for you fellows? Roffle replied.

Mr. President, would you have some time in the next few week or so?

Some of us down here would like to iron out some issues and possibly forge a better understanding of the current situation.

President Cabbot's voice was friendly and compelling.

Well, I think I can clear a few hours for you, Roffle responded just as friendly.

Mr. President, we were hoping to come up before the end of the month.

Actually, now that you are President, we hoped we could revive a sense of cooperation that was, umm, difficult before.

Jim, I would be happy to meet with you. Who all did you wish to be at this meeting?

I mean to say, how extensive a meeting are you hoping to arrange, President Roffle asked as sincerely as he could.

Well, Mr. President, just you and me and Vice President Payne. We just would appreciate any time you can spare as to review and develop an understanding to go forward, Cabbott replied, just as sincerely as he could.

Okay, Jim, let me confirm with the White House staffers but let's plan on the twenty-eighth, Saturday, say one p.m. in the afternoon, come on into Andrews and we'll get you over here.

All right, Mr. President, we'll look forward to it, Cabbott replied.

After they hung up President Roffle began to wonder what they were after.

The conversation was too brief and casual to be worthy of a serious meeting.

Ah, they just want to wiggle out of the money they agreed to pay to Delacorte, that's got to be it, he said to himself.

Well, if that's the case, this will be a truly short meeting, imagine that, thinking they can pull that on me. He was sure that was the case.

I've got other pressing issues to be working on and reneging on their deal to this country is dead on arrival.

He was sure he was right. He didn't think about the meeting again.

*****

Friday evening of the twenty-seventh, Roffle's assistant, Julie Brossard reminded him about the meeting the next day.

Mr. President, you have President Cabbott and Vice President Payne coming in to meet you tomorrow. Julie was Roffle's right hand and was the liaison in most matters.

She was svelte and witty and full of energy. She was the woman who lit up a room with her presence. Her ash blonde hair complimented her intense blue eyes.

The arrows from her stare at those who made disparaging remarks about her boss could cut them in half. Most males in the press corps went out of their way to stay on her good side.

Yes, yes, I remember, he told her, but I think this is going to be a waste of their time.

What do you mean, sir? she asked him.

Well, I've got a notion they want to rework the deal they did with Delacorte, and if that's the case, they are wasting their time.

I guess we will find out when they get here, sir, won't we?

I'd bet the farm on it, Julie,

I guess we'll know tomorrow. She seemed to hope for a different outcome.

*****

Cabbott and Payne's plane arrived at right at noon and were whisked from Andrews to the White House.

Jim, good to see you again. Roffle grasped his hand with a firm handshake.

Turning, he did the same with the Vice President.

Lowell, it's good to see you both.

I hope your flight was pleasant, President Roffle cordially asked.

Come on and sit down.

Julie asked if the two visitors cared for coffee or a drink.

Julie, I would like coffee, light and two sugars, President Cabbott responded.

I 'll take coffee, black, one sugar, the Vice President replied.

Gentlemen let's address first things first, Roffle began.

I believe you have an interest in a discussion of the current situation and conditions.

What is the nature of your request to meet today? he asked in an all-business manner.

I must tell you that if you wish to rework the payments you had agreed to with Delacorte, this will be a short meeting.

Roffle was straightforward and firm.

Mr. President started President Cabbott, no, not at all.

I'm afraid you have read us all wrong.

Roffle's poker face gave way to a quizzical befuddlement. Well, gentlemen, then forgive me, why are you here?

Mr. President, broke in Lowell Payne, we are here out of respect to you.

The hell you say! Roffle barely was able to spit out the words.

You're kidding me, aren't you?

After all Delacorte put you guys through and you want me to believe you're here for tea and crumpets?

Come on, guys, what do you really want?

Mr. President, and I say that with all the respect due to the office and you, sir,

Jim Cabbott started as serious as possible, how much of a country do you have left because of Delacorte?

Before he could answer, Cabbott finished for him.

Not too damned much!

We have a system now that works, and it's getting better now that we have a few miles on the tires.

Sir, we didn't have to come here. But we wanted to share with you what we have learned as a gesture of good will.

We will be fine, and we are beginning to experience a sense of stability.

I don't think you are able to say the same at this moment.

Roffle jumped in.

Now look, gentlemen, tell me something I don't already know.

Yes, we have some major league issues, not a one has a simple solution. But we will work our way through it, of this, I am sure.

Look, Mr. President, we are here to offer a hand, a step in a direction we hope you might find useful, Lowell Payne offered, like he was offering him a map to the fountain of youth.

Roffle's demeanor began to shift from befuddled to perturbed.

Fellas, I know you're not here to lecture me, are you?

I'm a little too old to be *lectured*. He started to raise his voice noticeably.

Mr. President, Lowell Payne jumped in, you really have this all wrong, we are here to try to agree on a foundation to build on. There is no need to second guess our intentions; we feel the country has needlessly been torn apart with the leadership of Delacorte.

Wait just a minute, now ! Roffle retorted.

Yes, he was an egotist and extreme, but he was at one time my friend.

Payne couldn't help himself and blurted out, ***Yeah, well your friend left you with a giant mess and half a country!***

The silence was deafening…. the pause endless.

Finally, Roffle got up and said, Gentlemen, our conversation is concluded.

While I will consider this meeting an offer of helpfulness, I will continue to forge ahead in a manner that walks a similar path of the previous occupant of this office.

Roffle continued as he walked them to the door of the oval office,

When my term is up, then the people can decide what direction they wish for the country, and not until then.

But gentlemen, thank you for your time and good day.

Julie, please have them escorted to the limo and to Andrews.

He shut the door and the meeting was over.

There was barely a word spoken between them all the way to Andrews. The two men slowly climbed the stairway to their aircraft and the jet's door was pulled closed. They didn't expect to be returning any time soon.

The jet slowly rolled from the tarmac and taxied to the runway, held for a moment, and then roared off.

Jim, the Vice President leaned over after they were leveling off at altitude.

How do you see this thing playing out? I mean, he's dead in the water without us.

Lowell, you, and I have figured that out, he responded.

Apparently, George wants to think he can work his way out of this dung pile. And if we keep the stream of cash coming, he'll probably last through his term. Once they think we won't cut them off, and they start promising more freebies to keep the votes coming, then they'll want more from us.

I can see it as sure as God made little green apples. They'll start to threaten this, that, or the other, raise some fee or some other bullshit, all the while knowing we can pull the plug and then they're in a world of hurt.

Lowell, we will just go about doing what works for the RTW states. There is no sense trying to convince those who don't want to listen.

To tell you the truth, I'm more interested in that thing they got going down in Dominica, the President responded.

We may have a thing or two to learn from the grand experiment. Yep, best thing we ever did was cooperating with those guys. Hell, they could be the point of the spear for a whole new way of looking at doing things. Every time I go down there, they got something new going up or building something. And everyone is so damn happy, I can't get over it.

Well, damn, Jim, Lowell broke in, we ain't exactly chopped liver, neither.

Yep, we have done a lot in a little time, but we sure the hell don't want to believe we know all there is to know. We will have our share of shit storms, and I'm not smart enough to know how to handle everything thrown at us.

I guess so, Jim, Lowell responded. But we're getting there and faster than I would have believed.

That may be true, so far. I just want to keep all options open, Lowell, that's all.

I get your point, I get it, he replied.

The fracturing was done. The broken country was to stay broken. It was up to those who believed they knew best to see who would be proven right or wrong.

But in the long run, would it even matter?

A REACH OF THE HAND

Abbey, it's time to get to the doctor's office and get this cast off, James reminded her.

Oh, thank God, I can't wait to get this itchy damn thing off. She was exasperated dealing with the cast.

Hey, take it easy, it's not like you're going to be playing tennis tomorrow. He couldn't help but rib her a little bit.

I know, but it sure will feel good to feel normal again.

Well, come on, it's time to go, he told her.

From her bedside, she raised her hand for him to reach for her like so many years ago. He paused for a second and all those memories flooded back to him like a wave. He stopped for a second and smiled at her.

She looked up and slowly smiled back like she understood, they were back at the beach all those years ago.

This time it might be different.

CPSIA information can be obtained
at www.ICGtesting.com
Printed in the USA
LVHW081750271221
707271LV00010B/73/J